1777: THE YEAR OF DESTINY

1777: The Year of Destiny by Edward M. Cuddy III

Copyright © 2023 Edward M. Cuddy III

Cover and interior design: Jacqueline Cook

ISBN: 978-1-61179-409-0 (Paperback)
ISBN: 978-1-61179-410-6 (e-book)

10 9 8 7 6 5 4 3 2 1

BISAC Subject Headings:
FIC002000 FICTION / Action & Adventure
FIC014070 FICTION / Historical Colonial America & Revolution
FIC032000 FICTION / War & Military

Address all correspondence to:
Fireship Press, LLC
P.O. Box 68412
Tucson, AZ 85737
fireshipinfo@gmail.com

Visit our website at:
www.fireshippress.com

To Patty, my wife and forever love.

Acknowledgments

The novel's fictional characters Brian O'Brien and his son Tom were inspired by my brother Dr. Brian G. Cuddy, and my son Thomas M. Cuddy, the finest men I know.

The members and presenter Nick Johns of the Mahwah Library Writers' Collective, whose constructive feedback was most appreciated.

Historical Note

Historians credit the victories of the continental army in Saratoga, New York, in September and October 1777 as the turning point of the struggle for American independence. Those victories embodied a five-month-long campaign involving six battles and two sieges concluding with a British army's defeat, capture, and imprisonment.

Saratoga shattered the perception of British military superiority, persuading France and Spain to ally with the Americans in their War for Independence.

This is a story of those who fought.

1777: THE YEAR OF DESTINY

EDWARD CUDDY

FIRESHIP
PRESS

CHAPTER ONE
The Year of Destiny 1777

Washington Headquarters
Morristown, New Jersey
January 1777

As the high-spirited congratulations began to subside, he rose, drawing the attention of his guests. Then, as the room quieted, he locked his gaze for a solemn moment, into the eyes of each of his field commanders. Standing at the head of a table in front of a roaring fire in the private room of a recently liberated tavern, George Washington felt a deep and abiding respect for this handful of men.

Naturally, a reserved and private man whose formality was often mistaken for arrogance by subordinates and timidity by enemies, George Washington saved the American colonies from unconditional surrender in the final days of 1776.

The horrors of the last year's defeats had reduced an army of thousands to the few who chose not to countenance defeat: St Clair, Stark, Glover, Gates, Sullivan, Greene, Knox, and Hamilton . Instead, their spirit had inspired and led the remnants of his army to cross the ice-chocked Delaware River to Trenton, New Jersey, not once but twice to achieve three separate victories.

Raising his glass of Madeira, General George Washington toasted his inner circle, "Gentlemen, we have won a respite. We have stung General Howe and his field commanders, taking full advantage of their overconfidence and disdain for our resolve."

"The boys are well pleased that we served those Hessians out after the massacre of the militia at the battle of White Plains!" shouted Colonel Stark. In his late forties, John Stark, a New Hampshire farmer known for his irascibility but tolerated due to his military skills, forged as an officer of Roger's Rangers in the French and Indian War.

"Yes, Colonel. Our victory at Trenton has stripped the King's Hessian mercenaries of their aura of invulnerability and avenged our dead," replied Washington.

Although encouraged by his officers' renewed confidence and optimism, he felt compelled to remind them of the realities of the current military situation. "Colonel Rall, the best commander of the King's mercenaries, killed, and nine hundred of his men made prisoners in the battle of Trenton, New Jersey. Then, Howe's best commanders – Cornwallis and Mawhood defeated and embarrassed at Assunpink Creek and Princeton. But, make no mistake, 1777 shall be a battle year. Howe sits in New York City with fourteen thousand regulars supported by the British Navy. He is an aggressive and ambitious commander seeking the favor of the Crown."

"You are correct, General. But, gentlemen, we are all condemned rebels that the Crown shall hang as traitors. Our victories shall restore confidence, stimulate enlistments, and preserve our lives, at least for now," intoned Horatio Gates. An acquaintance of Washington and a retired British officer, Gates had been commissioned by Congress as a Brigadier General for his experience in military administration, not combat.

In response to the catcalls and boos of the other men, Washington lifted his hand for silence which was slowly respected. Then waiting until he had the attention of his commanders, Washington said, "Our shared heritage shall elicit no mercy from the British Crown. Every surviving signatory of the Declaration of Independence, member of Congress, and General officer of the Continental Army or militia shall be condemned and hung!" Gazing at the sobered faces, Washington relented and again raised his half-filled glass and said, "I know we are in the right. I toast to you as extraordinary men capable of turning the world upside down to the utter shock of George the Third. We shall provide indisputable proof to history that independence is achievable if a people are willing to pay the price."

Simultaneously rising as one, each man lifted his glass in salute and drank to honor the man who had chosen to be the first to risk the gallows to fulfill his beliefs.

Kensington Palace, London
January 1777

One month later and three thousand miles away, Washington's victories in Trenton and Princeton had drawn the attention and ire of George the Third, Europe's most powerful Sovereign. His fit of temper and spiteful reaction to these acts of defiance would initiate a series of events resulting in a world war and an aberration in the time of the Empire.

Wearing the uniform of a General officer of the British army, George the Third stood in his private apartments, a handsome suite of rooms adjacent to the Palace gardens. That morning the King was particularly agitated after reading a lengthy military dispatch from his rebellious American colonies. His Majesty summoned his Prime Minister to his apartments for a private meeting to vent his spleen out of the public eye.

Hearing a knock on the door, his valet, Jervis, stepped into the room and said, "Lord North has arrived, Your Majesty."

"Enter Lord North. Jervis, we are not to be disturbed until I ring."

Waiting until he heard the door had closed, the King finished reading the dispatch, handed it to his Prime Minister, and said, "Have you read this?"

"Yes, your Majesty."

"This is intolerable! Rebellion merits death. Our blood and gold saved the colonists from the French. Their response is to kill my soldiers, destroy my property, imprison my royal governors, and refuse to pay my lawful taxes." His face becoming flush, the King continued, "Boston must burn. New England must be isolated and humbled. The signatories of the Declaration of Independence must be captured, imprisoned, and hung as traitors."

Frederick North, Prime Minister of Great Britain, sighed quietly and mentally tabled the hundreds of pending issues focusing exclusively upon his Sovereign. Aged thirty-nine years, George the Third stood above average in height, was clean-shaven, and formally wigged for Court. George's unremarkable facial features were cast in an impervious demeanor of absolute privilege and formal unapproachability as befits a monarch for over seventeen years.

After six years as the King's Prime Minister, Frederick North, known by his courtesy title of Lord North, was a professional politician resembling his Sovereign. Accustomed to such outbursts, Lord North endured the King's glare and, after waiting a moment to allow his Majesty time to regain his composure, stated.

"Your Majesty, General Howe has matters well in hand. He has defeated Washington on every battlefield, reducing the rebel army to a rag-tag rabble isolated and sulking in New Jersey. The Royal Navy is safe and protected in the greatest harbor in the New World. The army is quartered out of the elements in New York City, ensuring that your soldiers shall maintain their health and martial spirit to sally forth in the spring to crush any armed resistance which may survive the winter."

George the Third turned slowly away from his Prime Minister and looked at the palace grounds before continuing, "Lord North, what year is it?"

"Seventeen seventy-seven, Your Majesty."

Turning again to face his Prime Minister, the King thrust his finger into his face and shouted, "Do you have an excuse why I am required to suffer a rebellion of farmers and shopkeepers for over two years?"

"Your Majesty...."

Lord North noticed the King's color had again heightened as his Majesty moved to within mere inches away and shouted, "Washington has not been defeated! He and his rabble still fight, Prime Minister—

achieving victory at Trenton, Assunpink Creek, and Princeton! My Hessians, Europe's most feared and expensive mercenaries, were defeated, captured, and their senior officer killed. My General Cornwallis hoodwinked, and his troops repulsed with unacceptable casualties by starving and ragged rebels!"

Maintaining his calm and professional demeanor, Lord North replied, "Your Majesty. These were mere skirmishes with isolated garrisons in the dead of winter."

The King leaned forward and grated, unappeased, "My army has suffered hundreds of casualties in these mere skirmishes!"

Taking a step back, Lord North said, "Your Majesty. General Carleton has driven the rebels from Quebec."

"My point, Lord North! My Province of Quebec was invaded by rebel farmers and shopkeepers. Montreal and Crown Point were captured and occupied. The rebel General Montgomery came within a hairs width of taking Quebec if a cannonball had not killed him and demoralized his men. How is this possible in the first place?"

Desperate to conclude this most unpleasant audience, Lord North repeated, "General Carleton has driven the rebels from the Province of Quebec, and the Crown's northern territories are safe." He confidently added, "General Howe will run Washington to earth in the spring."

Continuing to stare at his Prime Minister, George rang for his valet and sent him for a chair and two glasses of wine. Returning from his errand Jervis held the chair as the King sat, and a second servant proffered two glasses of wine on a dazzling silver tray. George took one of the offered glasses and took several sips gazing silently at Lord North. After a minute, he irritably motioned North to take the second glass. Then, dismissing the servants, the King calmly began.

"These farmers and shopkeepers have cost the Exchequer millions of pounds. My loyal subjects have been driven from their homes and their property. I will not countenance any negotiated peace. All resistance is to be crushed. Every traitor tried and hung. All rebel property seized and sold until the Crown's cost to crush this rebellion is reimbursed in full!"

"Yes, your Majesty."

Finishing his wine, he stood, handed the empty glass to his Prime Minister, and said, "I have been informed that General Burgoyne has a plan which will subject the entire colony of New York to the Crown's control. New England shall be isolated from the breadbasket of the South. The rebellion will collapse within the year."

"I am familiar with Burgoyne's plan," said Lord North. "To carry out the proposed campaign will require a massive reinforcement of troops transported from England to Quebec. Considering the necessity to protect the Empire's other territories, your army will provide half of those troops, and the balance will be Hessian mercenaries. General Burgoyne will lead an army of ten thousand south to capture Albany. Lt. Colonel St. Ledger will lead five hundred regulars reinforced by Butler's rangers across Lake Ontario, landing in Oswego, New York. St. Ledger will march west supported by the warriors of the Iroquois Confederacy to burn every rebel settlement in the Mohawk River Valley. General Howe shall sail north on the Hudson River, trapping Washington in between. The rebellion shall be crushed in one stroke!"

The King smiled for the first time, saying, "Washington's rabble will be surrounded and surrender or cease to exist! You will direct Lord Germain to interview General Burgoyne immediately. I agree with Burgoyne's intention to go for the jugular of this rebellion and crush it."

The Savoy Hotel, London

"Darling, please sit down. There is nothing to be the least bit nervous about."

The Lady Charlotte Stanley, daughter of the Earl of Derby, and wife by her elopement with Major General John Burgoyne, slowly turned back to the dressing mirror in her cushioned chair and resumed applying rouge to her flawless skin untouched by the sun or the cares of the world. Attired in a floor-length silk dress made in Paris, fitting her petite form to perfection.

Gazing at this woman, Burgoyne could not imagine her existing anywhere other than the palatial Stanley five-room suite, well-appointed with furniture crafted to Charlotte's specifications in Paris and imported as a birthday present from the Earl to his daughter.

"My dear, I am to see Lord Germain within the hour. This interview, if successful, shall result in my obtaining the Lordship, whose absence your father has deemed so objectionable since I became his son-in-law," replied Major General John Burgoyne.

In his middle fifties, a handsome and robust cavalier decorated for valor, Burgoyne was an accomplished playwright known in the army as "Gentleman Johnny" and accepted in London's highest social and political circles.

Smiling into her mirror, Lady Stanley turned, pouting charmingly, and replied,

"Enough, my love. I like you, and my father has softened since the birth of our daughter. Remember he has arranged this interview so you may attain that Lordship through the opportunity to carry forward your brilliant plan to bag that fox Washington and bring this shameful rebellion to a close for both King and Britain."

Grimacing slightly and resuming his pacing, Burgoyne calmly continued, "Your father told me my plan was simple and obvious."

Lady Stanley pointed out in her matter-of-fact manner, "Of course, he did. All military adventures to succeed must be simple." Turning from her mirror, Charlette frowned prettily at the love of her life and repeated for the tenth time that morning, "For all our sakes, do not mention the Battle of Minden! Germain properly faced a court-martial for his cowardice! But it would be bad manners to remind him of that today."

Bending and kissing his wife on the top of her head, Burgoyne straightened his immaculate dress uniform, proud he was entitled to wear the spurs of the cavalry. His natural confidence now firmly in place, he drew on his leather riding gloves and departed for his meeting. Burgoyne responded over his shoulder, dutifully agreeing to his wife's request, "Yes, dear – Minden will not be mentioned!"

White Hall, London

Lord George Germain, a white-haired distinguished aristocrat in his early sixties, godson of George I, the son of the Duke of Dorset, first

Viscount of Sackville, whose earlier military career led to politics later in life.

Personally appointed by George the Third as Secretary of State for the colonies, he stared out of his office window onto the wintery street below, annoyed that a minor disagreement over taxes could reduce the Empire's valuable territories to profitless chaos. Publicly extolling the Crown's ardent opinion that military force was the only response to rebellion inevitably led to this appointment.

Lord Germain's responsibilities included the strategic planning for suppressing the rebellion and promoting or relieving the military commanders responsible for implementing the campaigns to defeat the rebels.

Warned by Lord North of the King's approval of Burgoyne's plan for the immediate employment of overwhelming force to crush the rebels, Germain eagerly awaited this meeting to add his endorsement.

"Gentlemen Johnny," he mused aloud, a fellow military man whose career had begun to rise as his ended in dishonor. Germain refused to waste his men in a futile cavalry charge at the Battle of Minden and was tried by court-martial and found guilty. Gentlemen Johnny became the darling of the light cavalry, with his reckless courage and daring – the "perfect cavalier."

Germain had been cashiered from the army at the demand of his godfather, George I. Then, Germain's entry into politics had been funded by his unexpected inheritance of a vast fortune. Germain reflected upon Burgoyne's equally fantastic luck. Burgoyne's elopement with the daughter of a peer had brought him influence in Court instead of condemnation and social banishment. Son-in-law of the Earl of Derby Burgoyne was being given the command of the best-equipped army fielded by the Crown in America. Germain mused that *Burgoyne was being gifted the opportunity to eclipse the Howe brothers and become the savior of British honor and prestige in the new world.*

In response to a soft knock on his office door, Germain left the window and sat behind his vast mahogany desk, choosing to commence Burgoyne's interview as a Secretary of State and not a fellow military man.

"Come in, General."

Burgoyne casually strolled into the office, dashing as always, in the glistering dress uniform of a Major General, caped and spurred, living up to his nickname Gentleman Johnny. Although Germain had received the exact impression he had anticipated, he was suddenly struck by the thought, *is such confidence seemly in one who had never commanded an army in the field?* Suddenly annoyed by the blatant patronage which denied a more qualified General the command, Germain said, "General, I have been told you intend to present a plan to crush the rebellion. I have an urgent appointment in thirty minutes."

Unaffected by the brusque greeting, Burgoyne sauntered to a chair and sat without invitation in front of Germain's ornate desk. Noticing Burgoyne pointedly contemplating the stacks of correspondence and miscellaneous documents cluttering his office, Germain thought, *Burgoyne, has decided I am now a Clerk rather than a General.*

His annoyance growing, Germain endured Burgoyne leisurely removing one of his riding gloves, relaxing back into his chair before replying, "The Hudson River is the jugular of the colonies, and its control is the key to ending all future resistance by dividing the fanatics of New England from the breadbasket of the south."

Lord Germain felt deeply disappointed that his King considered Burgoyne's plan a novel strategy to conclude the rebellion. "General, you point out the obvious. General Howe has already proposed this strategy. Even George Washington has grasped the paramount strategic value of the fulcrum colony of New York and its navigable waterways of the Hudson River. The rebels have fortified the river above New York City and have garrisoned Fort Ticonderoga against any thrust from Quebec. Washington sits in the middle, poised to rush the remnants of his army either north or south in reinforcement."

Lord Germain felt himself begin to fidget as Burgoyne slowly removed his other riding glove before responding. "Yes, my Lord, the strategy is simple and quite apparent. The distinction shall be its implementation! My military reputation, martial spirit, and leadership are known, and I have reassured the King that my plan will succeed with the Government's complete support. I drove the rebels from

Quebec. This year I will drive them from the Hudson Valley to fulfill the King's command."

Germain gaped at Burgoyne inwardly, shocked that Gentleman Johnny had claimed the credit due to General Carlton, Commander of all British forces in Quebec. Carlton, not Burgoyne, defended Quebec and routed the surviving rebels from the country. It was only bad luck that winter froze the rivers preventing Carlton from invading New York and crushing the rebellion.

Anxious to conclude this farce, Germain said, "Please continue, General."

Burgoyne smiled, stood, and walked to stand before a wall map of the American colonies. "His Majesty has approved the formation of a new army to conclude this sorry affair. My army will thrust south from Quebec as General Howe marches north from New York City. Washington's rabble shall be trapped between. Any possibility of Washington's reinforcement by the rag-tag militia of the Mohawk Valley will be eliminated by General St. Ledger's assault from Lake Oswego supported by the warriors of the Iroquois Confederacy. My Lord, unflinching leadership and resolve will end the rebellion this year as his Majesty demands."

Leaning back in his chair, Lord Germain was obliged to acknowledge that Burgoyne possessed a successful cavalry commander's arrogant confidence and reckless courage in full measure. However, Germain knew such arrogance blinded Burgoyne from the possibility that Howe would not march north. Germain seriously doubted that Howe would allow his brilliant campaign of capturing New York City and Fort Washington to be eclipsed by an adventurer like Burgoyne.

Germain chose not to endure the pompous Burgoyne any longer. Picking up a random military dispatch from a pile on his desk Germain said in a monotone, "Let me be the first to inform you that I am in complete accord with the King's decision to adopt your plan and appoint you as the Commanding General."

Remaining seated, Germain stoically endured Burgoyne's interminable ceremony of lethargically putting on the riding gloves and rising to his feet.

"You will forgive my hasty departure, but I must attend to my duty to our King."

Germain met Burgoyne's eyes in silence and watched Gentleman Johnny amble from his office.

With fifteen minutes until his next appointment, Germain leaned back in his chair and re-visited his nagging concern of the unpredictability of the resolve and spirit of the rebel "farmers and shopkeepers" held in such disdain by the King and his commanders. Nothing was a certainty in war.

Palace of Versailles, France

Comte de Vergennes, foreign minister of Louis XVI, stood silently in the Salon of War adjacent to the Hall of Mirrors, waiting patiently for his King to inspect his latest portrait. On this occasion, Louis was depicted as a martial equestrian. Satisfied with the presentation, Louis addressed him, "I am growing weary of the expense of your surrogate company, Hortal Ez & Cie, funneling my gold, arms, and munitions to the American rebels."

Vergennes had been a professional diplomat for over thirty years in the service of France. A trusted intimate of the King, he confidently replied, "As your Majesty may recall, the origin of that company was your Majesty's enthusiasm after receiving notice of the rebellion of the ancient Enemy's New World colonies. Your recognition of the golden opportunity to use Hortal Ez to funnel money and munitions to the rebels to repay the British for the humiliating terms imposed upon France in the 1763 Peace Treaty of Paris."

Twenty-three years of age, and absolute ruler of France for the past three, Louis had inherited over twenty million subjects still angered by their defeat and economic loss in the Seven Years' War with the British Empire.

"True. Two years. Millions of francs were spent. What does France have to show for it?"

"Your Majesty, the transferred money and war materials have prolonged the rebellion for over two years! Trade with England's most valuable colonies has been disrupted by rebel privateers. The enemy has incurred monstrous debt to resupply and reinforce the flower of its army. Consider, your Highness, that that army is three thousand miles away from France's borders. The desperate strain on their military is further demonstrated by the outrageous cost of hiring Hessian mercenaries to replace the thousands of casualties inflicted by the rebels."

Watching his King grow quiet and stare fixedly at him before saying softly, "Vergennes, I am not a child..."

"Your Majesty..."

"Vergennes, you are not to interrupt again!" Following the King into the Hall of Mirrors, returning to his chambers located off the Hall, Louis continued to address him, "The rebels have gifted thousands of my muskets, tons of my gunpowder, tents, and cannons abandoned to the British in Washington's defeats on Long Island, White Plains, and in the disgraceful capture of Fort Washington. What, may I ask, have you purchased with my money?"

Returning Louis's stare unflinchingly, Vergennes replied, "France's aid to the rebels has disrupted and weakened the British without the cost of the life of a single French soldier or sailor. The British forces are overextended, and India and the West Indies are vulnerable to seizure by France. The Spanish have expressed an interest in allying with your Majesty to take possession of Gibraltar and Florida."

Vergennes observed Louis XVI's eyes grow distant, perhaps dwelling upon more pressing problems as he walked towards his apartments. As the King reached the door, he suddenly turned back to face him and said, in a soft but firm voice, "Results, Vergennes. I will not commit France to American independence until the rebels demonstrate the will and ability to defeat a British army in the field."

"Your Majesty shall have your answer before years end. Howe in New York, Burgoyne in Quebec. If fortune favors the rebels, they will face one of those armies at a time. However, if the British are wise, which is rare, but unfortunately does occur, a joint operation of both those armies must end with annihilation."

"Vergennes, I am content to allow God to decide."

Headquarters of Northern Department
Albany, New York, June 8th

Major General Philip Schuyler, Commander of all continental forces from Albany to the border of the Province of Quebec, was worried. Looking north from his office window in his Albany mansion, Schuyler contemplated how best to use his force of continental regulars to defend the Hudson River Valley against the anticipated British invasion.

Information received from Phillip's commercial contacts in Quebec confirmed rumors of the arrival of a significant reinforcement of British regulars and German mercenaries from London commanded by General John Burgoyne, a recent favorite of the King.

Philip Schuyler was the scion of Dutch aristocracy in America, tall and slender in his early forties. Philip was related by blood and marriage to the van Cortlandt and the van Rensselaer, the most powerful families, together with his own, in the colony of New York. A veteran of the French and Indian War, Schuyler became a member of the Continental Congress and was appointed Major General in command of the Northern Department.

In 1775 Major General Schuyler planned and launched a successful invasion of Quebec. Poor health prevented Schuyler's participation. But his chosen Commander, Richard Montgomery, captured Fort Ticonderoga, "the Gibraltar" of America.

Winter icing of the northern lakes and rivers gave time for Schuyler to garrison Ticonderoga with three thousand continentals preventing its re-capture.

The current Commander of Ticonderoga, Major General Horatio Gates, had departed the fort in protest of General Washington's refusal to relieve Schuyler and appoint Gates to the command of the Northern Department.

Major General Arthur St. Clair had been assigned by General Washington to assume command of Ticonderoga and was arriving tomorrow to discuss his assignment with Schuyler.

As Philip focused upon his meeting with St. Clair, he thought, *Is this the invasion? If so, Fort Ticonderoga is all that stands between the British and Albany.* Startled by a knock on the door, Schuyler saw Peggy, his youngest and favorite daughter, burst in and heard her say, "Dinner is ready, and I am starving." Grabbing his hand, Peggy pulled him to his feet, dragging him toward the dining room.

Hiding his concern, Philip laughed and said, "I will race you!" As Peggy sprinted ahead, Philip felt better, promising to enjoy the evening with his family and face tomorrow with a clear head.

Headquarters of Northern Department
Albany, New York, June 9th

Seated comfortably in his mansion's parlor, Philip Schuyler briefed St. Clair concerning the current situation at Fort Ticonderoga.

Major General Arthur St. Clair was a robust highlander forty years of age, a French and Indian War veteran, and an unsuccessful claimant to a Scottish Earldom.

"General St. Clair, my contacts in Quebec have reported a steady reinforcement of the British garrison. In the last few weeks, local fishermen on Lake Champlain report that the British are seizing anything that will float. The warships which defeated Benedict Arnold last year at Valcour Island have been observed being provisioned and their crews preparing to leave port."

"Invasion," muttered St. Clair, his eyes staring into the distance and his hands tightening on the arms of his chair.

"Frankly, I expected it sooner. When the British captured New York City, I believe the Crown expected our unconditional surrender. General Washington shocked them. You were with Washington at Trenton and Princeton?"

"Yes. The weather was worse than where I was raised in the Scottish Highlands."

"You participated in a miracle, and that experience may serve you at Fort Ticonderoga."

Frowning, St. Clair leaned forward and said, "That remark calls for an explanation General."

Schuyler stood, walked to the sideboard, and poured two glasses of whiskey, handing one to St. Clair. Resuming his seat, he replied, "Since this will be your first posting at Ticonderoga, the fort's reputation for impregnability is a mere invention of the British newspapers. The Crown needed to justify the British army's failure to capture Fort Ticonderoga during the French and Indian War."

St. Clair lit his pipe, blew out a stream of smoke, removed it from his mouth, gestured it toward Schuyler, and said, "I wasn't in that fight, but the officers who were said the commanding General was a fool for ordering a frontal assault without artillery support."

"We cannot count on the British making the same mistake again. Fort Ticonderoga's garrison comprises most of the continentals assigned to the Northern Department."

"General Washington met with me when he assigned me to Ticonderoga and expressed his concern that the garrison must be preserved at all costs. He firmly believes that resisting a siege or winning a battle is not worth the high cost of casualties."

"I am glad we are all in agreement. Considering the increased military activity in Quebec, I have arranged for Brian O'Brien, the Northern Department's teamster, to transport you and your staff by batteaux convoy to assume your command as soon as possible."

"General Washington introduced me to Mr. O'Brien."

"O'Brien has been delivering supplies and soldiers to the fort since we captured it in 1775. He will know what supplies are needed and include them in convoy."

"My staff are all in Albany and prepared to depart once the convoy is ready."

Chapter Two

Ticonderoga

Lake Champlain
June 12th

Cruising with the wind abaft the beam, the unfurled sails of a column of heavily laden batteaux flew across the lake's surface to the convoy's destination. Brian O'Brien stood shoulder to shoulder with Major General Arthur St. Clair on the bow of the lead batteau, enjoying the relief from the heat from the spray of the bow slicing through the waves. Brian pointed to the lake's narrowing, "Your new command, General."

Brian wore a linen shirt and deerskin leggings comfortably rooted despite the rougher water encountered closer to the shore. A middle-aged frontiersman, Brian possessed the piercing blue eyes of his Celtic ancestors, a full head of nut-brown hair speckled with grey, a clean-shaven weathered face, and the trim, muscular carriage of a younger man.

St. Clair relished the sight of the surrounding mountains covered with virgin forest reminiscent of Scotland. Farsighted, St. Clair perceived the star-shaped fort built upon a spur of land jutting out into the water near the south end of Lake Champlain.

"Mr. O'Brien, why has a bridge of batteaux been built to the eastern shore?"

"General Gates, the previous Commander, had me provide the batteaux for its construction. Gates wanted a means for the garrison to retreat when the British returned to re-capture the fort."

"Not optimistic, was he?"

"No. Gates prepared for a retreat by building a fortified battery of cannons at the foot of Mount Independence to defend the bridge, which ends at the beginning of the military road to Hubbardton, Vermont."

Looking at the approaching granite walls, St. Clair replied in his soft Scottish burr, "Fort Ticonderoga is certainly impressive approaching from the south. That is hardly surprising since the French built it to defend Quebec. Quebec is now British. How formidable are the northern defenses?"

Brian replied, "Since the Green Mountain Boys captured the fort in 1775, each garrison has built redoubts and entrenched batteries to defend against the inevitable invasion from Quebec. Unfortunately, the current garrison is woefully insufficient to man those defenses."

"That is General Washington's and General Schuyler's understanding of the situation. Our spies in Quebec have reported ten thousand British regulars, and German mercenaries landed since May. With the recent imprisonment of thousands of continentals after the British capture of Fort Washington, General Washington could not send a sufficient garrison to defend Ticonderoga. Its loss has become inevitable. To reduce the resulting ire of Congress, Washington sent me to hold the fort long enough to force the British to assault the defenses. Once the British are blooded, I am responsible for successively retreating, preserving the garrison to reinforce the Northern Army's defense of Albany."

"Do you know who the British commander is?" asked Brian.

St. Clare answered, shielding his eyes from the sunlight reflecting from the water, "General Burgoyne, a favorite of George the Third, known at Court as 'the perfect cavalier.' He is credited with developing the British light cavalry and leading a charge critical to repulsing a Spanish invasion of Portugal. He is also famous for successfully eloping with Lady Charlotte Stanley, the daughter of Lord Derby. Our spies credit the patronage of his father-in-law for Burgoyne leading the invasion without ever previously commanding an army."

"Does Washington hope that Burgoyne's aggressiveness as a calvary commander may result in the hoped-for assault?"

"Perhaps," responded St. Clair. "Our spies report Burgoyne arrived in Quebec in early May and expect him to set sail down Lake Champlain in mid-June."

"I will immediately conduct a thorough inventory of the munitions stored in the fort's arsenal."

"I want you to supervise that each man of the garrison receives their full allotment of sixty rounds of ammunition and powder. In case of evacuation on short notice, distribute the fort's provisions equally to each regiment's commissary."

"Evacuation by batteau would be ideal. I will inspect the condition of the fort's batteaux and organize their mooring to expedite departure should it become necessary."

"Keep me informed, Mr. O'Brien."

Fort Ticonderoga
July 5th

Brian, approaching the fort's headquarters, observed a steady stream of staff officers entering and leaving the building. Met at the entrance by St. Clair's adjutant Brian was escorted directly into the General's office.

Sitting at his desk writing dispatches, St. Clair looked up and said, "Mr. O'Brien, my lookouts report that since the British investment of the fort on July 2nd, Burgoyne has succeeded in installing a cannon on Mount Defiance capable of bombarding the garrison. Our cannons are unable to sufficiently elevate their barrels to respond. Before the British complete their preparations to attack, I intend to evacuate immediately. Have you finished the distribution of the munitions and supplies?"

"Yes. Will the withdrawal be by batteaux?"

"The families and patients in the infirmary will be carried by batteaux convoy with a small escort. The garrison shall cross the bridge of boats to Mount Independence and march down the military road to Hubbardton, Vermont. I have chosen Colonel Ebenezer Francis to command the rear guard. He is not familiar with the area. I will need your assistance as a guide."

"I am surprised you didn't choose one of the local commanders. Francis must be pretty special."

"He is Mr. O'Brien. I cannot order you to do this. But, when Washington gave me this command, he told me you could be depended upon to do what was necessary."

"I heard the same said about you. That is why we are both here. I will guide the Colonel. Send for me when I am to meet Francis. I will be supervising the loading of the batteaux convoy and the pack animals for the march south."

***

After calling his three senior commanders and Colonel Francis to his office, St. Clair stood behind his desk as they filed in and stood at attention.

In his early forties, Enoch Poor was a successful shipbuilder and Brigadier General in command of the New Hampshire Brigade.

John Paterson commanded the Massachusetts brigade and fought in every major battle in the north.

Matthias de Rochefermoy was a foreign volunteer commanding the Massachusetts and New Hampshire militia.

Colonel Ebenezer Francis, thirty-three years of age, was well known for his excellent sense, calm demeanor, and courage under fire. Ebenezer Francis had been recommended by General Paterson to command the rear guard.

Agitated by the situation, St. Clair began his briefing without the usual courtesies. "The British have accomplished what our engineers have repeatedly opined as impossible! An enemy cannon has been installed on the top of Mount Defiance, exposing this garrison to bombardment. Our position is untenable." Meeting the sober stares of the assembled brigade commanders, he continued, "What is the readiness of your men to evacuate the fort when darkness has fallen?"

"With respect, surrendering the strongest fortress in the Americas without a shot fired is dishonorable," intoned General John Patterson. Perhaps the most professional General in the continental army, he had been with St. Clair and Washington at the Battle of Trenton.

"General Patterson, you were at the siege of Boston when the British Army and Navy evacuated the city," stated St. Clair. "Were the British dishonored for evacuating Boston without resistance instead of being bombarded by our cannons on Dorchester Heights?"

Shaking his head, Patterson dropped his eyes to the floor. St. Clair turned his attention to his other commanders and inquired, "General Poor and General de Rochefermoy?"

"The New Hampshire brigade is ready to march," answered Poor crisply.

Nodding, de Rochefermoy said, "Ready, sir."

St. Clair motioned them to the map table, "The British batteaux convoy carrying Burgoyne's army were escorted by warships. Our dependents and sick shall go by batteaux convoy. Unwilling to burden their advance with non-combatant prisoners, there should be no danger that the British would interfere with their passage to Fort Edward. The garrison shall cross the bridge of batteaux to Mount Independence and march south down the military road. Once the British learn Ticonderoga has been abandoned, we shall be hotly pursued by the enemy. Your brigades must not camp until reaching Castleton, Vermont, to avoid capture.

Colonel Francis, I have chosen you to command the rear guard. Your 11th Massachusetts will be reinforced by men chosen for their tenacity in combat by each Brigadier from their command. Send the chosen men to Colonel Francis' headquarters. General Patterson, your brigade will lead the evacuation soon as night has fallen. Gentlemen, rejoin your men. Francis, please remain for a moment."

After the others had left his office, St Clair invited Francis to take a seat and said," The rearguard will withdraw after midnight through unfamiliar territory. Mr. O'Brien will be accompanying you as a guide. He is the teamster of the Northern Department and is thoroughly familiar with the area."

Stepping out of his office, St Clair called, "Come in, Mr. O'Brien. I want you to meet Colonel Francis."

Entering the office, Brian shook hands with Francis, who had risen from his chair, and said, "Mr. O'Brien and I have met. He and my quartermaster have worked together distributing ammunition and supplies to my regiment. Good to see you again."

"You have a fine regiment, Colonel," replied Brian.

"Will there be a 'forlorn hope?'" asked Francis.

"What's that, Colonel?" asked Brian.

"A forlorn hope is a military tactic in siege warfare, such as a frontal attack upon a breach in the enemy's lines or fortification, or the last stand in defense," explained Francis.

St. Clair answered, "Yes, Colonel. The forlorn hope will be a cannonade from the battery overlooking the floating bridge between Ticonderoga and Mount Independence. The mixture of solid and case shot fired at point-blank range shall destroy the bridge of batteaux and any pursuing enemy troops."

"Do I need to ask for volunteers?"

"No. Four gunners in that battery have already volunteered," replied St. Clair.

"The British light infantry shall be the first unit to attempt the crossing," remarked Francis.

"Those elite troops are capable of capturing the entire garrison if not delayed and blooded," agreed St. Clair. "Those cannons must be fired."

"Of course, General, we'll do our best."

Mount Independence
Shore Battery
July 5th, 7pm

After inspecting the loading and priming of each of the four cannons of the battery, Colonel Francis addressed the volunteer artillerymen. "Your courage shall provide the garrison time to withdraw."

Sergeant Ross, a thirty-year-old, practical Scotsman, and gun captain in the siege of Boston replied, "Colonel Francis, every one of us has lost friends and family in the invasion of Quebec. We intend to bleed the lobsterbacks. I can promise you; we'll make every shot count."

"Sergeant, how have you loaded the cannons?"

"Three cannons are loaded with case shots to thin out those lobsterbacks chasing us. The fourth is double-loaded with round shots to shatter and sink the bridge of batteaux."

"You know your business, sergeant. After destroying the bridge, spike the cannons and fall back to join the rearguard in Hubbardton."

***

Sergeant Ross began to regret his volunteering for what would most likely be a suicide mission. Colonel Francis and the rear guard had marched over the bridge disappearing into the darkness two hours ago, and he had checked the priming of the four cannons thrice since.

"Sergeant, look what I found!"

Agitated by the shout that shattered the lightless silence, Ross snapped, "Jenkins, I'm surprised you returned from inspecting the fort for stragglers. I expected you to run."

John Jenkins, a scrawny eighteen-year-old recruit from the streets of Boston with a child's attention span, giggled and replied, "That's not fair. I want to pay the lobsterbacks for bayoneting my brother William when the grenadiers overran Breed's Hill." Motioning to the other two privates in the gun crew, Jenkins continued, "Boys, look what I found in the officer's quarters! A full cask of Madeira that is simply begging to be drunk."

Sergeant Ross knew that drinking was forbidden when handling gunpowder and munitions. Fear and the realization of his mortality caused him to disregard years of discipline and say, "We will all have one stiff drink, and then the cask goes into the lake. Agreed?"

All three men nodded vigorously and promised simultaneously, "Yes, sergeant, one drink. Then we will send the bastards to hell."

Jenkins pulled a soup ladle from his backpack, "I hoped you would agree, sergeant. I brought this to pour our drinks into."

Holding up Jenkins' choice of drinking vessel, Ross said, "A soup ladle?" Laughing, Ross resumed, "Well. We certainly earned it if this is our last nip!"

Burgoyne's Army

The operational field unit in the British army in America was the battalion comprising ten companies with an authorized strength of six hundred fifty men. Eight were regular line companies, and the remaining two were "flank" companies. The flank companies were all combat veterans chosen for their unique attributes. Grenadiers for their size and fearlessness under fire. Light infantry for their intelligence, endurance, and tenacity.

All British infantrymen wore red brick coats, the lapels folded back to reveal long facings of a specific color, depending upon their regimental designations. The line companies wore brimmed tricorn hats, grenadiers, tall bearskin headdresses, and leather caps by the light infantry.

The battalion was also the operational field unit of the Hessian mercenaries employed by George the Third. Identical to the British battalion in the number of men and their attributes, composing the line companies, grenadier, and light infantry. Attached to each Hessian regiment was an independent company of elite jaeger hunters known for their superior woodcraft and aggressiveness. The Hessian regulars wore light blue coats trimmed with regimental colors like the British uniforms. The grenadiers wore tall, mattered hats with brass facings, and light infantry leather caps. The jaeger hunters wore dark green uniforms and black campaign hats.

During the Saratoga campaign, Burgoyne stripped the British battalions of their flank companies and formed one composite battalion of the grenadiers and one of light infantry, each numbering six hundred men.

Major Alexander Lindsay was the twenty-five-year-old 5th Earl of Balcarres and *de jure* 23rd Earl of Crawford, commanding Burgoyne's army's light infantry composite battalion.

Major John Ackland was the thirty-one-year-old heir of the Baronet of Killerton, and Petherton, commanding the grenadier composite battalion.

Brigadier General Simon Fraser commanded the advance corps of Burgoyne's army, a forty-eight-year-old highlander who served under General Wolfe in the French and Indian war. Known for his demanding standards of discipline and training, Fraser also commanded the 24th Foot. Fraser often addressed his subordinate, Major Lindsay, by his title, "Balcarres."

Major General William Phillips commanded the right wing of Burgoyne's army. Phillips conceived the method of placing the cannon on Mount Defiance and was a trusted adviser of Burgoyne. Thirty of forty-seven years of his life were spent in the British military. Thomas Jefferson described him as "the proudest man of the proudest nation on earth."

The left wing was composed of Hessians commanded by Major General Baron Frederick Riedesel. General Riedesel was a professional soldier whose military career began at the age of seventeen. He commanded a brigade at twenty-three, decorated for distinguished service at the battle of Midden. The duke chose Riedesel to lead the first division of his troops sent to America. In his early forties, he had a short, stout stature, known for his astuteness of battlefield tactics and a reputation of unquestioned courage. Riedesel's only common language with British command was French, in which the senior British officers were fluent.

Just before midnight on July 5th, Fraser led fifteen hundred chosen men of the 24th Foot, a company of marksmen, and the composite battalion of the light infantry to infiltrate the perimeter fortifications of Fort Ticonderoga.

Fort Ticonderoga
Perimeter Fortifications
Pre-dawn, July 6th

Major Lindsay advanced silently with two light infantry companies until he reached the fort's outer trenching and the redoubts earthen walls, which rose from the cleared land leading to shadowed thirty-foot high granite bastions.

Materializing out of the darkness, a grey-haired sergeant, his face painted black, reported, "They are gone."

"How far did you go?"

"All the way through the fortification to the bridge of batteaux."

Nodding, Lindsay said, "You have done well. Is the bridge intact?"

"Yes, sir."

"There is a battery of cannons on Mount Independence overlooking the bridge. Did you see any activity?"

"No, sir."

"Take your men and use the ropes holding the batteaux bridge together to cross the lake to Mount Independence. Determine whether the battery is occupied or abandoned. Light three touches to signal if it is safe to cross the bridge. Otherwise, send me a messenger with a detailed report of the situation."

As the scouts disappeared into the darkness, General Fraser joined Major Lindsay, returned his salute, and said, "Balcarres report."

"General, the damned rebels have scampered off without a shot fired!"

General Fraser smiled and replied, "Balcarres. This is our opportunity to bag the entire garrison. Send a messenger to General Burgoyne that I am immediately pursuing with half of the advance corps. The remainder is to occupy Ticonderoga until the main army arrives. Organize the men and follow me to the rebel's bridge of batteaux."

British Army Field Headquarters
Fort Ticonderoga
Dawn, July 6th

Lieutenant General John Burgoyne, elegant as always in full uniform, motioned to Riedesel to leave the assembled officers and share his view of the maps on a table under a tarp serving as his field headquarters. Erected in the forest a thousand yards from Ticonderoga's perimeter walls, Burgoyne and his staff closely followed the progress of the assault through the reports received from General Fraser's advance corps.

Burgoyne summarized the current situation. "Riedesel, the fort has been abandoned, and my advance corps occupies it. General Fraser is pursuing to capture the garrison."

"General Fraser intends to kill or capture three thousand men with seven hundred?" asked Riedesel.

Hearing a slight rustle among the assembled officers, Burgoyne thought, *I must put this mercenary in his place.* Staring momentarily at Riedesel, Burgoyne smiled and said, "I admire Fraser's initiative. We are not facing the French. These rebels are mere farmers and shopkeepers without honor. They ran without firing a shot."

Clearing his throat, Major General William Phillips said in his soft burr, "General Burgoyne, you appointed Fraser to command the light infantry due to his initiative. But should the rebels turn on him, he will be outnumbered over four to one."

Burgoyne turned to his executive officer, "Thank you, General Phillips. Sometimes I must be reminded that I no longer command a cavalry brigade. Odds are not as important when ordering a charge upon the enemy." Returning his gaze to Riedesel, he continued, "I summoned you to order your jaegers to immediately march to join Fraser's efforts to bag the enemy garrison."

General Riedesel continued studying the map ignoring Burgoyne's patronizing behavior recognizing the urgent necessity to provide an immediate reinforcement, and replying, "I shall send the Hessian advance corps in support."

Shaking his head with a slight frown to hide his concern at Fraser's impulsive action risking the loss of his army's best troops, Burgoyne replied, "Thank you, Riedesel. As always, I am most appreciative of your readiness. Your entire advance corps will not be necessary. Your jaegers and grenadiers should suffice."

Familiar with the British's habitual need to express their disdain for the rebels' fighting abilities, Riedesel was unsurprised by Burgoyne's order of insufficient reinforcements. Although his professional integrity prevented him from disobeying a direct order, Riedesel was outraged that the lives of his men were being risked to satisfy British vanity. Determined to minimize that risk, Riedesel said, "I shall assume personal command of the Hessian reinforcements."

Burgoyne bowed slightly, acknowledging Riedesel's evident desire to gain the personal glory of leading the King's Hessians in the first combat with the rebels, and said, "Godspeed, General, and good hunting."

Mount Independence
Bridge of Batteaux
July 6th

General Fraser crouched behind a perimeter wall looking through his telescope to study the rebel's bridge that had been abandoned intact. Fraser turned his attention to the shore battery on Mount Independence overlooking the bridge, "Balcarres, have you seen any activity?"

Lindsay replied, "No, General. But it's obvious that the rebels want us to march over the bridge exposed to their cannons."

"Agreed. When did the scouts leave to infiltrate the battery?"

"About forty-five minutes ago. Crossing hand over hand in the water along the securing ropes is slow work. Sir."

"To give them the best chance to succeed, it's necessary to distract the attention of any rebels in the shore battery. Form a company in the open at the foot of the bridge as if preparing to cross. The rest of the men will remain undercover behind you. What is the signal that the battery has been captured?"

"Three lit torches."

After what felt like hours, the shadowed enemy battery burst into light.

General Fraser shouted, "Major Lindsay led your men across!" Walking toward the assembled officers of his command, he continued, "The light infantry will lead, followed by the grenadiers and the 24th regiment. We are the spearhead of this army. It is our responsibility to capture the entire garrison. Join your companies and prepare to march."

Mount Independence
Shore Battery
July 6th

General Fraser stood on the walls of the captured shore battery watching his troops march beneath the silent cannons in pursuit of the rebel garrison fleeing on the road to Hubbardton, Vermont.

"Sergeant Wallace, report."

Snapping to attention, Wallace replied, "Sir! Upon entering the battery, I found all the rebel artillerymen drunk with one draped over a half-empty cask of Madeira. I guess they raided the officers' quarters after the garrison ran."

Noticing the burning lintels in their buckets adjacent to each cannon, Fraser asked, "Were the cannons loaded?"

Wallace looked accusingly at the four supine figures snoring noisily and said, "Yes, sir. Each was double-loaded. Three with case shot. One with round shot."

Frazer placed a hand on the sergeant's shoulder and said, "Well, Wallace, this is reassurance that the Lord favors us. Those cannons would have shredded us and shattered the bridge. Detail four men to secure the prisoners and lead the rest to track the rebel garrison. We have the opportunity to end this."

CHAPTER THREE
Hubbardton

Hubbardton
Early Afternoon
July 6th

General St. Clair paced back and forth anxiously outside the Bligh Inn adjacent to the road to Castleton in the center of the hamlet of Hubbardton. The commons and woods surrounding the modest settlement were filled with thousands of men sitting or lying asleep around a hundred cooking fires heating kettles of soup or porridge eagerly consumed by the retreating garrison. O'Brien's teamsters walked through the gatherings distributing loaves of bread baked the previous day in the fort's kitchen and carried by the pack train organized during the evacuation.

Unconsciously consulting his pocket watch every couple of minutes, St. Clair had reluctantly permitted the halt. Without their first meal in over twelve hours, St. Clair knew his men would be incapable of reaching Castleton, Vermont. Becoming aware of the presence of his aide, he heard him say, "General, please finish your soup. Colonel

Warner is here in response to your summons."

Returning his watch to his pocket, St. Clair focused on his surroundings, observing the cat-like approach of Colonel Seth Warner, commander of the Green Mountain continentals. Warner's first served his country as a teenager in the French and Indian War. A constantly active man thirty-four years of age, physically imposing, Warner had the respect and trust of the fiercely independent men of the recently recognized Vermont Republic.

"Colonel Warner. I can't wait any longer for the rear guard. We should have heard the cannon fire from the Mount Independence battery if the bridge of boats had been destroyed. I am concerned that the British pursuit has not been delayed, and Francis and his men have been seized. I must march now if I am to preserve this garrison from capture. I rely upon your experience as the rearguard's commander during the successful retreat from Quebec. If Francis does not arrive in the next several hours, you may assume his capture and continue to Castleton. If he does arrive, you will assume command. The British will be relentless. You must march to join me without delay. Once joined, any pursuing force will be of insufficient numbers to attack three thousand men."

Still angry about retreating without a shot fired, Wagner nonetheless drew himself to attention in silent recognition of his acceptance of St. Clair's orders.

Noting Wagner's silence, St. Clair continued, "Colonel Hale shall remain under your command. I will see you tonight in Castleton."

Hubbardton
Early Evening, July 6th

After hours of forced marches interspersed with sharp skirmishes with British light infantry, Colonel Francis' chosen men reached Hubbardton. Walking beside Francis, Brian O'Brien was relieved to see Colonel Warner step from the Bligh Inn's entrance, followed closely by Colonel Hale. Tired but pleased by the men's performance, Brian welcomed the completion of his responsibility to rejoin the command and asked, "Where is General St. Clair?"

Francis saluted Warner and said, "Good evening, Sir. Your pickets on the edge of town were a welcome sight. I want to report that British light infantry has harassed us for miles which should not have happened if the bridge of boats had been destroyed by the forlorn hope. We heard no cannon fire. I credit Mr. O'Brien for our safe arrival. He got us out of several tight spots."

Warner returned the salute, enthusiastically shook Brian and Francis' hands, and replied,

"General St. Clair has continued to march to Castleton and placed me in command. I have decided to call a halt here. Francis, your men are excused from picket duty and will camp with us on Monument Hill. Patrols will continue to warn us of any British pursuit."

Warner introduced Brian to Colonel Hale, who excused himself, and entered the inn. A few moments later, Hale carried a tray of glasses of rum from the inn. After each man took one, Hale placed the empty tray on one of the inn's outdoor tables, and Brian and the others slumped tiredly into the surrounding chairs.

Nathan Hale was a thirty-four-year-old graduate of Yale, a minuteman at the battles of Lexington and Bunker Hill, commissioned as a major in the continental army, and commanding officer of the 2nd New Hampshire continentals.

Watching Francis take a deep breath, close his eyes and let out a long sigh, Brian heard him say, "I hope we have been through the worst of it."

Lifting his glass to the trio of Colonels, Brian said, "From your lips to God's ear."

Five Miles from Hubbardton
Late Afternoon, July 6th

General Baron Riedesel rode beside the marching troops until he reached the head of the stationary column. Riedesel gave silent thanks to the rebels for abandoning a half dozen horses in the fort's stables.

Observing General Fraser and his staff studying a map on a tree stump surrounded by his men sitting and eating rations of bread and cheese, Riedesel dismounted and joined them.

Addressing the assembled officers, Riedesel said, "General Fraser, my men and I congratulate your advance corps for capturing the shore battery and floating bridge to Mount Independence. We appreciate the opportunity to join you in bagging the rebel's rear guard."

Although annoyed by having to share the glory of defeating the rebels in the first battle of the campaign, Fraser appreciated a fellow professional's compliment and recognition of his men's courage and ingenuity in foiling the rebel ambush.

"General Riedesel, you and your men have made excellent time. Your reinforcement of my command guarantees the capture of the entire rebel garrison," replied Fraser.

Upon joining forces with the British detachment Riedesel, as a Major General, outranked Fraser and automatically became Commander of the entire force according to military etiquette. The Baron, though secure in his abilities and military reputation, chose not to challenge Fraser's assumption of command. Having campaigned successfully with Fraser in the past, Riedesel had become tolerant of the highlander's pride and simply replied, "My men and I are pleased to be members of this hunt. I suggest my men bivouac here, and you camp several miles ahead to create a defense in depth. Tomorrow we may proceed together to meet the enemy."

Fraser bowed and replied politely, "A fine idea General. Our respective scouts will have an opportunity to ascertain the location and strength of the rebels so that we may seize the lot."

Bowing in his turn, General Riedesel thought, *I must try to convey my advice one last time to ensure our men incur the least casualties.*

"If I may suggest, General, I intend to commence my march to Hubbardton at three a.m. tomorrow morning. I would be honored if your forces marched with mine to best plan and employ our combined forces in the assault once the scouts locate the rebels."

In response, General Fraser urged his captured mount forward, ordering his men to continue their march toward Hubbardton.

Hubbardton
Continental Camp on Monument Hill
Officer's Call, July 7th, 4 am

O'Brien accompanied Francis and Hale to Warner's campsite and heard Warner say, "I have just received orders from General St. Clair's messenger diverting our destination from Castleton to Rutland, Vermont. Burgoyne has pushed through to Skenesboro and captured the woman, children, and supplies evacuated by water from Ticonderoga by Colonel Long. General St. Clair intends to take a more circuitous route to the Hudson River."

Brian saw Colonel Francis's shoulders slump slightly upon receiving the news of yet another British success but was pleased when Francis quickly returned to the practical concerns of the current situation by asking, "Colonel Warner, when do you wish to break camp?"

Warner yawned and came slowly to his feet before responding, "We should be ready to march at first light. Your men should eat their rations as soon as possible and check the priming of their weapons. If Burgoyne is in Skenesboro, we should expect to meet the enemy before the day is over. We currently hold a defensible position on this hill with our picket line along Sucker Creek. Remind the men of the British pursuit and encourage vigilance. The standing order is to aim at the enemy's belt buckle. Return to your commands and begin preparations to continue our march south."

Three Miles from Hubbardton
Military Road, British Camp
British Officers' Call, July 7th

General Fraser stood in the darkness of a virgin forest and conveyed his orders to his commanders, "Our scouts have located and overcome the rebel outpost on the saddle of the military road just outside Hubbardton. No alarm was given. Major Grant's detachment from the 24th and Balcarres' light infantry will eliminate the enemy pickets along Sucker Creek. Major Ackland's grenadiers will circle the village and rebel camp and block the road to Castletown. I will not be satisfied unless we capture or kill the rearguard."

Hubbardton
Monument Hill
Continental Encampment
July 7th, 6am

Standing with the men amid the rising tendrils of white smoke of scores of dying cooking fires, Brian saw Colonel Francis raise his hand and commence his morning brief to the chosen men of the garrison and his 11th Massachusetts continentals. "Burgoyne has already advanced to Skenesboro, and General St. Clair has diverted the garrison to Rutland. We are being pursued by Burgoyne's advance corps. I expect enemy contact before the end of the day. Today everyone shall march with loaded and primed muskets as an exception to general orders...."

The morning's silence was torn by the crash of a volley of scores of muskets from the direction of Sucker Creek. Startled, Brian heard Francis yell, "Those are the muskets of our pickets! We will form our firing lines here on the hill, providing a rallying point for the pickets. Send a messenger to Colonel Wagner to form on our left flank. We must prevent the British from cutting us off from the road to Castleton. You are the chosen men of the garrison. It is up to us to provide time for the command to organize and repulse the enemy."

Turning to Brian, Francis said, "You stay with me. If we can't hold, I will rely on you to guide us to Rutland."

Retrieving his rifle, Brian watched Francis form his men into two firing lines. Brian observed the pickets fall back from Sucker Creek. As those men reinforced the firing line, Francis asked one of the officers, "What's the situation?"

Dressed only in a shirt and breeches without boots or weapons, the man replied, "I woke from a dead sleep by musket fire. I rolled out of my blanket and started to stand when I saw a flood of lobsterbacks with leveled bayonets emerge from the woods, pouring over Colonel Hale's camp."

"Colonel Hale?"

"Dead or captured."

"Go to the rear," Francis ordered, "there will be extra muskets and clothes before long."

As the minutes passed, other survivors from the pickets and 2nd New Hampshire's overrun camp joined Francis' firing line; some armed, others not.

Standing near Francis on the hill, Brian saw Warner walking over from his regiment to Francis's left and heard him shout at the formation, "We are the toughest men of the garrison. I almost feel sorry for those bastards charging up this hill into our musket fire!"

Brian joined in the laughter of the men responding to Warner's bravado when he heard Francis's roar, "Let's make them bleed."

Hubbardton
Military Road
July 7th, 6am

Major Grant and two companies of the 24th and Captain Fraser's marksman began the British advance upon the rebel pickets and camped continentals at Sucker Creek. The light infantry was advancing on his right flank. Expecting terrified militia half asleep at their posts, Grant stepped confidently from cover with the first line of the 24th, shouting, "Drop your weapons, you damned rebels, and—"

Grant's command was cut off mid-word by a thunderous crash, smoke, and flames which snatched him up and threw him back into darkness.

Following closely with the second company of the 24th, General Fraser reached the site of carnage and shouted, "Captain Smith, where is Major Grant!"

Captain Smith holding his left arm tightly to his side as it pulsed blood from his forearm, calmly replied, "The Major was killed in the first volley. The company has commenced volley fire. The rebel pickets are falling back."

Fraser shouted, "Major Lindsay, your light infantry is to drive the pickets back and attack the camp closest to the road. I will lead the 24th and attack the rebels on Monument Hill. Major Ackland, your grenadiers shall prevent the rebels from reaching the road to Castleton. Send a messenger to General Riedesel, inform him that we are in contact with the enemy, and request his assistance."

Hubbardton
July 7th, 7am

Circling behind Monument Hill, Major Ackland led the advance element of his grenadiers when he heard a sudden shout from ahead, "Major, we have a group of rebels who wish to surrender."

Smiling, Ackland remarked casually, "Quite understandable, sergeant."

Sauntering toward the rebel prisoners, Ackland observed that they had inverted or "clubbed" their muskets, a universal sign of surrender. He gestured to the rebels and said, "You dammed rebels! Place your muskets on the ground and your hands behind your heads."

When the two groups were only yards apart, the continentals suddenly reversed their muskets, firing at point-blank range and dropping the grenadiers' entire advance guard.

Enveloped in a suffocating cloud of gun smoke Major Ackland found himself flat on his back, unable to catch his breath. As consciousness slipped away, he gasped, "Grenadiers charge - no quarter!"

Running pell-mell into the forest, the surviving grenadiers closely pursued the continentals. Enraged by the rebels' false surrender, any who resisted were bayoneted. The main body of the grenadiers double-timed forward, seizing the road to Castletown and cutting off the rebels' retreat.

On top of the hill, Brian saw the rear guard was surrounded and thought *the only way to leave Monument Hill is with a victory.*

* * *

Reloading his rifle for the tenth time that morning, Brian observed Colonel Francis's calm professionalism and exemplary courage motivating his men to repulse repeated attacks by the British light infantry and the 24th. As Fraser gathered his men for a third assault, the grenadiers who had seized the Castleton Road broke Colonel Warner's left flank, driving his regiment down Monument Hill into open farmland. Brian joined Francis' counterattack, shooting a senior British officer, and repulsing the third charge of the British light infantry.

* * *

Standing on a slight elevation in the open two hundred yards from the melee, General Fraser observed the rebel counterattack see-saw between success and failure. Recognizing this as the pivotal moment in the battle, Fraser motioned to one of his marksmen and pointed toward Francis. Moments later, the continental officer was thrown to the ground, his left arm shattered by a rifle ball.

Catching Major Lindsay as he stumbled back to the British rallying point for the next attack, Fraser shook his subordinate and grated between clenched teeth, "Balcarres, take your men and break the rebels now!"

His uniform was holed by multiple musket balls, bleeding from his left arm and the right thigh; Lindsay drew his sword, straightened his shoulders, and yelled to his exhausted and bloodied men, "We are the best of the best. Fix bayonets, charge!"

***

Lifting Francis from the ground, Brian saw a broken bone protruding from his uniform jacket and a steady stream of blood flowing from the wounded left arm. Wrapping a supporting arm around the Colonel's waist, Brian supported Francis stumbling with the flood of continentals descending from the hill to the farm fields below.

As they reached the bottom, Francis looked around, pointed with his right arm toward a high log fence, and yelled, "Rally to me. Form a firing line behind the fence. Force the British to attack across open ground in the face of our volley fire!"

Propping Francis against the fence, Brian commenced loading his rifle when he heard the sound of battle drowned out by voices singing hymns in a foreign language and the music of a military band. Brian turned toward the singing and saw a rotund Hessian officer emerge on foot from the forest into the field, leading two columns of enemy reinforcements. The first column was green-coated jaeger hunters carrying rifles with fixed bayonets that sprinted to the left of the continental firing line. The second column of blue-coated Hessian grenadiers jogged to the right.

Brian recognized possession of the log fence as decisive to achieving victory. Lifting his rifle to his shoulder to shoot the Hessian officer, Brian saw both enemy columns charge shielding the officer.

The jaegers collided with Francis' men still forming on the log fence, and the grenadiers launched a bayonet charge on the right. Victory now rested upon who would organize and fire the first volley.

The jaegers won. Closing to within pistol shot, they knelt and fired, sweeping Francis' defensive line as grenadiers and light infantry collided with the center and right flank of the continentals.

In the ensuing melee, Brian checked Francis for a pulse. Finding none, he left Francis's body surrounded by the corpses of his men. Brian joined the survivors, who, together with Wagner and the remaining Green Mountain men, scattered into the forest.

Hubbardton
British Field Headquarters
July 7th

Ministering to a bleeding Lindsay, who had collapsed unconscious the moment the rebels had broken, Fraser addressed the approaching Hessian commander, "Riedesel, better late than never."

Shocked by the greeting of a man he had just saved from defeat and possible death, Major General Riedesel nodded tensely and dropped his gaze with no further thought of Fraser to the corpse of the rebel commander. His men had found the gallant enemy officer in a tangle of corpses at the site of the rebel's last defense. Standing on a battlefield littered with the wounded and dead of hundreds of Burgoyne's best troops, Riedesel mused, *I will never forget the sight of this commander continuing to lead his men after suffering a mortal wound.*

Overcome by his distress that his soldiers were obliged to kill this man, Riedesel's professional demeanor slipped. He snapped, "General Fraser, I intend to bury this officer with my men who died saving you today. In my opinion, this command cannot prudently continue the pursuit of the rebel garrison."

***

Fraser stared in disbelief at the Hessian commander. Riedesel had previously voiced no military advice or recommendations since the commencement of this campaign. *This fat mercenary dares to suggest the dead rebel had nearly defeated him!* Continuing to boil internally, his shock evolved into anger. *What would be Burgoyne's reaction if I challenged the Baron to a duel?*

The moaning of wounded Lindsay shifted Fraser's attention to the carnage surrounding him. Focusing on the present, he listened to Riedesel directing his men to gather the wounded and dispatch messengers to Burgoyne for wagons to transport the casualties and dead to Fort Ticonderoga.

Staring at Riedesel, who returned it unflinching, Fraser thought *the mercenary was right. I jeopardized the success of this campaign by the extent of the casualties suffered by the army's elite light infantry and grenadiers, including both battalion's senior officers.*

Reluctantly Fraser said, "General Riedesel, I agree with your assessment of the situation. The command will camp here to stabilize the wounded, bury our dead, and interrogate the prisoners. Messengers will be sent to Skenesboro to obtain wagons to transport the wounded, captured arms, and prisoners to rejoin the main army. As for your dead, their internment is solely your affair."

Headquarters Northern Department
Albany, New York, July 8th

Agitated but in control, seated together in his office in his Albany mansion, General Schuyler addressed his chief of staff with the worst possible news in an already hopeless situation.

"Fort Ticonderoga has fallen, and Burgoyne is marching south with nine thousand British regulars, Hessian mercenaries, five hundred Abenaki and Ottawa warriors led by our old enemy St. Luc. My God! How can Burgoyne and his staff suffer from being in the same camp as that murderer."

In his late forties, Colonel Learned, a no-nonsense New Englander commanding officer of the 9th Massachusetts continentals, asked, "General St. Clair had a garrison of thousands. How could this have happened so quickly? Has the garrison been captured or destroyed?"

"Colonel Learned, there is no time for speculation. Even if St. Clair successfully retreats with the entire garrison, we are seriously outnumbered. Washington must send reinforcements." Pulling a dispatch form from his desk, Schuyler hurriedly wrote a summary of the current situation, concluding with a request for more continentals. "Colonel, send Brian O'Brien's son Tom to General Washington with this dispatch."

"The last word is Washington's headquarters are in Middlebrook, New Jersey. O'Brien, the teamster?"

Looking up, Schuyler replied, "Yes. Since Independence was declared, his company has acted as a teamster for the Northern Department."

"Sorry, General, I have not met him."

"Brian has traveled all the roads and waterways in the Northern Department. He is a widower, so his son has accompanied him everywhere and possesses the same experience. I use Tom as a special courier when time is of the essence." Handing Learned the dispatch, Schuyler continued, "Please hand-deliver the dispatch immediately and convey to him the urgency."

Looking up from the dispatch he had just read, Colonel Learned replied, "General Washington is all there is blocking Howe's fourteen thousand British regulars and Hessian mercenaries in New York City."

As grim as Colonel Learned had ever seen him, Schuyler pointed to the map and responded, "Washington is thoroughly familiar with the threat Howe's army presents. This is a time for hard decisions and a fine balance of risks. His victories at Trenton and Princeton prove that Washington can think out of an impossible situation."

"Burgoyne?"

"Burgoyne remains my problem. Without any information revealing the fate and location of St. Clair and his garrison, I have one last card to play against Gentleman Johnny Burgoyne."

***

"Colonel Learned. General Schuyler told me you wanted to see me."

Learned saw a young man of average height with a lean, wiry build wearing a weather-worn uniform of a continental private and thigh-high leather riding boots. Motioning him to enter his office, the boy stood silently in front of his desk.

"Are you Tom O'Brien?"

"Yes, Colonel."

"Do you know where Middlebrook, New Jersey, is?"

"Yes, Colonel."

"What is the quickest way to reach there carrying only a dispatch?"

"Canoe down the Hudson to Newberg, New York, and horseback to Middlebrook."

"Where do you get the horse?"

"My father's company, O'Brien Freighting, has a stable and warehouse in Newberg."

"Here is a dispatch from General Schuyler to General Washington. Do you have a safe-conduct pass should you encounter any continental checkpoints and patrols?"

"Yes, Sir."

"Fort Ticonderoga has been captured. The fate of the garrison is unknown. The British army is marching upon Albany. General Washington must be informed, and the Northern Army must be reinforced as soon as possible. Do you have any questions?"

"No, sir."

"Godspeed, son."

CHAPTER FOUR
Skenesboro

British Headquarters
Senior Officers' Call
Skenesboro, New York
July 9th

Lieutenant-General Burgoyne stood at the head of a polished walnut conference table in the wood-paneled office of Philip Skene, the British Governor of Crown Point and founder of Skenesboro. Seated around the table were Burgoyne's senior commanders and Governor Skene quietly discussing the bloodless capture of Ticonderoga, the Gibraltar of the Americas.

Dressed in a tailored, newly pressed uniform wearing the light blue sash identifying him as Commanding General of the army, Burgoyne listened delightedly to his senior officers praising his plan and execution. His gaze sweeping the room, he noticed Riedesel and his regimental commanders sitting silently at the far end of the table, aloof from the celebration.

His mood sobering, Burgoyne rapped the knuckles of his right hand on the tabletop quieting the room to silence. Then, summarizing the first ten days of the campaign, he enthusiastically concluded, "The Crown is once again in possession of Ticonderoga, two hundred batteaux, one hundred cannons, and tons of munitions and food. General Fraser has killed or captured the chosen men of the garrison, suffering only nominal casualties. I have invited Governor Skene to attend this meeting to call upon his knowledge of the local area. Gentlemen, I wish to hear advice as to how to proceed. General Fraser, I will start with you."

Standing up from his chair, Fraser said, "I recommend that we take advantage of the rebels' panic and immediately sail my advance corps down Lake George to capture Fort George and Fort Edward. The army would follow by batteaux convoys. Fort Edward is fifty miles from Albany and would be ours before Schuyler and Washington could organize a continental force to oppose us."

General Burgoyne exclaimed, "Well said, General. When I commanded light cavalry, those would have been my exact words. I must consciously suppress my aggressive spirit and temper my judgment for what is best for the campaign. We have the rebels on the run, but our success has necessarily weakened the army by garrisoning Fort Ticonderoga with nine hundred men to secure our lines of communications, supplies, and reinforcements to Quebec. While this command's first victory came at a cost, your destruction of the garrison's rearguard at Hubbardton has weakened the rebels.

"We must remember that until General Howe's army joins us in Albany, we rely primarily on loyalist militia for reinforcement. General St. Ledger and his army cannot be counted upon until he crosses Lake Ontario and defeats the rebels along the Mohawk River west of Albany. Governor Skene, would you give us your opinion on how best to proceed."

In his early fifties, Philip Skene, a Scotsman, enlisted in the British army fighting in Europe and India before arriving in North America in 1756. He was wounded in the British attack on Fort Ticonderoga during the French and Indian War. Skene retired in New York, purchasing land at the head of Lake Champlain. In 1765 Skene obtained a royal patent for thirty-four thousand acres and founded Skenesboro, a tenant settlement of thirty families. Skene sold his commission in 1769 to build roads, mills, storehouses, and batteaux. With the commencement of the rebellion, Skene's loyalty was questioned by the rebel government. He fled to England, where he used his political influence to support the launch of General Burgoyne's expedition, which he joined when it sailed from England.

Standing and remaining in place at the table, Skene began, "Gentlemen, the rebels have stripped the horses and oxen from the area. The stock animals brought from Quebec are insufficient to transport the supplies, boats, artillery, and wagons across the portage of several miles from Fort Ticonderoga to Lake George. It is over thirty miles to the south end of Lake George and the second portage of ten miles to the Hudson River and Fort Edward. It is only twenty miles from Skenesboro to Fort Edward. I have built roads from Skenesboro to Bennington and Salem. With my engineers and the manpower of this command, it will be far faster to build a road to Fort Edward for passage by the main army. The artillery and supplies may be transported separately by batteaux down Lake George."

General Philips shook his head slightly and said, "I agree with Fraser. Supplemented by the captured batteaux, our fleet can immediately carry General Fraser's and General Riedesel's advance corps down Lake George in advance of the artillery and supplies. Those men will march the portages and do not require oxen or horses. Their capture of Fort George and Fort Edward will secure our next bases of operations. This will require a fraction of the time of building a road through twenty miles of trackless forest. With respect, the obvious economic value to Governor Skene's lumber and milling business of a road from Skenesboro to Fort Edward compels me to question the impartiality of his recommendation."

Sharing a brief look of annoyance with Skene during General Philip's challenge to the proposed road, Burgoyne smoothly regained his poise and said, "Governor Skene, thank you for your hospitality, advice, and assistance. General Fraser shall supervise the army's draft horses and wagons to carry the army's artillery, reserve munitions, tentage, and supplies across the portage to the La Chute River and by the captured batteaux to Lake George. The batteaux convoy will sail down Lake George carrying the horses to transport the equipment across the portage to the Hudson River. Tomorrow General Philip and the army engineers shall meet with Governor Skene to survey the road to Fort Edward. Once the route has been determined, the work begins. I expect this army shall complete the road and arrive in Fort Edward well in advance of the arrival of the batteaux convoy!"

***

Burgoyne sat with Skene at the conference table after the departure of his officers. Tapping his fingers on the table, he gazed silently at Skene for several minutes before stating, "Governor, Philips, and Fraser made a strong case for proceeding immediately by batteaux convoy instead of building your road."

Unfazed, Skene replied, "When we discussed an ownership interest in my company in London, I explained the obvious commercial benefits of a road from Skenesboro to Fort Edward and access the Hudson River. Nothing has changed."

Leaning forward in his chair, Burgoyne's eyes bore into Skene's. The General grated, "I now possess the opportunity to win the King's favor by capturing Albany in a matter of days by following my senior commanders' recommendations."

Fearlessly meeting Burgoyne's eyes, Skene re-filled the General's glass with wine and replied, "There are inadequate batteaux, horses, and oxen to timely transport your entire army any faster than building a twenty-mile road directly to Fort Edward. I have built roads through the same terrain, and your infantry shall be waiting in Fort Edward for the arrival of the batteaux convoy transporting your artillery and munitions."

Smiling in relief, Burgoyne sipped his wine and said, "I shall hold you to that Governor."

Howe's Headquarters
New York City, July 13th

It was a rare occasion when General William Howe, and his second in command, General Henry Clinton, discussed a subject upon which both were of a like opinion – Burgoyne's unworthiness to command an army.

Comfortably residing in a confiscated mansion on Queen Street, the men sat in the wainscoted parlor upon overstuffed chairs, amicably drinking port in their after-dinner jackets. Chuckling softly, Howe handed a dispatch to Clinton and said, "I know you are friendly with Burgoyne, but you must read his July 11th dispatch crowing about his capture of Fort Ticonderoga. Burgoyne recites an endless inventory of every pot, ladle, and blanket captured. A raw ensign could have captured Ticonderoga. The fort was defenseless against an attack from Quebec. General Philips deserves the credit for the victory, not Gentleman Johnny! Philips succeeded in mounting a cannon on a mountain overlooking the fort. It was simply Boston in reverse. Even "Earl" St. Clair recognized it was suicide to stay and fight."

Clinton nodded his agreement that the capture of Ticonderoga was not a notable military victory. His friend Burgoyne had been fortunate that he had not been subject to harsh criticism. Fraser and his men would have been killed, and the bridge of boats sunk but for the drunken rebels who failed to fire the shore battery's cannons. Clinton could not suppress his resentment of Burgoyne's unwarranted luck and brood. *Burgoyne's command should have been mine as the senior General in the colonies after Howe.*

Lighting a cigar, Howe continued, "You know I recommended you for the command. The King's decision was strongly influenced by Burgoyne's father-in-law, the Earl of Derby. I simply cannot understand how a man can elope with a peer's daughter and receive the Crown's favor!"

Clinton was aware of the reason, as did most English social and military establishments. The grandchild produced from the union and the Earl's daughter's loyal support for his dashing friend had convinced Derby to acknowledge the reality of the situation.

Unaffected by Clinton's silence, which was quite welcome, Howe broached the reason for this rare private meeting. "I am relying upon this dispatch of his resounding success as the basis of my decision not to march my army north to join Burgoyne. Instead, I intend to proceed by sea to capture Philadelphia, the rebel capital, and bag the entire Congress of traitors for presentation to his Majesty for justice."

Clinton anticipated that Howe had no intention of supporting Burgoyne. Nevertheless, he was shocked that the Crown had agreed to lose the opportunity of splitting New England from the South by not simply marching half the garrison north, trapping the rebels between two British armies. Leaning forward in his chair, Clinton frowned and asked, "General, New York City, is far more important than Philadelphia. You would risk its loss to Washington's forces?"

Howe gestured his glass toward Clinton and said dismissively, "Of course not. I am leaving you in command." Smirking, Howe mused, "I am confident that those traitors' screams of terror will compel Washington to attempt to defend Philadelphia." Howe's face hardened, leaning toward Clinton, and he grated, "Once Washington and his rag-tag army are out in the open, I shall destroy it! No one shall remember the embarrassment of Trenton and Princeton."

On July 17, 1777, Burgoyne received a dispatch informing him of General Howe's intentions which read as follows. "By advancing on Philadelphia, I expect to be attacked by Washington, but should he go northward instead, you can keep him at bay until I return to relieve you."

On July 23rd, Howe sailed from New York harbor with his army of fifteen thousand regulars.

Middlebrook, New Jersey
Camp of Rifle's Regiment, July 13th

In his early forties, Colonel Daniel Morgan sat on a stool in front of his tent, looking across the flames of his small campfire at the shadowed face of his finest marksman Tim Murphy. Both men wore the off-white buckskin hunting shirt and breeches uniform of the Continental Rifle Corps.

Morgan served the cause of independence as a senior commander in the invasion of Quebec. He was captured and imprisoned after the failure to capture Quebec City. Exchanged in January 1777, he returned to the army, where General Washington promoted him to Colonel to command an elite corps of riflemen, which Morgan personally recruited.

In his mid-twenties, Murphy was a brawny six-footer, raised on the frontier, who enjoyed the confidence of his solitary commander borne of mutual respect and ferocity in combat.

Inviting Murphy to his fire, Morgan asked, "Tim, what's the kid's name who's been your shadow? Last year, I saw him in that hellish battle in the snow outside Quebec."

"His name is Tom O'Brien, Colonel. He carried a message from General Schuyler to General Washington requesting reinforcements. I invited him to join my camp while he waited for Washington's reply."

"I noticed him during the siege of Quebec City. He could not have weighed more than one hundred pounds soaking wet."

"He's grown and filled out in the two years since the siege of Quebec. Two of the boys challenged Tom to wrestle. He knocked the first one out. The second submitted rather than having his arm broken."

"You have me interested, Murphy. He still looks like a kid. Do you think he's worthy of becoming a Rifle?"

"Well, Colonel, you boys lost that fight in Quebec. Montgomery killed, Arnold wounded, and you and the others captured."

"Murphy, if you weren't the best shot in the regiment, I might take serious exception to that last remark," snarled Morgan rising to his feet and closing his hands into fists.

Murphy stammered, rising and retreating from the fire, "Colonel, my point is the boy's a survivor. I have been working with him, and his shooting is as good as anyone in the regiment. His woodcraft is superior to mine."

Crossing his arms and leaning against a tree, Morgan said, "That's what's bothering me. Depending on how he answers my questions, I may give your shadow some more time in camp."

In response to the Colonel's nod, Murphy gestured to the object of the discussion over to the fire. The boy looked sixteen but possessed the sinewy look of the warriors Morgan and his cousin Daniel Boone had fought while serving as civilian teamsters during the French and Indian War.

"Have I seen you before, O'Brien?"

"Yes, Colonel. I was with Arnold and Montgomery outside Quebec."

"Were you captured?"

"No, I fell in with some Green Mountain boys. We got out in that snowstorm before the British could cut us off."

"You got lucky, O'Brien."

"Yes, sir."

"You carry a tomahawk. I don't recognize the design."

"It is Oneida. I received it from my godfather, Tehawenkaragwen Han Yery, an Oneida sachem of the wolf clan. I am a blood brother to his sons, Paulus and Cornelius. We were taught to read and write by the Reverend Samuel Kirkland, missionary to the Oneida."

"O'Brien, the Oneida is one of the member tribes of Six Nations, allies of the British."

"The Six Nations ratified the pledge of neutrality before Independence was declared. Recently there was a Great Council when all the Nations except the Oneida and Tuscarora joined the British. To my knowledge, the Oneida have allied with us in this war."

"All right, Murphy, I am satisfied. What are you teaching him?"

"The mixture of measures of gun powder propositional to the weight of the ammunition to maximize distance and accuracy."

"Well, O'Brien, you must be worth the trouble. Murphy is my best. You are welcome to join the Rifles if you are a mind.'

"Thanks, Colonel. If I had a choice, I would be proud to join your outfit. I have been ordered by General Washington to immediately return to General Schuyler's headquarters because of my familiarity with the land between Albany and Fort Ticonderoga."

"What's General Schuyler's concern?"

"I'm not sure, Colonel. British armies were poised at the opposite ends of the Hudson River for the first time in the war. General Schuyler's certain the enemy will invade New York from Quebec. He is considering delaying their advance from Quebec until reinforcements reach Albany."

Morgan nodded and said, "That makes sense to me, but British generals have been known to make mistakes. One of them sentenced me to four hundred ninety-nine leashes because of my unwillingness to be bullied by a lobsterback officer. The bastards expected me to die, and I didn't. Before I am done, the British will pay for each of the scars on my back. Good luck, O'Brien. If there's trouble, the Rifles will be there. Remember what Murphy taught you and keep your powder dry."

"Murphy, the next time I see O'Brien, it is your responsibility that he is in a Rifle's uniform. O'Brien, you are one of us when General Schuyler releases you from his service."

"That's smart, Colonel. Enlist him before someone else does," volunteered Murphy.

"I glad you agree, Murphy," scoffed Morgan.

"Thanks, Colonel. I am proud to be a member of the Rifles."

Fort Edward
Commanding Officer's Office
July 12th

"General St. Clair, you have saved three thousand men from capture by the British. Your leadership has made it possible to defend Albany," repeated Philip Schuyler for the third time to an exhausted and despondent Arthur St. Clair.

St. Clair sat slumped in a chair, blankly staring at the floor, his hand wrapped around an untouched glass of whiskey Schuyler had poured for him a half-hour before.

Standing beside the bedraggled man, Schuyler placed a hand on his shoulder and said softly, "General St. Clair."

Lifting his head to look into Schuyler's eyes, St. Clair mumbled, "I ordered the Gibraltar of the Americas abandoned without a shot fired!"

Relieved that St. Clair had become responsive but disturbed by the tears in the eyes of the veteran commander, Schuyler asserted, "We talked about the possible necessity to abandon Ticonderoga when I assigned you to the command. The French built the fort to defend Quebec. Ticonderoga required a garrison of ten thousand men to defend against an attack from Quebec."

"I failed to even bloody the British. My honor is lost."

"You saved your men. General Nathaniel Greene failed to evacuate the continentals garrisoning Fort Washington, and those men are now wasting away on British prison hulks moored in New York harbor. Once the British installed a cannon on Mount Defiance, your position was untenable."

"I should have garrisoned troops on Mount Defiance to prevent that," snarled St. Clair.

"Ticonderoga was captured in 1775. Since then, no commander or military engineer has seen the need to take such precautions because of the sheerness of the slope. General Gates, the most recent commander, saw no need. You commanded the fort only three weeks before the British arrived."

"I will face a court-martial nonetheless."

"Yes. Congress shall insist. I shall appear at those proceeding as your commanding officer and testify in your defense. I owe you a debt for the three thousand men you lead to safety. Those men will defend the people against the invading British and their Ottawa and Abenaki allies. Now finish your whiskey and join me for dinner with the fort's officers to inform them of your heroic march, reinforcing the defenses of Albany."

Fort Edward
Commanding Officer's Office
July 13th

"Major, please show Mr. O'Brien in." As Tom entered the office, General Schuyler recognized the meticulously maintained fringed hunting shirt and buckskin leggings of Colonel Morgan's Rifles Corp, which Brian's son wore like a second skin. *The boy looks tired but ready for a new challenge*, Schuyler thought. Motioning Tom to sit in a chair in front of his desk Schuyler said, "My adjutant has informed me of your report. Well done, Tom."

Slowly settling himself into the ornate chair, Tom replied, "Burgoyne's capture of Fort Ticonderoga did not surprise General

Washington. He was prepared to reinforce the Northern Army. Morgan's Rifles and two regiments of continentals are marching from Middlebrook, New Jersey, within the week."

"When did you become a member of the Rifles?"

"I met the Colonel when delivering your dispatches to General Washington's camp. My hunting skills and marksmanship impressed him. The Colonel invited me to join his command when the fighting started. He made me a member of the Rifles on detached duty to you."

"Middlebrook is over two hundred miles from here. I must have time for those reinforcements to arrive. I plan to delay the British, and you must play a critical role."

General Schuyler called out to his adjutant, "Major Smith, please come in with Paul and Colonel Kosciuszko to join us at the map table."

Complying, the men found places around the table while Schuyler unfolded a map depicting the territory north to Quebec. Other than the General's adjutant, the men were unknown to Tom.

Tom recognized the embroidered dark green robe worn by the warrior identified as Paul as distinctive of a Mohican of Stillwater, New York. The soldier, introduced as Colonel Kosciuszko, was a tall, powerfully built man, clean-shaven, wearing a tailored uniform of a foreign military. From Tom's experience at Washington's headquarters, he surmised that Kosciuszko was one of the European specialists recruited by Benjamin Franklin as the Congress' ambassador to France.

"Gentlemen, Colonel Kosciuszko is a military engineer assigned to the Northern Department by General Washington." Nodding toward Kosciuszko, Schuyler continued, "The Colonel designed and oversaw the construction of the fortifications at West Point, which have so far blocked the British advance up the Hudson River from New York City."

Colonel Kosciuszko politely nodded to the assembled men and asked in unaccented English, "How can I be of service?"

In response, Schuyler introduced Tom and said, "Paul was a scout assigned to Fort Ticonderoga. When the fort's garrison retreated, he stayed in the vicinity to observe the British advance south."

Paul raised a hand to the other men with the quiet dignity of his ancestry, gestured toward the map on the table, and said, "General

Burgoyne is building a road from Skenesboro, New York, to Fort Edward."

Schuyler nodded his thanks to Paul and continued the briefing, "Gentlemen, this information cost the life of Paul's brother killed by Burgoyne's Ottawa scouts."

"James gave his life to protect the people of the Hudson Valley from invaders," Paul added solemnly.

Schuyler said to the group, "The British have made a mistake. Burgoyne has chosen to build a twenty-mile road through a trackless forest instead of sailing unopposed down Lake George and the Hudson River to Fort Edward. Colonel Kosciuszko, your mission is to delay the completion of that road. My adjutant Major Smith has the authority to muster the local militia to supply any required labor. Mr. O'Brien was raised on the frontier hunting and trapping the area Burgoyne's road must transverse to reach Fort Edward."

Colonel Kosciuszko, who had been listening without expression, broke into a smile. Approaching each man, he vigorously shook their hands before turning to face Schuyler, saying, "You have provided me with the perfect staff to fulfill this mission! We begin tomorrow."

British Field Headquarters
Senior Officers' Call
Burgoyne's Road, July 17th

Standing on a raised platform of wooden planks placed upon closely grouped recently hewed tree stumps, General Burgoyne sweated in full uniform, holding a dispatch. Raising it toward the mob of partially dressed and filthy officers milling among scores of fallen trees and piles of cleared brush, Burgoyne verbalized its contents.

"Gentlemen, General Howe has informed me of his intentions to draw Washington south by a seaborne attack upon Philadelphia. I am convinced Washington shall march his army to defend Congress in Philadelphia and leave Albany to fend for itself.

"My friend General Clinton is now in command of the garrison in New York City, expecting reinforcements from England. In separate correspondence, General Clinton has assured me he shall capture the rebel forts on the Hudson River to aid in our campaign to seize complete control of the Hudson River."

Standing together in the foremost rank, General Phillips and General Fraser exchanged glances of surprise and concern. Phillips whispered to Fraser, "Howe has abandoned us in this wildness without hope of reinforcement or resupply!"

Oblivious to his senior officers' reactions, Burgoyne continued addressing the assembly, "In light of the current circumstances. I have decided to employ our Ottawa and Abenaki allies to suppress the local population of the Hudson River Valley. Without the militia, Schuyler is limited to the demoralized regiments of continentals salvaged from the garrison of Fort Ticonderoga. More than a thousand continentals can't be left after General Fraser's destruction of the three continental regiments of St. Clair's rearguard in our victory at Hubbardton."

Fraser and his officers knew the losses suffered by his irreplaceable light infantry and grenadier battalions inflicted by the rebels and ignored Burgoyne's reference to Hubbardton as a victory.

Surprised by Fraser's silence in response to his compliment, Burgoyne's smile slipped from his face and, clenching his fists, snapped, "Only a few miles stand between us and the capture of Albany. I expect this road to be completed within the next five days!"

Masking his emotions, Fraser glanced at Philips to confirm the possibility of the army's engineers accomplishing such a task. He saw the man who had succeeded in placing a cannon on a mountaintop frown in disbelief.

Burgoyne's Road
British Army Officers' Call
South of Senesboro, New York
July 22nd

The officers of the finest British army sent to the colonies gathered impotently as their progress remained blocked by a swollen, fast-moving river, the product of the rebels' redirection of local streams. Stripped to their filthy and sweat-stained shirts and uniform breeches, they watched two scores of engineers frantically building a bridge.

Joined by Lieutenant-General Burgoyne, similarly shorn of his uniform coat by the forest's oppressive humidity, Burgoyne wore only his light blue sash of the army's Commanding General over his linen shirt and breeches. Staring at his officers in silence, Burgoyne grew steadily more frustrated. He bitterly thought *my victories at Crown Point and Fort Ticonderoga had been eroded by this unacceptable delay in completing a mere twenty-mile-long road.*

"Gentlemen, a single mile of road is built per day! Eight thousand men supervised by the finest engineers in the world. There is no rebel army to defend Albany. Empty forest stands between us and the victory the King has demanded."

Red-faced Brigadier General Fraser, commander of the advance guard, sputtered, "General, the rebels have turned the surveyed route to Fort Edward into a swamp."

Burgoyne ignored Fraser, nodded to his adjutant, and said, "Captain, please summon St. Luc."

As Chevalier St. Luc de La Corne entered the clearing and stood beside Burgoyne, an involuntary wave of hostility radiated from the British officers. These men had all lost relatives and friends in ambushes planned and executed by St. Luc during the French and Indian War. The French Crown had awarded him medals for committing those atrocious acts, which he proudly displayed on his uniform jacket.

"Chevalier, our progress is being impeded by rebel farmers felling trees and damming creeks. You and your Ottawa warriors are to clear those woods of every living soul."

St. Luc performed a slight bow and smiled at the assembly. Placing his hands behind his back and visibly relaxing his posture, he met the hostile glares with a calm demeanor waiting for Burgoyne to continue. His thirty-year business relationship with the Ottawa had conditioned St. Luc with the stamina and strength of a man half his age and gave him a fur trade monopoly. He had become one of the wealthiest men in Quebec.

Taking a sheet of parchment from his adjutant, Burgoyne handed it to General Fraser and continued, "Your scouts are to post this proclamation in every settlement in advance of our line of march.

General, please read it aloud."

Using his battlefield voice, Fraser complied. "I have but to stretch out my hand with the five hundred Ottawa and Abenaki warriors under my command. As messengers of his Majesty's justice and wrath will rain down devastation, famine, and every concomitant horror on all who oppose us."

Fraser, a tough and battle-hardened highlander, looked up from the parchment and, seeing his officers' shocked expressions, questioned his commander. "General, this may be interpreted as being directed at women and children, in addition to rebel combatants."

Smiling for the first time, Burgoyne replied, "I have spoken at length to the Chevalier and explained his Majesty's desire to employ the warriors to terrorize the rebels within the parameters of common decency. I have every confidence in him. Chevalier, you have your orders. All further interference with the construction of my road to Fort Edward is to be purged."

St. Luc bowed and replied, "If your King desires terror, I shall not disappoint him."

***

Unaware of the wave of death just unleashed by Burgoyne, five miles south, Tom walked through scores of men, women, and teenage children chopping trees, digging ditches, carrying baskets of food and pails of water deep in the Adirondack Mountains of northern New York. He was awed by the tapestry of ceaseless motion united in a common cause directed by the man he had come to see.

In his shirt sleeves, breeches, and black riding boots, Colonel Kosciuszko explained to a group of local militia leaders where to direct their people and what tasks each group would perform.

Nearby, Major Smith studied a map tacked up on a tree. Smith stoically wore his continental wool uniform with the collar buttoned despite the thick humidity of the forest.

Tom was thankful that the Rifles wore the loose-fitting deerskin hunting shirt and leggings in this oppressive humidity. Tom stood silently until Kosciuszko had finished conveying his instructions and said, "Colonel, the Mohican scouts observed a war party of Ottawa warriors leaving Burgoyne's camp."

Major Smith pointed down at the map and said, "This morning, Captain Younger's rangers found the bodies of one of our work crews who had been damming streams several miles north. They had been scalped. Younger had to threaten his men with court-martial to compel them to return to camp instead of immediately tracking and killing those responsible."

"Major, what is the militia's reaction?" Kosciuszko asked.

"Scared, Colonel. Unless we can stop that war party, they will disperse to protect their families."

"Tom, do you have a recommendation?"

"Colonel, I have spoken to Paul. The Mohican and Ottawa are ancient enemies. We have agreed that a successful ambush of the Ottawa may give us the time to finish the spoliation of the land between the British army and Fort Edward."

Looking at the map, Smith asked, "Has an ambush site been chosen?"

Tom placed his finger on the map and answered, "Yes, a mile north. We must leave before the war party passes through that point."

Colonel Kosciuszko shook his head, saying, "I need you to scout and supervise the work crews."

"Colonel, I have already scouted the area and prepared this map." He handed Kosciuszko a hand-drawn sketch. "I have marked where best to drop the trees and dam the streams."

Studying the drawing for several minutes and aligning it to Major Smith's map of the surrounding terrain, Kosciuszko said, "Excellent work. Good luck. Don't get yourself killed. This war is not done with us yet."

Burgoyne's Road
Continental Army, July 22nd

After Tom and the ambush party departed, Kosciuszko recalled the militia leaders and asked them to gather their people to receive important news.

Less than an hour later, with the militia and their families surrounding him, Colonel Kosciuszko informed the people of their neighbors' deaths and the current situation they faced.

"Your work has frustrated a British army of thousands. Burgoyne has retaliated by sending the King's Ottawa warriors to kill us. I will not let that happen. The rangers and Mohicans have left camp to kill the raiders."

"Is Tom O'Brien with them?" asked one of the militia leaders, a burly, brown-faced, grizzled farmer who had brought his wife and children to the work site two days before.

Smiling, Kosciuszko replied, "He's taking the first shot."

"That is good enough for me. Let's get back to work. If the Ottawa breakthrough, we are better off fighting them together than separately on our farms."

***

While Colonel Kosciuszko addressed the militia, Major Smith met with the ambush party half a mile north of the work site in an overgrown grove of oak trees. The party consisted of Captain Younger's rangers dressed in the hunting shirts of the Rifle regiments and Paul's kilted Mohican warriors, their chests painted black and their faces green. Major Smith stood in front of the men sitting in a half-circle on the ground.

"The Colonel has chosen you to stop the Ottawa raids on our work parties. Tom, please continue the briefing."

Tom took Major Smith's place and said, "The Ottawa and Abenaki are known to rely for their morale and aggressiveness upon their chosen leader. The raid leader is always in a trailing position behind the scouts and advance party of veteran warriors for his protection. Paul, would you carry on."

Paul rose and said, "I have fought the Ottawa. The raid leader will be at least several hundred yards behind the scouts. Tom and I have chosen the ambush site with a large clearing for Tom to shoot the leader before the scouts reach our position."

"Thank you, Paul," Tom said. "We do not know the size of the war party. There will be only twenty of us. I had asked you to bring a musket and your rifles to double our firepower." As one, the men lifted a musket in response, and Tom's chuckle was joined by the group releasing the men's tension. Tom concluded, his demeanor sobered, "Time is of the essence, so we will proceed to the ambush site. Major Smith will return to report to the Colonel."

***

Several hours later, hidden in a hollow above the ambush site, Tom and the others watched and waited silently. Three hundred yards in length, the clearing was bordered by a sheer cliff face to the west and flooded woods to the east.

As the sounds of the forest died away to silence, a trio of Ottawa scouts materialized from the forest. Their faces, painted red and wearing only deerskin kilts, moved individually in short runs across the clearing, randomly zigzagging or falling flat. Lightly armed with spears and belted knives or tomahawks, their identity as veteran raiders became apparent from the speed of their choreographed advance.

Paul had warned the ambush party that the Ottawa employed this tactic to draw fire. He stressed that Tom must take the first shot. As the main body of the war party began to lope from the woods into the clearing, it numbered over thirty warriors. Twice what Paul had anticipated. Armed with either muskets or rifles, the Ottawa raiders possessed superior numbers and firepower to Tom's party.

"Now, what do we do?" Captain Younger whispered.

Staring at the forest's perimeter, Tom caught sight of a European in the green leather uniform of the British rangers emerging into the clearing. He was accompanied by half a dozen warriors wearing deerskin leggings and silver officer gorgets.

Captain Younger whispered, "My God, it's St. Luc! I recognized him from my service on the frontier."

Focusing on the apparent raid leader until he advanced within two hundred fifty yards, Tom let his breath out slowly, squeezed the trigger, and saw his target somersault to the ground. Tom dropped his rifle in one continuance motion, turned on his side, picked up his musket, and fired a second time, killing an Ottawa scout throwing a tomahawk.

Simultaneously with Tom's second shot, the rangers and Mohicans fired their rifles, cutting down the remaining scouts and several of the leading warriors of the main band.

As the rangers reached for their muskets and Tom began to reload his, the surviving Ottawa let out a murderous howl and exploded into a dead run toward the powder smoke. Tom knew that his command would be overwhelmed once his men fired their muskets, taking his tomahawk from his belt.

A shrill whistle suddenly pierced the war cries of the Ottawa.

Tom looked on in amazement as the charging warriors skidded to a stop, screamed in rage, turned as one, and ran back to the forest from which they had emerged.

Tom raised his hand, signaling his men not to fire their muskets. Putting his primed musket aside, Tom began reloading his rifle. Following his example, each man completed the task and silently lifted his hand, signifying readiness to resume combat.

Captain Younger leaned toward Tom and whispered, "What the hell just happened?"

Tom sighed and replied, "When you identified St. Luc, my first reaction was to avenge all the deaths he has caused. The size of the Ottawa war party he led saved his life. I shattered St. Luc's right knee preventing him from leading the raid. He shall bleed to death without immediate medical care. That was his whistle which called off the attack."

"If we had fired our muskets, the warriors would have ignored St. Luc and attacked anyway," Captain Younger said.

Tom and Paul nodded.

"That was my thought, too," Tom added. "And by not firing, the Ottawa cannot be certain of our exact numbers. The raids will cease until a new raid leader is chosen. Once Burgoyne's Road reaches this position, the British will be further delayed by thoroughly scouting the area to determine whether the ambush is still in place. Paul, send your scouts out to be certain the Ottawa is gone."

Two hours had passed when the Mohican scouts returned and

reported no enemy within a mile of the ambush site. Removing all traces of their occupation from the hollow, Tom and his men returned to Colonel Kosciuszko's camp.

***

Burgoyne's warriors failed to eliminate the rebel's interference. The British army required twenty-four days to complete the road to Fort Edward. General Washington's reinforcements arrived in time to join in defense of Albany.

Burgoyne's Abenaki and Ottawa warriors descended upon the Hudson Valley, unleashing a reign of death and destruction upon the entire civilian population without regard to gender, age, or political affiliation.

On July 27, 1777, Jane McCrea, a young woman affianced to a loyalist officer, was slain and scalped in the vicinity of Fort Edward by warriors carrying out the campaign of terror in advance of Burgoyne's army. News of McCrea's murder was reported in newspapers throughout the region, and the militia turned out in thousands to avenge her death.

When the murderers of McCrea were identified, General Burgoyne chose not to punish them. His reliance on their scouting outweighed justice for a murdered girl.

Despite Burgoyne's attempted appeasement, most Ottawa and Abenaki warriors abandoned the British soon after returning to Quebec with their loot and captives.

CHAPTER FIVE
Bennington

General Court of New Hampshire
Exeter, July 17th

President of the General Court of New Hampshire, John Langdon, rapped his gavel several times upon the pastor's pulpit calling the attending members to order. Langdon addressed the assembly in the pews in the town's meeting house, whose primary purpose was a house of worship.

"I have called this emergency meeting to respond to an urgent request for military support from Vermont's Committee of Safety. Their sole military protection from the British invasion of Quebec is Colonel Seth Warner's Green Mountain Continentals. After the Battle of Hubbardton, Warner's command was reduced to only one hundred men. Should we grant them aid?"

In response to the summons, William Martin, Vice President of the Assembly, had come armed directly from working his fields. Standing but remaining in his place in the pews, Martin replied, "I have no issue with the settlers of the New Hampshire Grants choosing to form their own state, Vermont, instead of remaining part of ours. I vote to help them!" Receiving applause from the other members, he continued, "But John, we can barely afford to keep General Poor's New Hampshire brigade of continentals in the field. Where's the money going to come from to aid Vermont?"

John Langdon leaned forward and replied firmly, "Bill, the farmers from the New Hampshire Grants were with us at Concord and Lexington. Those men formed the Green Mountain regiment, and their leader Ethan Allen captured Fort Ticonderoga. We have been safe and allowed to farm in peace for two years. The British have brought hundreds of Ottawa and Abenaki who don't care whom they're killing or whether the farms they burn are in New Hampshire or Vermont!"

The Vice President of the Assembly voiced the harsh truth in reply. "John, we agree with you, but New Hampshire has no money!"

To signify his recognition of the facts, President Langdon replied in a conversational tone, "Bill is correct. However, as you gentlemen remind me on occasion, I am a wealthy man by the grace of God's bounty." He received the expected chuckles from his friends and neighbors. "I will finance the provisioning and equipping of a militia brigade to assist our neighbors in repulsing Burgoyne."

After the applause died, President Langdon continued, "In my opinion, there is only one man we all trust to protect our families and property from the ravages of the invaders. I propose that the General Court unanimously commission John Stark as a General of the New Hampshire militia to command the brigade."

After a resounding "Aye," the members passed a resolution confirming Stark's commission and authorizing him to raise a force of fifteen hundred men.

Reducing the commission and authorization to parchment, signed by the attending members, Langdon rolled it up, placed it in a message cylinder, and said, "I will personally deliver this to General Stark since time is of the essence. Bill, please arrange for messengers to advise the militia captains of the General Court's decision to muster their men."

Deerfield, New Hampshire
July 18th

John Langdon rode into the yard of the Stark farm, pleased to have waited until the following morning to escape the heat of the day. Invigorated by his unaccustomed role of courier, Langdon gazed about, impressed by the fastidious condition of the modest home, barns, and corral, praying to find its owner in a good mood.

"John Langdon. If you are here to order me to allow that thief Benjamin Lincoln to steal the militiamen I have trained like he stole my commission as a continental General, get off my land!"

Dismounting from his horse and tying the reins to a fence post, John thought, *oh, well,* and said, "It is news to me that General Lincoln is in New Hampshire. Colonel Stark, New Hampshire, is in danger. I offer you the General Court's appointment to recruit and command a militia brigade. You are authorized to muster and deploy fifteen hundred men in the field as soon as possible."

Frowning, John Stark sneered, "Langdon, who has the money to pay for that?"

Smiling, Langdon replied, "I do. May I trouble you for a glass of water before you throw me off your property?"

Not known for his humor, Langston saw Stark smother a smile and heard his reply, "Come take a seat on the porch for a glass of rum while I read what the General Court has to say."

While Stark read his appointment, Langston took the opportunity to observe this accomplished but combative man. A French and Indian war veteran, Stark served as an elite Roger's Rangers officer. An acknowledged expert in frontier warfare, Stark had been commissioned a Colonel in the Continental Army and fought with distinction at the Battles of Breed's Hill and Trenton. When Congress promoted Colonel Benjamin Lincoln to General, and not him, Stark resigned his continental commission. Deeply disappointed and embittered that his service and success in the field had not been recognized, Stark had remained aloof from the war.

"Before I accept, I want it understood that my militia brigade is outside the Continental chain of command and authority of Congress," demanded Stark.

His musing interrupted, Langdon looked into the skeletal face of Stark, which reflected the trials he had overcome in his forty-nine years, tall, gaunt, but radiating pulsating aggression belaying his frail appearance. Langdon understood why Major Rodgers had made him his senior captain and replied, "Agreed."

"Has the General Court called out the militia?"

"Yes. I sent out the summons to all the captains."

Once the militia learned of the brigade's formation and Stark's appointment as its commander, a flood of volunteers enabled him to organize and provision the authorized four battalions in a mere six days.

Few in the brigade had formal military training. The majority were farmers and townspeople from Vermont and New Hampshire who reported wearing their work clothes and carrying their personal weapons to the muster. Despite appearances, many were veterans who had followed Stark during the French and Indian War and fought under his command after independence. Stark's reputation as a former ranger resulted in his further recruitment of two hundred Vermont rangers.

General Stark marched his command a hundred and twenty miles to Manchester, Vermont, to join the Green Mountain regiment and confer with Colonel Warner on how best to confront Burgoyne.

Continental Army Headquarters
Northern Department
Albany, New York, August 1st

Ushering Tom O'Brien into his office, General Schuyler gestured to a Continental Major General sitting in front of the desk and said, "Tom, I want to introduce General Benjamin Lincoln. General Washington assigned him to the Northern Department to recruit militia in Vermont. Tom is Brian O'Brien's son, the Northern Department's military teamster. He is well known in the territory where you intend to recruit. I recommend him as a guide and escort for this mission."

Lincoln was in his mid-forties, a portly but energetic man who had followed his father into local politics. Active in the Massachusetts militia for twenty years before Independence, he was promoted to General in the continental army soon after its declaration. "Well, Tom, General Schuyler has briefed me on your fine work delaying Burgoyne's advance. Your Rifle's uniform tells me you are capable. Colonel Morgan doesn't suffer incompetence or fools. We will be leaving in two hours for Bennington. You are dismissed."

Lincoln returned O'Brien's salute when Schuyler said, "Tom, replenish your gunpowder and ammunition from my arsenal. I am sorry that Peggy is visiting her mother's relatives. She was looking forward to your visit."

Pausing for a moment, Tom replied, "Thank you, General. Please pass on my kindest regards to Peggy."

After Tom left, Lincoln frowned in surprise and asked, "You have introduced your daughter to that boy?"

"Yes, General. He is an extraordinary young man, as you will learn."

Lincoln replied, "Useful, I agree. O'Brien's familiarity with the territory and its people will accelerate my mission to recruit a local militia force. I intend to disrupt Burgoyne's attack by employing them to raid the British supply lines from Fort Ticonderoga. But whether O'Brien would be worthy of introducing him to my daughter? I shall reserve my opinion."

Burgoyne's Field Headquarters
Fort Edward, August 5th

Burgoyne was relieved that the continentals had abandoned the fortifications without a fight. However, he could not hide his disappointment that the rebels had stripped it of all supplies, munitions, and cannons. Although his natural confidence remained undaunted, Burgoyne felt a tenuous concern for the increasing necessity to resupply his army now that Howe would not be joining him in Albany.

Surprisingly the fort had not been burned, but the palisades and buildings would require significant repairs to render them defensible and habitable.

Standing in the center of the fort's parade ground, watching his men restore the walls and bastions, his adjutant caught his attention and said, "Excuse me, General. Ensign Sturgis has arrived by batteau with a message from Lt. Colonel Ledger."

"Captain, please bring him to me."

In response to a gesture from the General's adjutant, Ensign Sturgis walked through the fort's open gates, crossed the parade ground to face Burgoyne, snapped to attention, and saluted. Burgoyne was familiar with St. Ledger's reputation and knew his military career had been exclusively on the American frontier. Curious about how St. Ledger trained his officers, Burgoyne looked forward to meeting one. Burgoyne returned the salute and took a moment to see the man in the uniform. Consistent with his junior rank, Sturgis was a teenager, but he possessed a mature and capable demeanor typically instilled by frontier service.

"Ensign, you look like a man who has sailed the Mohawk River night and day without pause."

"I have, Sir."

Impressed by Sturgis' attention to duty, Burgoyne asked, "When may I expect St. Ledger's arrival?"

"General St. Ledger's advance has been blocked by a rebel fort guarding the portage between Lake Oneida and the Mohawk River. He has commenced a siege."

Slapping his riding crop sharply against his leg, Burgoyne's barked, "I was informed the fort was in ruins! The success of my campaign relied upon St. Ledger's destruction of the rebel settlements along the Mohawk River. I relied upon St. Ledger to resupply my army with captured cattle, food, and horses!"

Sturgis continued stoically, "We successfully crossed Lake Ontario and found Fort Oswego abandoned. After crossing Lake Oneida, General St. Ledger was met by Sir Johnson, the loyalist commander. Sir Johnson informed us that Fort Stanwix had been rebuilt, garrisoned by continentals, and armed with cannons."

Exasperated, Burgoyne grated, "Is that all, Ensign?"

Red-faced, Sturgis stammered, "Before I left, our scouts informed General St. Ledger of a brigade of rebel militia marching to relieve the fort's garrison. When I departed with this message, actions were being taken to ambush the traitors."

Regaining his composure, Burgoyne asked in a conversational tone, "When can I expect St. Ledger? Weeks, months, when upon your honor!"

Shaking and perspiring, Sturgis had been reduced to a terrified teenager. He whispered, "General St. Ledger told me he was confident that the ambush would succeed. But General Ledger does not possess the men to carry the fort by assault. He has commenced a siege digging trenches to safely install our mortars within range to bombard the garrison with explosive shells."

"That shall require weeks and possibly months since the rebels have cannons."

"Yes, sir."

Burgoyne placed a hand on the shaking boy's shoulder and said, "You have done well to provide me this information with admirable dispatch. My adjutant shall arrange for quarters and your return to St. Ledger by batteau tomorrow. Inform Lt. Colonel St. Ledger that I expect regular reports of his status. You are dismissed."

Burgoyne saw his staff officers and Colonel Skene crossing the parade ground, walking toward him, and heard them discussing the number of men to garrison the fort. Motioning Skene to join him, they strolled together toward the river. When they were alone, Burgoyne casually asked, "Colonel Skene, I wish to continue our previous discussion concerning finding cattle and horses to replenish the army's provisions and mounts for Colonel Baum's dragoons. St. Luc and his warriors have abandoned this army betraying their duty to the King. The success of this campaign now relies upon the reconnaissance of Baum's dragoons to ascertain the rebels' location, strength, and movements."

Smirking, Skene replied confidently, "General, I regularly purchase livestock in the territory which recently became a new colony called Vermont."

Annoyed by Skene's habit of imparting irrelevant information, Burgoyne snapped, "Are you willing to guide an expedition commanded by Baum?"

Surprised by Burgoyne's sharpness but mindful that his retaining ownership of Skenesboro depended upon defeating the rebels, he replied politely, "Of course."

"Are you capable of acting as Baum's translator? He speaks no English."

"Yes. To conduct business, I have become conversant in French and Hessian."

"Excellent." Despite his usefulness, Burgoyne blamed Skene for manipulating him into jeopardizing the campaign by building that infernal road and said dismissively, "Thank you, Colonel. I will send for you to finalize the details after speaking to Colonel Baum."

Naturally longwinded but politically sensitive, Skene bowed slightly and walked swiftly toward his campsite where his servants would prepare his meal.

Burgoyne's field headquarters, while on a campaign, was a tent lovingly designed by his wife. Always considering her husband's comfort, Lady Charlotte had directed the installation of partitions to divide the tent into separate spaces for office, sleeping, and dining.

Alone in his office, Burgoyne contemplated the complexity of the inevitable delay and possible defeat of St. Ledger. *If the rebel settlements of the Mohawk River Valley were not destroyed, would the rebel militia leave their homes to defend Albany?*

Abandoning the unanswerable, Burgoyne had reconsidered an earlier recommendation by Riedesel to raid the rebel farms and villages for cattle and food. Burgoyne had automatically rejected the proposal simply because Riesdesel had made it. Later, when discussing the idea with his senior officers, Burgoyne reasoned it was unnecessary to delay the army's advance. St. Luc's warriors could be relied upon for scouting, and St Ledger's looting of the farms of the Mohawk Valley would resupply the army with food. St. Luc was gone, and St. Ledger was not joining him in the foreseeable future. The current situation made the raid imperative. With reluctance, Burgoyne summoned Riedesel to his quarters.

Burgoyne, his thoughts interrupted when he heard the voice of his adjutant, "Excuse me, General Burgoyne, General Riedesel has arrived."

"Thank you, Major. Please show him in."

Assuming his most sincere smile, Burgoyne invited Riedesel to sit and served him a cognac before saying, "General Riedesel, you shall be pleased I have decided to accept your recommendation. With the desertion of St. Luc and his warriors, Colonel Baum must raid Vermont for horses to mount his dragoons for scouting and screening the army's movements. Skene informs me that the area also abounds in cattle and mills full of food for the taking. Colonel Skene shall act as guide and translator. Wagons will accompany Baum's detachment to transport all food seized to supplement our supplies now that General Howe may be delayed."

General Riedesel nodded in silent acknowledgment of Burgoyne's orders. He had recommended a raid by the Hessian and British light infantry days ago and had been ignored by this incompetent egotist. Baum's dragoons were equipped to ride, not conduct a raid on foot into enemy territory. Burgoyne squandered the bloodless capture of Ticonderoga to waste weeks building that folly of a road through a godforsaken swamp.

"The requisition of several hundred horses will mount my dragoons and jaegers. I am relieved that this army shall no longer rely upon that renegade St. Luc and his undisciplined murderers of women and children," Riedesel replied gruffly.

Burgoyne's smile froze. *This mercenary dares to vocalize the unspoken opinion of every officer of my command.*

Burgoyne regretted the poor girl's death and his decision not to punish the murderers, which cost him loyalist militia support. Frustrated by his mistake, Burgoyne admitted to himself what made the situation more galling was that the savages and St. Luc had abandoned him anyway. "Yes, General. I trust you will not be insulted if I meet with Colonel Baum to discuss my expectations of the mission."

For the good of the command, Riedesel ignored Burgoyne's insult, blatantly flouting the chain of command, and waited without expression for him to continue.

Observing no reaction Burgoyne grew bored with baiting the mercenary and picked up and began to read correspondence from his desk. Burgoyne looked up after several minutes of silence and saw that the stiffly formal Riedesel had walked out instead of waiting for permission from a superior officer to leave a formal meeting.

Riedesel's Field Headquarters
Fort Edward, August 7th

General Riedesel returned to his campsite feeling more agitated than usual after dealing with Burgoyne. His instinct told him this raid unnecessarily endangered his men and the campaign's success without the participation of the British light infantry. Turning toward his adjutant who had accompanied him, Riedesel said, "Captain, please summon Lieutenant Colonel Baum to me as soon as possible," and entered his tent.

Sitting behind his field desk, Riedesel considered the change which had come over Burgoyne since receiving notice of Howe's decision to capture the rebel capital of this godforsaken wilderness. The juvenile jealousies of the British Generals were unnerving to Riedesel. Briefed by his Duke, this campaign was simply a coordinated march south from Quebec and north from New York. Two professional armies totaling twenty thousand soldiers and the Royal Navy's unchallenged superiority would control the entire waterway between Quebec and New York City, dividing the rebel colonies.

"General, Lieutenant Colonel Baum has arrived."

"Thank you, Captain. Please come in, Baum, schnapps?"

"No, thank you, General!"

Friedrich Baum was a burly, fifty-year-old professional whose legs were permanently bowed from decades of riding.

"You have met with Burgoyne?"

"Yes, sir.

"What is the composition of your command?"

Surprised that Riedesel had not been informed previously, Baum replied, "I will command my two hundred dragoons, a detachment of our light infantry, and jaegers. Burgoyne's command provides Captain Fraser's marksmen, the remaining Ottawa and Abenaki scouts, and a force loyalist militia. Seven hundred men in all."

"I have been informed by Colonel Skene, who will accompany you, that Vermont is stocked with hundreds of horses that would provide mounts for your men and a company of jaegers. Your mission is to capture the village of Bennington, which Colonel Skene informed me is a rebel supply depot. The strength of your detachment should deter any resistance from the local militia. But do not initiate combat. We can afford no unnecessary casualties. No British armies are joining us despite the agreed-upon plan of this campaign."

Baum blurted, "What of St. Ledger's thousands of British regulars, Mohawk warriors, and loyalist militia joining us in Albany?"

Frustrated, Riedesel replied sarcastically, "Our employer's reconnaissance missed a garrisoned rebel fort equipped with cannon blocking St. Ledger's advance. I do not believe St. Ledger shall ever join us!"

Baum asked, "What of Warner's Green Mountain continentals?"

Calmed by the practical question, Riedesel replied, "General Fraser reports that Wagner's regiment suffered at least fifty percent casualties during the Battle of Hubbardton. Fraser believes less than one hundred continentals may oppose you in the area. Given the losses incurred, there is also a chance Warner's regiment has been disbanded."

Knowing that continentals attracted militia, Baum nodded, relieved that local resistance should be non-existent, and asked, "When do I march?"

"Immediately upon receipt of my written orders. This army needs your men mounted as a scouting and screening force. Good luck."

After Baum had left, Riedesel returned to his concern about the tenacity and skill of the enemy commander his men had killed. He had buried that gallant officer at Hubbardton and concluded that *these rebels were not mere farmers and shopkeepers.*

Riedesel ignored Burgoyne's bravado and prepared to send a relief force if Baum encountered another rebel officer of the same quality.

"Captain, please ask Lieutenant Colonel Breymann to report to me."

Drawing a blank dispatch from his desk draw, he drafted orders to Baum's detachment. He signed the dispatch and heard his adjutant say,

"Sir, Lieutenant Colonel Breymann is here."

"Show him in. Deliver my orders to Baum immediately."

Breymann marched into the tent, snapped to attention, and stood silently in front of Riedesel's desk.

"Lieutenant Colonel Breymann, I have ordered Baum to conduct a raid on a rebel supply depot in Bennington. You are to take all steps necessary to ready your grenadiers to march upon an hour's notice to his relief."

Breymann was surprised by his general's intensity and consciously suppressed his dislike of Baum, asking, "Do you expect Baum to encounter a superior continental force?"

Riedesel stood, began to pace to release some of his tension, and replied, "No, Breymann, quite the contrary. Colonel Skene, accompanying Baum, has assured me there are less than a hundred continentals in the area. I am more concerned with the local militia. Baum's men will be isolated from the army. I want you to be prepared to support him if Baum runs into something unexpected."

"Yes, sir. My grenadiers will be ready to march immediately upon receiving your order."

Manchester, Vermont
Red Lion Inn, August

Colonel Seth Warner sat at a table on the porch of the village's only inn, a modest trading center amidst a cluster of prosperous farms. The Red Lion Inn was situated at a crossroads of commercial transportation between New York and New Hampshire, with rooms for lodgers, stables for their horses, and a surprisingly sizeable common room.

After the Battle of Hubbardton, General Schuyler ordered the remnants of his Green Mountain regiment to garrison the Bennington supply depot. Warner found himself cooling his heels on guard duty until he received a message from General Stark requesting a meeting in Manchester to discuss a new mission.

According to the messenger, General Stark's militia brigade would be marching in today with reinforcements. Warner knew Stark had been a Colonel in the continental line who resigned his commission when Congress had promoted Benjamin Lincoln to General instead of him.

Major General Lincoln, who happened to be staying at the Red Lion Inn, had also asked Warner to meet with him. From Lincoln's guide, Warner learned that the General was recruiting a militia force to disrupt the British supply line to Ticonderoga.

Colonel Warner gleefully looked forward to the inevitable confrontation when Lincoln demanded that Stark place his brigade under his command.

"Colonel Warner, when is Colonel Stark due to arrive?"

Startled, Warner hid his grin, turning toward the voice, snapped to attention, saluted, and responded formally, "Good morning General Lincoln. I was informed by a mounted messenger that General Stark and his militia brigade are due before noon."

Lincoln, a no-nonsense commander one trifled with at their own peril, had been promoted to senior command for his willingness to do what was necessary to succeed.

Lincoln stared at Warner for a moment and asked, "General Stark? Has Congress recently promoted Colonel Stark?"

Suppressing a suicidal urge to smile, Warner painfully maintained a straight face and responded, "That was how the messenger identified the brigade commander, sir."

Ever a practical man, Lincoln chose to abandon any further inquiry on what rank Stark currently claimed. Instead, he focused on how best to use the fortuitous arrival of the militia to accomplish his mission. "Warner, what is the brigade's strength and constitution?"

"I am told that General Stark is leading about fifteen hundred men. John Langdon, President of the New Hampshire General Court, equipped and provisioned the brigade."

Lincoln appreciated Warner's candor that this force was privately raised and financed, foiling his intention to assume command. Avoiding a futile and personally embarrassing confrontation with Stark, Lincoln said, "Thank you, Colonel. I shall be foregoing the pleasure of meeting with Colonel Stark." Motioning to Tom, who had walked from the stables and joined them, Lincoln continued, "Warner, I will be leaving

O'Brien with you and continuing on my own. You will inform Stark that General Schuyler has sent O'Brien to introduce me to the local militia leaders, now accomplished. Find a reason for O'Brien to join Stark's brigade. I want to know what *General* Stark is doing."

Tom nodded and looked at Warner, who saluted Lincoln and stood silently at attention.

As one of the stable boys walked Lincoln's horse from the stables, the General mounted and said, "O'Brien, you did well. I will return to Pawlet, Rutland, and White Hall to brief the militia captains you persuaded to muster their men and assign their targets. Stark was a ranger in the war against the French, and frankly, I think you two will get along." Putting his spurs to the horse, Lincoln rode north to Pawlet.

Smiling at the back of the departing rider, Warner relaxed for the first time since Lincoln's appearance that morning. Warner returned his attention to Tom and said jokingly, "Good luck to both of us. I was with Stark when we captured Fort Ticonderoga and invaded Quebec. Stark will know you are Lincoln's spy, but he will appreciate your Rifles' uniform and respects Morgan's opinion of fighting men."

Later that afternoon, General Stark rode into Manchester, leading his brigade. Colonel Warner welcomed Stark with an honor guard of his Green Mountain continentals.

"General Stark, welcome to Manchester," greeted Colonel Warner.

Mounted on a prancing sixteen-hand thoroughbred in front of a mile-long column of men, General John Stark silently looked down his nose at Warner, radiating disappointment and annoyance. Standing with the inn owner and Tom O'Brien on the road in front of the building, Warner desperately maintained his stern emotionless visage enduring Stark's scrutiny.

***

Stark had last seen Warner and the boy rifleman in the swirling snow in Quebec when General Montgomery was killed. Stark sneered, staring at his welcoming committee for a moment, "Where is Major General Lincoln? I was told he was here. I looked forward to his attempting to steal my brigade just like he stole my promotion."

Unable to prevent his smile, Warner coughed, covering his mouth with his hand, and replied, "General Lincoln departed this morning. My regiment is protecting the supply depot in Bennington. I rode over this morning to ask how my men may support you."

Mollified by Lincoln's retreat and Warner's deference, Stark said, "Colonel Warner, I am pleased to inform you that two hundred Vermont rangers are marching with me. I have assigned them to your regiment to restore its full combat strength."

Warner grinned from ear to ear and replied, "That is the best news you could have given me, General! After Hubbardton, my men were concerned the regiment would be disbanded."

Warner looked shocked when Stark returned his smile and revealed an emotional side rarely exposed by replying, "I knew we would win independence after learning of Colonel Francis and your courageous stand at Hubbardton. No General worthy of the rank would tolerate the disbanding of a fighting regiment such as yours!"

Turning his gaze to Tom, Stark asked, "When did Colonel Morgan start recruiting boys into the Rifles?"

Straight-faced Tom met Stark's eyes and replied, "Colonel Morgan invited me after I crippled St. Luc at three hundred yards."

Overhearing the exchange Colonel Herrick, the brigade's senior Colonel, shouted, "I didn't hear 'Sir' at the end of that answer. You will address the General properly or—"

"That will be all, Colonel Herrick," shouted Stark and, continuing to look at Tom, asked, "You were with Arnold at Quebec?"

"Yes, General."

Chuckling in appreciation of the boy's reply despite the lack of a 'sir,' Stark said, "I heard one of General Schuyler's chosen men made that shot. I will take Colonel Warner to teach the lobsterbacks a lesson. Can Colonel Morgan spare you for several weeks?"

"Colonel Morgan always encourages his men to learn from the best, and I am sure he would not mind me joining your command, sir."

Relieved that he didn't have to justify O'Brien joining the campaign, Warner asked, "General would you join me in the Red Lion Inn for a meal and a pint?"

"Thank you, Colonel Warner. Bring O'Brien. I want to hear why he decided not to kill St. Luc, that murdering bastard."

***

Later that night, sitting companionly in the empty public room of the inn, Stark reached out his hand to Tom and said, "Son, please give me the tomahawk you were thinking about using on Colonel Herrick this afternoon."

Smiling, Tom complied, slowly drawing and passing the weapon to Stark, handle first.

Taking the tomahawk and looking closely at the form of the blade and engraving on the handle, Stark said, "This is a fine weapon. Perfectly balanced for throwing."

"My godfather is an Oneida sachem. He gave it to me for my eleventh birthday and taught me how to use it, sir."

Returning the tomahawk to Tom, the conversation was interrupted by a soft knock on the inn's front door, and a man's voice heard to say, "I am here to speak to Colonel Warner. May I come in?"

In reply to a nod from Stark, the innkeeper admitted a broad-shouldered man, a few years older than Tom, in the uniform of a Continental officer. Walking to the seated men, he stood at attention and saluted Stark and Warner. Warner said, "General, may I introduce my adjutant, Lieutenant Stafford."

Stark looked up from the plate of bread and cheese he had been eating and instinctually recognized Stafford was the rare junior officer a commander could trust to act independently of his orders, think for himself, and take the necessary action regardless of the consequences. Standing, Stark offered his hand to Stafford, receiving the bone-crushing grip he expected and returned. Stafford broke out in a shy smile, clearly delighted by the friendly gesture from the reputedly taciturn Stark, and said, "It is a pleasure, General, to meet a man who soldiered with Major Robert Rodgers."

Nodding, Stark paid his highest compliment by saying, "Stafford, I remember your father, good ranger. You remind me of him."

"Thank you, sir."

"Stafford, what is it?" asked Warner.

Removing a dispatch from his pocket and handing it to Warner, he answered, "Colonel, I just received this by a messenger from General Lincoln."

Sitting back in his chair, taking a long swallow from his mug of rum, Stark grimaced and said, "Lincoln!"

Warner nodded, looking up from the dispatch he had just finished reading, and said, "General Lincoln has ordered the regiment to remain in Bennington until further orders."

Stark sighed softly and said, "I can live with that, Warner. You, however, will accompany me to find a suitable place to intercept any raiders from Burgoyne. Stafford can be trusted with the regiment. Remember, Stafford, orders are orders, but a man must think for himself. In combat, each man's actions will affect victory or death, so he owes it to his comrades not to blindly follow orders."

Stafford and Warner nodded, sobered by the words of a man who had repeatedly proven himself to be one of the most successful combat leaders in the Continental Army.

Breaking the solemn mood, Stark grimaced and said, "I will tell you a story about Lincoln. During the siege of Boston, my men and I were short of supplies, and the nights were getting cold. One evening a wagon pulled up to our campsite and stopped. Lincoln was standing on the wagon's bed, handing out provisions and blankets gathered personally and on his own initiative. My men and I have never appreciated anyone more than Colonel Lincoln."

Stafford smiled and said, "I appreciate what you're saying, General. You can count on me to possess the initiative to do what's needed."

Reverting suddenly to the man that fifteen hundred men had trusted with their lives and their families, General Stark stood and issued his first orders of the Bennington campaign.

"Warner, you are familiar with the terrain and shall accompany the brigade. Place your men and my Vermont rangers under Stafford's command." Looking eye to eye with Stafford, he said, "You shall obey General Lincoln's order holding the regiment in Bennington guarding the supply depot. Remember, I reinforced your regiment to prevent disbandment and act as a ready reserve to my militia brigade. If needed, I expect to see you, Stafford. Your father never disappointed Major Rogers or me."

Bennington
Stark's Field Headquarters
New Hampshire Militia Brigade
August 13th

Standing around a map spread upon a camp table with Warner and his militia battalion commanders, Stark asked, "Colonel Warner, has the enemy been located?"

"Yes, General. O'Brien located a raiding party of about seven hundred soldiers accompanied by a small band of Ottawa and Abenaki warriors. The warriors terrorize the people of Cambridge and kill their livestock. If Burgoyne counted on recruiting local Tory support, he wouldn't get it. Everyone is hunkering down in their villages and farms, protecting their families and property."

"Colonel, what is your recommendation for the best place to intercept the raiders?"

"O'Brien has shown me a place to halt the enemy's advance East of the Walloomsac River. There is a place with a bridge and a small hill covering the crossing."

"Warner, that sounds like our camp should be on top of that hill."

"Not this time General. That hilltop is solid granite impervious to digging earthworks and can't be adequately fortified."

"I see where you are going, Colonel."

"When the enemy observes that the brigade outnumbers them two to one, I want their commander to camp protected by the river and send for reinforcements."

"How do you suggest we delay them sufficiently to achieve what you suggest?"

"I recommend a small force occupy the mill at Sancoick and that the contents not be destroyed."

"You propose provisioning the enemy?"

"No, General. I propose to use the mill and its contents as a lure so they advance to the river where the ravagers may be surrounded and destroyed."

"Your recommendation is accepted."

Vicinity of Cambridge
Baum's Detachment
August 13th

Lt. Colonel Baum believed he had reached the third level of hell after a full day of the march since leaving the fort. From the sound of his men's groans, they were sure of it. The Hessian dragoons were burdened by a heavy cavalry saber, thigh-high boots designed for riding, and wore a cap with a thick brass crest.

Walking beside Skene, he complained, "My men are not equipped for this raid. The speed of this column is pitiable. The savages who were supposed to be scouting are burning the crops and killing the cattle that should replenish Burgoyne's army."

An avid hunter and explorer, Skene enjoyed his role as guide, suitably attired in cotton breeches and shirt at home in the seasonal humidity. He replied jovially, "Since St. Luc returned to Quebec, his warriors have become uncontrollable. I recommended to General Burgoyne not to send them on this expedition."

Turning to Skene, Baum gave him orders to translate his commands to the British and loyalist contingents.

"Colonel Peters' Queen's rangers will replace the Ottawa and Abenaki as scouts. Major Pfister's loyalist militia will form flank guards west and east of our line of march. Captain Fraser's marksmen and jaegers will act as the rear guard. My dragoons will form the main column, and the warriors shall join us. I shall control them!"

Sancoick Mill
Morning of August 14th

Smiling for the first time since commencing this mission, Colonel Baum proudly signed his dispatch, reporting to Burgoyne the capture of a mill filled with food and several prisoners for questioning by Colonel Skene.

Baum had loaded the captured supplies aboard the freight wagons by midday, which he intended to return to Burgoyne under escort. Seeing Colonel Skene approaching from the huddle of prisoners he had been questioning, Baum asked, "What have you learned, Colonel?"

"We face a militia force of fifteen to eighteen hundred men. The militia has no cavalry or cannon. Warner's continentals are reportedly at Bennington."

Frowning slightly, considering the unexpected opposition, Baum smoothly resumed his professional demeanor and said, "Thank you, Colonel Skene. I will add your description of the enemy's strength to my report with a request to return the wagons once the captured supplies are delivered to General Burgoyne. We will continue our march to Bennington as soon as I have dispatched the wagon train and escort."

Stepping in front of the departing Baum, Skene grated, "The prisoners confirm we face a force at least twice our numbers! I insist reinforcement be requested, and we fortify the mill and await their arrival."

Without breaking stride, Baum picked Skene off the ground, removing his sputtering interpreter from his path, and said gruffly, "I have my orders and shall not tolerate your interference. You possess no authority. Translate my orders or leave!"

Terrified by the possibility of returning to the army unescorted, Colonel Skene visibly shriveled and said, "If my advice is no longer wanted, I shall return to my campsite."

New Hampshire Militia Brigade
Field Camp at the Intersection of
Bennington and Cambridge Roads
August 14th

Standing with his battalion commanders on the shore of the Walloomsac River, General Stark said, "Colonel Warner, you have guided me to perfect ground to deal with these invaders. The brigade will camp on the elevated ground blocking the road to Bennington. The river shall protect our flanks. To assault us, the enemy must march uphill into the fire of fifteen hundred entrenched muskets."

Warner replied, "Actually, Tom O'Brien showed me this spot. He and his father often used it as a campsite when freighting by wagons through this area."

Turning to look at Tom, standing outside the immediate circle of senior officers, Stark motioned him to join the group and asked, "Are you familiar with the terrain across the river? In particular, the hill overlooking the other side of the bridge."

"As a boy, I would explore the woods while my father and his drivers set up the camp. I would climb that hill for the view and figure out the fastest way to reach the top," replied Tom.

Stark said, "Colonel Warner, what is your opinion?"

"The enemy's leadership has been identified as Hessian dismounted dragoons. They have put the militia to flight in every battle in this war and reportedly consider them cowards and beneath contempt. After dispatching a wagon train filled with contents of the Sancoick mill, the raiders remained. In my opinion, their commander will build field fortifications and send for reinforcements. Once reinforced with cannons, they will attack."

Addressing his senior officers, Stark said, "We will watch the enemy prepare their defenses. Then, we will form a plan of attack."

Warner asked, "General, you intend to attack?"

"Colonel Warner, once our scouts had determined the size and composition of the marauding force, I decided that this was the perfect opportunity to destroy an isolated contingent of Burgoyne's army. The thieves are not regulars, elite light infantry, or grenadiers. Colonel Herrick and Hobart, you will take two hundred of your best men and skirmish with any who have crossed the Walloomsac River and drive them back to the fortified cabins at the bridge."

Herrick, the senior Colonel, and a veteran commander nodded and asked, "Do you want the cabins captured?"

Stark looked up from his map and shook his head, "No, I want your men and Hobarts to pin the enemy in the cabins. Once you have accomplished that, O'Brien will guide you to the nearest ford across the river and be prepared to attack their rear. Send O'Brien back once your men are in position. Hobart, you will lead an attack on the left flank to support Colonel Stickney's attack on the fortified cabins."

Colonel Nichols looked up from the map and asked, "General?"

Stark looked at Nichols and barked, "Afraid you'll miss the fight?"

As a familiar of Stark, Nichol took no offense to his brusque manner and replied, "Where do you want my men, General?"

Stark nodded, mollified, and continued, "Nichols, you and your men will be scouting the woods to our front, driving any enemy forces back to their camp. While you are about it, plan your route for a frontal attack if the enemy builds a redoubt upon the hill. Your assault will be launched once you hear the musket fire of Herrick's attack on the enemy's rear. Consult with O'Brien once he returns."

Straightening to his full height, Stark looked at Warner and said, "It is time for you to send for your regiment and the Vermont rangers. Tell your messenger to remind Stafford that his father never let me down, and I don't expect him to. Have them march to our camp. They will join me and the reserve. I anticipate the enemy will be reinforced by Burgoyne. Your men shall tip the balance in our favor."

Warner replied, "I will do whatever is necessary to avenge Francis and the men lost at Hubbardton."

Stark grimaced slightly at the mention of Francis, whom he knew as a fine officer, and said, "I intend to teach Burgoyne that his disdain of the militia will cost him his army. The loss of his looters shall become his first lesson."

Baum's Detachment
Field Camp, August 14th

Since departing the captured mill, Baum received constant contact reports between his jaeger scouts and rebel militia. Professionally unconcerned, Baum remained confident that the cowardly rebels would not dare assault his column of professional soldiers. As the day progressed, skirmishing increased until his scouts could not pierce the enemy picket line.

Baum addressed his adjutant, "Captain Schmidt, please ask Colonel Skene to join me at his earliest convenience." Moments later, a worried

Skene appeared with two riflemen, and Baum asked, "Have our scouts succeeded in crossing the river?"

Skene replied, "Yes. These men are from Colonel Peter's command. The Queen's rangers have broken through the militia skirmishers, crossed the bridge, and dug in on a small hill on the far side. Peter reports strong forces of militia occupying a fortified camp blocking the road to Bennington. No continentals have been seen, but the rebel militia is at least twice our numbers. Peters recommends stopping our advance to request reinforcements and cannons to attack the rebel camp."

The confirmed strength of the rebels and his Ottawa and Abenaki warriors' fear of engaging them convinced Baum to accept Colonel Peter's recommendation.

"Colonel Skene, return to General Burgoyne and request that Colonel Breymann's grenadiers and cannons be immediately dispatched to our relief. Advise General Riesedel I am in a strong defensive position and await Breymann's arrival. My jaegers shall escort you to ensure compliance with my instructions."

Before leaving camp, Colonel Skene communicated Baum's orders to the commanders of the individual contingents to build field fortification.

Baum's dragoons fortified the hill overlooking the bridge with a redoubt of logs that lacked earthworks because of its granite façade. Baum designated the field fortification as the dragoon's redoubt. To maintain a close watch on his baggage train and his undisciplined Ottawa and Abenaki warriors, he placed both at the foot of the fortified hill. Baum kept half of Fraser's riflemen with him in the redoubt. The remainder were stationed with the batteau men who occupied the fortified cabins on either side of the bridge. Across the river, the Queen's rangers constructed and occupied small log-reinforced earthworks designated as Tory's redoubt.

Baum's inability to communicate directly in the absence of Skene prevented his coordinating the construction of the defensive line resulting in significant gaps. The rebels probed and skirmished throughout the day until the Queen's rangers were isolated inside

Tory's redoubt.

As evening fell, Baum was confident that the following day would find the militia dispersed to their homes and the arrival of reinforcement.

New Hampshire Militia Brigade
Field Camp, Officers' Call
August 15th

Standing in the middle of the clearing surrounded by scores of rough shelters of branches and brush built by his men the previous evening, Stark's farmer's instinct was sure of rain. Commencing in the late afternoon and continuing through the day, Stark postponed Herrick's night march to attack the dragoon's redoubt and addressed his men regarding what precautions were necessary to protect the camp that evening.

"Gentleman, this rain prevents any assault today. I anticipate the enemy commander will use his warriors and jaegers to infiltrate our lines to terrorize what the enemy perceives as untrained farmers." After the laughter died, Stark continued, "To counter this threat, all skirmishers and outposts will pull back to the camp. A log rampart will encircle the camp's perimeter, pierced by rifle pits with three-man teams stationed every ten yards apart throughout the night. Each team shall include a hunter with a crack shot who can keep his powder dry in this constant rain. The other two men will be prepared with knives and tomahawks to kill any attacking warriors who rush the shooter after firing. Major Rogers trained us in this tactic, and it works. Assign only your most experienced men. The rest of the command will remain in camp until we need their muskets in tomorrow's attack."

***

As darkness fell, thirty Ottawa warriors led by their chief Negwagan crossed the Walloomsac River. They proceeded northeast through the forest to eliminate the rebels' picket and approach their camp from the south.

Twenty Abenaki warriors led by their chief Massasoit left the dragoon redoubt, moving southeast to eliminate the rebels in the woods on the other side of the river.

Moving noiselessly through the forest, Negwagan could see the winking of the rebel's campfires and thought *fifty more yards, and these fools were within musket range.*

Tongues of flame lit the darkness in a curved line in front of the campfires, followed by the crash of rifle fire revealing the location of the rebel defenses. Negwagan blew his whistle signaling his warriors to initiate a rush attack upon the revealed sentries. As the screaming warriors reached the sources of the rifle fire, shadowed figures rose out of the darkness, and the interrupted silence of the night descended again.

Negwagan blew his whistle three times, signaling to break off the attack and retreat to camp. His signal was echoed by Massasoit as the Abenaki war party fell back to the dragoon redoubt before launching its attack.

Later in camp, Massasoit confronted Negwagan, tending to one of his men gasping for breath with a sucking chest wound, and demanded, "Why did you call off the attack? My men were almost within musket range of the camp."

"So were we. But the rebel riflemen fired first." Tears running down his cheeks, Negwagan sobbed, "My son will not survive the night."

"You coward! Riflemen never survive a rush attack!" snarled Massasoit.

Negwagan replied softly, "I saved your men from a trap. Those who rushed the riflemen never returned. I saw each one mobbed and struck down."

Reduced to silence, Massasoit sat down next to the grieving man and listened to the last minutes of the labored breaths of the dying boy. After an hour, Negwagan said, "The rebel leader is to be feared. After burying my son, I will return to Quebec with my war party. It will be safer to travel together."

Massasoit nodded and helped Negwagan dig a shallow grave to bury his son.

The surviving Ottawa and Abenaki deserted Baum in ones and twos that night to rendezvous and return to their homes in Quebec.

Bennington
Stark's Camp
August 15th

Stark's face, lit by the flickering fire, listened to his commanders sharing the reports of the successful repulse of the night attack with only several wounded in hand-to-hand combat.

After the reports had concluded, Stark nodded and said, "They won't try that again. Replace the pickets with new men. Remember, the veterans will be needed to stiffen the attacking columns tomorrow. Colonel Nichol and Colonel Herrick, have you scouted and chosen your routes for tomorrow?"

Colonel Nichol nodded, and Colonel Herrick, whose column had the furthest to travel, said, "O'Brien guided me to the rear of the dragoon's redoubt and returned without detection. But two hundred men may be discovered because the route is close by Tory's redoubt guarding the southern approach to the bridge."

"That is a legitimate concern. Colonels Hobart and Stickney will position their men in front of Tory's redoubt and the fortified cabins and maintain harassing fire to keep the enemy's attention. That should permit Herrick's men to safely reach their positions. Tomorrow when O'Brien returns from leading Herrick's men to the rear of the dragoon's redoubt, I will order the firing of three-volley, each one minute apart, to signal all columns to attack their assigned targets."

Suddenly from the darkness came an imperious voice, "General Stark, I have marched five hundred Massachusetts militiamen away from their homes to support you in defense of Bennington. I demand that we be included in any attack upon these invaders, or we will never come again!"

Stark grimaced and replied calmly, "Parson Thomas Allen, you and your men are welcome. Would you go now on this dark and rainy night? Rejoin your men and tell them to get some rest. If the Lord gives us dry weather tomorrow, I guarantee your congregation their fill of fighting."

"I shall hold you to that, brother Stark," groused Parson Alen.

In the early morning of August 16th, Stockbridge Mohicans joined

Stark. He assigned warriors to each of the assault columns to assist in infiltrating the Hessian's defenses.

Bennington, Stark's Camp
August 16th, Noon

With the cessation of rain, Stark ordered the four columns to engage Baum's defenses.

Colonel Nichols marched north from the camp with two hundred fifty men to circle northeast through the forest to a position north of the dragoon's redoubt to launch a frontal assault once Herrick initiated his attack upon its rear.

***

With three hundred fifty men accompanied by O'Brien and his friend, Paul of the Mohicans, Colonel Herrick crossed the river, circled south into the forest behind a wooded ridge, and re-crossed the river to attack from the west.

Three hours later, Tom assisted Herrick in settling his men under cover two hundred yards behind the dragoon redoubt and whispered to Herrick, "Colonel, Paul will be staying. I will be returning to General Stark. Any message…sir?"

Breaking into a grin in response to Tom's pregnant pause, Herrick said, "Good work Tom, just call me Sam. No message."

Smiling in return, Tom replied, "Good luck, sir," and silently disappeared into the forest.

Forty-five minutes later, Tom was led to Stark, watching the continuous volley of fire of hundreds of muskets splintering the fortified cabins and log walls of the Tory redoubt.

"O'Brien, is Herrick prepared to attack the rear of the dragon's redoubt?" Stark asked.

"Yes, General."

Turning to his adjutant, Stark ordered, "Commence firing the signal volleys to launch the assault upon the dragoon redoubt."

Standing with Stark, Tom heard musket fire in the direction of the attack points identified during the senior officers' planning meeting. Tom watched Nichol's column, reinforced by Parson Thomas' Massachusetts militia, commence a continual fire on the dragoon's redoubt from his vantage point.

Simultaneously, Hobart's column charged the bullet-riddled fortified cabins. Taking advantage of the brief interruption of the rebel fire, the terrified occupants emerged from shattered windows and burst from splintered walls and doors. They dropped prone on the ground in submission or stampeded toward the dragoon redoubt in retreat.

***

Colonel Stickney stood and yelled to his men after capturing the cabins, "Charge the Tory redoubt. Let's end this." Joined by his men, Stickney saw the flashes of a dozen rifles and, feeling burning on his right arm, shouted, "We withstood their fire. No mercy."

Drunk with the adrenaline of survival, Stickney and his companion screamed their defiance of death and flowed over the log ramparts of the redoubt, flattening the Queen's Rangers with musket butts, tomahawks, and fists. Those rangers not killed were quickly captured. Prodded by musket barrels to Stark's reserve force, the prisoners were bound. Those men not tasked with guard duty joined Colonel Nichols and Colonel Herrick's assault on the dragoon's redoubt.

***

Twenty years of war on the battlefields of Europe had left Baum unprepared to cope with these nightmare circumstances. His command had been reduced to his dragoons and a handful of survivors who miraculously reached his redoubt.

Cursing, Baum whispered to himself, "You fool! Building a redoubt upon a bald granite outcrop. No earthworks. No loopholes to fire from!"

Men he had led for ten years were forced to stand above the chest-high log walls to fire their cavalry carbines exposed to rebel fire, harvesting them without mercy.

Drawing his saber Baum addressed his command, "Each squadron will defend a wall and fire by squads. Continuous, disciplined volleys shall break the spirit of the rebels, and they will run."

As the dragoons returned fire, Baum was reassured by his men's flawless performance firing three rounds a minute and rotating their positions to replace the fallen and thought. *My men shall defeat this rabble!*

Startled by a body falling at his feet, Baum stepped backward, glanced down, and saw the stricken dragoon spurting blood splattering his polished boots. Scanning the redoubt's interior, he was stunned by the scores of his men littering the stone floor with fatal head or chest wounds.

"Captain, can you explain this catastrophe?"

"The rebels are firing volleys from every direction," answered Baum's adjutant, a hint of hysteria in his voice.

"From the rear?"

"Yes, sir. Many hundreds of muskets from everywhere!"

"My God."

Baum addressed the survivors using his battlefield voice, "We are the duke's dragoons and shall never surrender." Relieved to hear a responding growl, the redoubt walls were fully manned, and the disciplined fire resumed.

The rebels' fire intensified, and the responding fire dwindled to silence. Their ammunition exhausted the remaining defenders gathered in the center of the redoubt.

Standing in blood pooled around his boots seeping from the corpses of his proud dragoons, Baum chose his command's fate and shouted, "You have preserved Hessian honor. There is a final duty to perform." In a firm voice, Baum bestowed a rare smile upon thirty surviving troopers and said, "Draw sabers. Wedge formation." Assuming the apex position, Baum ordered, "Double time, stop for nothing until breakthrough. Follow me!"

Emerging from the redoubt, the Hessian phalanx startled militia who scattered or were sabered by the enraged dragoons. Retracing their march from the British encampment Baum and his men slowed, exhausted by hours of combat and their heavy thigh-high boots. The rebels flanked the spent Hessians and fired point-blank into the stumbling and diminishing mob.

Baum shrieked a primeval cry cutting down another rebel farmer, and stepped forward into a cloud of smoke and flame, knocking him to the ground and sending his saber spinning from his hand.

Unable to rise, Baum stared at a ring of rebel faces and uttered in Hessian, "Peasants!"

Looking down at the corpse, one of Stark's veterans remarked, "I'm glad we won't be facing these bastards again!"

***

Standing next to Colonel Herrick, Tom, who had joined him during the attack, shivered, hearing the Hessian officer's death rattle, and asked, "Sam, what did he say?"

Herrick replied, "It wasn't complimentary." Lifting his arm and drawing his men's attention, he ordered, "Colonel Hobart, your regiment will gather the wounded and transport them to camp. The rest will be joining General Stark. If Burgoyne has sent a relief force, he will need all of us to defeat them."

Bennington
St. Luke's Bridge, August 16th, 5 pm

Upon crossing the bridge, Colonel Breymann's relief column of grenadiers met Captain Fraser leading his surviving marksmen, Queens Rangers, and loyalists of Baum's command. Addressing Breymann in French, Captain Fraser reported, "Colonel Baum's encampment has been overwhelmed by rebel militia. I saw Baum and his dragoons shot down before we could reach them. My rearguard has reported pursuers occupying the high ground to our left." A veteran of a dozen European battlefields, Breymann shouted to the crews of his cannons, "Unlimber the guns, and we will blow those rebels out of that position. Grenadiers fix bayonets and prepare to advance."

Bennington, Baum's Camp
August 16th, 5:30 pm

Walking through the ruins of the captured enemy camp, Stark observed his officers assign their men to secure the prisoners and gather the dead for burial. Scattered everywhere was detritus of battle: discarded weapons, abandoned tents, and assorted boxes and barrels of supplies and munitions. A veteran of such sights, Stark remarked to his companion, "Parson Allen, you are to be congratulated for holding your men in discipline despite the opportunity to loot the enemy's camp. God has allowed you and your men to smite the enemy's relief force which my scouts' report is fast approaching."

Facing his men, Parson Allen intoned as if from his pulpit, "God has given our people a great victory. Now is the moment to advance and drive them from our land!"

Stark placed his hand on Parson's shoulder and addressed the Massachusetts militiamen, "My reserves are four hundred chosen New Hampshire men. Join me in a blocking force to stop the enemy's advance until the attack columns return. A messenger has been sent to Colonel Wagner's continental regiment to march to our relief. Are you with us!"

After the cheering quieted, the men formed into two ranks to engage the approaching column of Hessian grenadiers, the most feared shock troops upon the European battlefield.

Bennington
West of Baum's Field Camp
Astride the Road to Sancoick's Mill
August 16th, 6 pm – 8 pm

Half deaf from the unremitting exchange of volleys and engulfed in smoke, Stark shouted into Parson Allen's ear, "True to your word, your men have matched the Hessians volley for volley. Thwarting every attempt to launch a bayonet attack."

Loading his musket, Allen chanted, "God be praised the Canaanites fall by the sword of justice."

"General, where do you want us?"

Turning toward the source of the voice, Stark looked into the smiling face of Lt. Stafford of the Green Mountain continentals and replied, "Mr. Stafford, you've come in good time as I expected. Whom have you brought?"

Stafford replied, "The entire command."

Joining them from the firing line, Colonel Warner said, "Stafford, if asked, you are to say you were following my orders—"

Interrupting, Stark shouted, "Warner. Your regiment is to attack the enemy light infantry guarding the flanks of the firing line of the grenadiers. Parson Allen and I will advance upon the grenadiers holding the center of the line. Colonel Francis and his men will be avenged."

Bennington
Breymann's Detachment
Astride the Road to Sancoick's Mill
August 16th, 8 pm

As darkness fell, Colonel Breymann thought ten more spring up for every rebel killed. *My men are now engaged with thousands of demons who have captured my cannons and scattered my light infantry.*

Resolved on the price which must be paid to prevent a rout, Breymann shouted, "Major Stein, begin a fighting withdrawal. Fall back two strides every thirty seconds facing the enemy with bayonets leveled and muskets loaded. Captain Meyers, your remaining light infantry, stay in contact with the flanks of the grenadier's line until we break contact with the enemy. It will soon be too dark to tell an enemy from a friend, and the rebels will be forced to cease their attack."

Breymann knew his command would have already joined Baum's dead or captured dragoons but for the elite grenadiers' pride, discipline, and fighting prowess.

Minutes after the withdrawal, Captain Meyers was carried into Breymann's presence. Squatting down next to his cousin and childhood playmate, Breymann bent his ear to the ashen face and heard his boyhood friend's dying words. "My lights routed from a bayonet charge by rebel continentals. You are outflanked…."

Breymann sprung to his feet and shouted, "Form square. We meet these peasants with steel!"

However, before the grenadiers could form, Warner's continentals struck. They bayonetted several Hessians, including Breymann, who was swept up in the rout supported by two of his officers.

Nightfall brought hostilities to an end.

***

The following morning a wounded Breymann and his surviving grenadiers limped into Burgoyne's camp. Breymann's relief column had lost a third of his men and personal cannons to the rebels.

Met by General Riedesel and the Hessian medical staff, Breymann struggled to straighten to attention, saluted, and said, "The rebels are not mere farmers!"

Supporting Breymann as he slumped forward, Riedesel spoke softly, "Baum?"

Breymann replied in a whisper, "Unknown. We never reached him. My column was ambushed by continentals supported by veteran militia outnumbering us three to one."

Motioning to the waiting stretcher-bearers, Riedesel helped position Breymann, who was carried away to the hospital. Experiencing a moment of pride from the professionalism demonstrated by his medical staff handling this disaster, Riedesel realized *that I am obliged to report this loss to the duke and write to the loved ones of those who shall never return home.*

Fort Miller
Burgoyne's Headquarters
August 17th

Burgoyne had been focusing on readying his army to cross the Hudson River when he received word of the fighting at Bennington. Reacting as a fearless cavalry commander, Burgoyne ordered the entire army to prepare to march to reinforce Baum and Breymann. Before a second relief force could be dispatched, word arrived that the remnants of Breymann's command were approaching.

As the day passed, survivors continued to stagger into camp, spreading the details of the defeat throughout the army.

After de-briefing Breymann with Riedesel, Burgoyne learned that the rebel militia had been reinforced by a strong force of continentals, heavily outnumbering the Hessians. His army had lost hundreds of elite professionals who could not be replaced.

Sitting alone in the fort's headquarters building, pondering how to solve the debacle. Burgoyne despaired that his failure to immediately sail south, made possible by the improbable bloodless capture of Ticonderoga, may cost him the Crown's favor. On the verge of panic, the loving face of Lady Charlotte flooded his consciousness, and she was smiling. The center of his universe since they met at court years ago, her confidence in him had always inspired him to accomplish the impossible. Steeled by her love and his wish to earn the lordship he wished to gift her, Burgoyne experienced a moment of lucidity. *I now know how to regain the confidence of my commanders.*

"Major Brown, please come in here."

Entering the office, his adjutant said, "Sir."

"Inform Generals Phillips, Fraser, and Colonel Skene to attend a conference in my office in thirty minutes."

"General Riedesel?'

Winking, Burgoyne replied, "British only, Major."

Brown smiled, "Of course, sir."

***

Sitting behind his desk, Burgoyne had waited until all the participants had arrived before permitting them to enter his office and assume their seats. As Skene began to sit, Burgoyne snapped in his battlefield voice, "Colonel, remain standing! You are on notice that this is a Court of Inquiry to determine whether you are responsible for the grievous casualties suffered by the King's Hessians and loyal militiamen. If so, I shall recommend your prosecution for negligently weakening this army, endangering the victory promised to our King!"

Burgoyne enjoyed his senior staff's shocked faces, particularly that of Skene.

Skene sputtered, "What nonsense! I volunteered to translate for Baum and almost got killed for my trouble."

"Silence. You are here to answer questions. Your life is in the balance, so listen." Confident that he had his Generals' attention, Burgoyne asked Skene, "Did you assure us that Vermont was devoid of any continentals or militia force which would endanger Baum's command?"

"Yes, General Burgoyne, to my knowledge."

"Colonel, what was the basis of that knowledge?"

"Word of mouth."

"When was the last time you were in the territory you recommended raided?"

"Before the rebellion."

"Colonel, did you share your complete lack of personal knowledge with anyone? With Baum?"

"No."

"Colonel Skene, I find you solely responsible for the unnecessary losses to this command and your road, which made Baum's raid necessary. You are dismissed from this camp. I will inform the Crown of your role in threatening the success of this campaign."

Skene stormed out of the room, slamming the door behind him.

Returning his focus to Phillips and Fraser, Burgoyne asked, "Questions? Comments?"

Shaking their heads in reply, Burgoyne continued confidently, "Fortunately, the British core of the army is unaffected by Skene's dereliction of duty. General Phillips send a messenger to take my report to General Carlton detailing Governor Skene's involvement in our setback at Bennington. Detail two of your officers to escort Skene back to Skenesboro. Gentlemen, you will accompany me to announce my intentions to continue the campaign to the officer corps."

Walking from the fort's headquarters building into the parade ground, followed tentatively by the army's senior officers, Burgoyne faced a formation of the entire officer corps organized by his adjutant to be held after the meeting. Smiling brilliantly, Burgoyne began, "Gentlemen, our stalwart Hessian allies scattered the rebel rabble. All that stands before is the remnants of the garrison of Ticonderoga. Those cowards ran once and will again! Once we reach Albany, General Clinton shall join with reinforcements and supplies. We shall crush this rebellion together. General Fraser, your light infantry shall screen our encampment from rebel eyes until we are ready to march. Dismissed!"

**General Court of New Hampshire
Exeter, September 1st**

John Langdon, President of the General Court, stood behind the minister's pulpit addressing the twenty members of the General Court dressed in their finest seated in the pews in the town's meeting house. Gesturing toward the man standing at his side Langdon said, "Gentleman. I give you General John Stark, the Victor of Bennington!"

Standing at attention, dressed in a suit of clothes, becoming his rank provided by the General Court as a reward for 'the memorable Battle of Bennington,' Stark replied, "Thank you for recognizing the victory won by your relatives, friends, and neighbors, not I. We are further beholden to Parson Allen and our Massachusetts neighbors. Together we destroyed the Hessian mercenaries who slaughtered our men on Long Island and their Ottawa and Abenaki allies who murdered the innocents of the Hudson Valley."

Unsurprised by Stark's terse response, John Langdon pulled a letter from his jacket pocket and said, "General Stark and members of the General Court, your attention, please." Holding an envelope up, Langdon removed the contents. "I received this letter from John Hancock, President of the Continental Congress, expressing the thanks of that body to John Stark for his service to the cause and in recognition of his victory at Bennington has elevated him to the rank of Brigadier General in the Continental Army."

As congratulatory applause commenced, Langdon handed Stark the letter and watched him read it silently and without expression. Observing Stark folding the letter and putting it in his pocket Langdon heard him whisper, "It's about time."

**Fort Miller
Burgoyne's Headquarters
Senior Officers' Call, August 19th**

Burgoyne stood on the porch of the fort's headquarters' building dressed in full uniform, wearing his military award for valor at the Battle of Minden, and spoke to five ranks of officers, all motionless as statues in the freshly raked dirt of the parade ground.

"Gentlemen, Lt. Colonel Baum has been killed in an ambush by a continental brigade reinforced by Vermont Rangers. Despite a forced march, Lt. Colonel Breymann's relief force was too late to save Baum's command. In retaliation, our allies' grenadiers and light infantry decimated the ambushers. General Riedesel has recently received reinforcements from Quebec, restoring his division to full strength."

The British officers stole a glance at Riedesel to see his reaction to Burgoyne's falsehood. Only two hundred and fifty Hessian regulars had arrived from the garrison of Fort Ticonderoga, not Quebec, to replace the loss of one thousand elite Hessian soldiers. But anyone who expected a dramatic response from Riedesel was disappointed. His eyes fixed on the horizon, Riedesel stood at attention, maintaining a stern but emotionless visage.

Grinning at the silent Riedesel for a moment, Burgoyne resumed confidently, "Although one may question the choice of Breymann as the commander of the relief force in light of his rivalry with Colonel Baum, the raid succeeded in capturing sufficient supplies to sustain this command for another month. I consider that adequate to continue the advance and prepare your men to cross the Hudson River at Saratoga and engage the remnants of the continental army encamped at Stillwater.

If the rebel commander has the good sense to retreat, we won't be delayed by the necessity of killing his men before capturing Albany. We possess exclusive control of Quebec's supply lines, further augmented by our road from Fort Edward to Skenesboro. I expect to be resupplied from Quebec momentarily."

On September 13th, Burgoyne crossed to the West Bank of Hudson and advanced south toward Albany.

General Lincoln's Headquarters
Pawlet, Vermont, August

General Lincoln had just purchased a third round of rum for militia Colonels Benjamin Woodbridge, John Brown, and Samuel Johnson, sitting at a table in the tap room of the town's only tavern. Lincoln raised his mug, "Gentlemen, I am pleased that our combined recruitment efforts have successfully enlisted two thousand militiamen. We are now in a position to deny Burgoyne food or reinforcements from Quebec."

Nodding to Colonel Wagner and young O'Brien, who had joined him for the last meetings with the militia leaders, Lincoln recounted their report of the stunning militia victory at Bennington. The overwhelming defeat of the Hessians had galvanized the Vermont and New Hampshire militias to mount an offensive against Burgoyne.

Colonel Woodbridge was a thirty-eight-year-old lawyer, physician, and farmer who had fought as a minute man at bunker hill and was active in the Massachusetts militia.

Colonel Brown participated in the capture of Fort Ticonderoga and was an active militia leader in defense of the New York frontier.

Colonel Johnson raised and commanded a Massachusetts militia regiment that participated in the siege of Boston.

Rapping his knuckles on the table for attention, Lincoln said, "Gentlemen, each of you will command a column of five hundred men with the following objectives. Colonel Woodbridge will capture and burn Skenesboro and Fort Ann, destroying supplies and munitions. Colonel Brown shall raid the portage at Fort Ticonderoga and destroy all wagons and batteaux. Colonel Johnson shall summon Fort Ticonderoga to surrender, supported by Colonel Brown.

"Your accomplishment of these three objectives shall cut off Burgoyne's supply line, fatally weakening his army. The defense of Albany depends on your success. The balance of five hundred men shall march with me to Stillwater to reinforce the Northern Army."

Colonel Warner completed the briefing.

"Gentlemen, my orders are to garrison Manchester and continue patrolling to detect any further raids from Burgoyne's army or the local loyalists to safeguard your families until you and your men return."

General Lincoln shook everyone's hands, then grimaced in anticipation and said, "Now I must meet with General Stark and pass on General Gate's orders to march his brigade to join the Northern Army at Stillwater. Wish me luck!"

Taking leave of Wagner and the militia Colonels, Lincoln turned to Tom and said, "O'Brien, you are to accompany me to Stillwater.

Colonel Kosciuszko has been assigned to prepare a fortified position blocking Burgoyne's advance upon Albany. He has asked that you assist him. Why?"

"My father and I traveled that route a hundred times freighting cargo. I have several sites which Colonel Kosciuszko might approve."

"Excellent. Let's be on our way. No time to waste."

CHAPTER SIX
Saratoga

Northern Army
Gates' Field Headquarters
Saratoga, New York, August 19th

Major General Horatio Gates rode into camp escorted by a brace of General Washington's Lifeguards and a pack train of three mules. Gates was accompanied by three servants and a pair of Marquees' tents gifted by the grateful citizens of Charles Town, South Carolina. Gates had successfully repulsed a British attack against that city in 1776 as Commanding General of the Southern Continental Army,

He was met by a mounted Officer of the Day who guided Gates' party into the Northern Army's encampment that engulfed the village of Still Water, New York. Gate's confidence grew as he rode past hundreds of tents, lean-tos, and huts housing thousands of continentals and militiamen hugging two miles of the west shore of the Hudson River. On a slight elevation near the village's river piers was an open space where Gate's servants unpacked the mule train erecting the Marquees and arranging his personal effects therein. In short order, the new headquarters of the Northern Department was put in order, and Gates snug at his office desk.

Major General Gates, a fifty-year-old retired British Major, had served the Empire in America during the French and Indian War in an administrative rather than a command capacity. Seriously wounded in that war, Gates had a pronounced limp, which with his wispy grey hair and thick spectacles, lent him a frail appearance. He was affectionally nicknamed "Granny Gates" by the soldiers because of his concern for their welfare and his elderly physical appearance.

Gates summoned his Deputy Adjutant General, Lt. Colonel James Wilkinson, and said, "Request Colonel Kosciuszko to report to me at his earliest convenience."

"Yes, sir," replied Wilkinson, who dropped the office partition at Gate's gesture, restoring his privacy.

Sitting back in his chair, Gates read the letter appointing him to the Commanding General after Philip Schuyler had been replaced by order of Congress on August 14, 1777. Smiling to himself, his promotion had resulted from ceaseless correspondence to the New England members of Congress condemning Schuyler's loss of Ticonderoga. Chuckling, Gates thought, *the distinguished members of Congress ignored that I had a much longer tenure in command of the Ticonderoga than the unlucky St. Clair, who held the position mere weeks before the British attack.*

Gates was unsurprised that the New England members of Congress had placed the total blame for the catastrophe upon St. Clair, known as a favorite of Washington. Secretly Gates was awed by St. Clair's ability to successfully evade the British pursuit saving thousands of veteran Continentals from capture. Those men now served him as the core of the Northern army.

That reminded him of General Lincoln's dispatch reporting the successful recruitment of two thousand militia in Vermont. Preparing and sending a message by mounted courier, Gates ordered Lincoln's return to Saratoga with five hundred men and approved the plan to use the balance to attack the British supply lines to Quebec.

Gates excitedly awaited his meeting with Colonel Kosciuszko, the Polish engineer who designed and built the West Point defenses formidable enough to stop the British's northern advance from New York City up the Hudson River. Gates's years in the British army had convinced him that only his defensive strategy would stop Burgoyne's invading army.

"Excuse me, sir, Colonel Kosciuszko is reporting as ordered."

Startled by Wilkinson's voice, Gates stammered, "Yes, please show the Colonel in."

As Wilkinson raised the partition, Kosciuszko strode in clean-shaven, with a robust military bearing, the physical opposite of the frail and round-shouldered Gates. Clicking his booted heels together and with a short head nod, Kosciuszko said, "General Gates, you sent for me?"

Staying seated, Gates gestured to Kosciuszko to stand at ease and commenced, "Yes, Colonel. You are critical to my plan to defeat Burgoyne. My twenty years in the British army have convinced me that our continentals don't have the training or discipline to defeat the British regulars and Hessian mercenaries in open battle. The militia shall run at the first sign of a line of British bayonets, and Albany shall fall."

The silent Kosciuszko waited for Gates to continue. Disappointed by Kosciuszko's lack of enthusiasm, Gates decided to get to the point.

"I want you to locate the strongest defensive site between Albany and Burgoyne's advancing army." After a soft chuckle, Gates continued, "I was told by General Schuyler that you were instrumental in delaying the building of Burgoyne's' ridiculous road from Skenesboro to Fort Edward."

Not joining in the merriment, Kosciuszko replied, "General Gates, I will do what you ask with the help of one of Colonel Morgan's men who possess intimate knowledge of this area. He assisted me in delaying the British advance. His name is Tom O'Brien, and I request that he be assigned to me for this mission."

Pleased but put off by Kosciuszko's brusque style, Gates thought, *Engineers.*

"Morgan's rifles are under my command, so O'Brien is yours," Gates replied. "The army's teamster is named O'Brien, any relation?"

"His son."

"I will inform his father of the assignment. That will be all, Colonel. Keep me informed."

Schuyler Mansion
Albany, New York, August 20th

Sitting quietly at his desk, Major General Schuyler finished reading the dispatch received that morning from a congressional courier. Removing his light blue sash, he folded it and the dispatch neatly and placed them in his desk drawer. Pulling a sheet of monogrammed writing paper from the drawer, he closed it and began to write a note addressed to his wife, Catherine Van Rensselaer.

> *My Dearest Kitty,*
> *I feel betrayed and misused by the men with whom we have risked all pursuing independence. Today Congress notified me that General Horatio Gates has replaced me as Commander of the Northern Army over the objection of General Washington. Congress cited my decision to employ half of the Ticonderoga garrison saved by General St. Clair to break the siege of Fort Stanwix threatened the defense of Albany. Washington rejected this because Burgoyne was building a road whose advance, I had successfully delayed sufficiently to receive reinforcements from the main army. My relief force broke the siege compelling the British to retreat to Quebec, saving the people of the Mohawk Valley, and freeing its militia to join the defense of Albany.*
> *I never sought or wanted this command. Nevertheless, for two years, I focused on nothing but the defeat of the British to the cost of lost time with you and the girls. For Congress to relieve me was blatant politics!*
> *My darling, I cannot prevent being overwhelmed by resentment that the extent of my commercial and political influence, seeded by envy of our wealth, had motivated this injustice.*

On the verge of losing control, he stood and began to pace to calm down. He passed a window and saw his daughters walking on the lawn with their lapdogs. His children's carefree innocence reminded him of his duty to safeguard them, and the settlers of the Hudson Valley from the devastation that would follow should the British not be stopped. Schuyler thought. *Get hold of yourself. The battle to defend Albany is inevitable and must be won.*

Resuming his seat, he folded the note and placed it in the drawer with the dispatch and sash. *Thank you, Kitty, for centering me.*

As a veteran military commander, Schuyler knew that only an army with adequate munitions had a chance to stop the British invasion. *Your wealth may defeat the British.*

"Captain Wolf, please come in."

When his aide poked his head into the office, Schuyler asked, "Have you reviewed the latest inventories of supplies and munitions?"

"Yes, sir."

"Come in and give me your opinion of the Northern army's readiness to stop this invasion?"

Stepping into the office, Captain Wolf answered, "Based on scouting reports, the invasion force is at least eight thousand regulars, supported by an extensive artillery train. All the continental division and brigade commanders in the Northern Army have requested a further supply of gunpowder and munitions. The Albany arsenal is inadequate to fill these requests."

Schuyler scribbled a note on his stationery and handed it to Wolf, saying, "I want you to send this by express messenger to my factor Mr. Jones in Albany."

"Yes, sir."

As Captain Wolf quietly closed the door behind him, Schuyler stood and resumed looking out his office window. *Mr. Jones will purchase the needed munitions from foreign merchants attracted by the war, and Brian will deliver them. I am honored to bear that expense as my contribution to driving the British back to Quebec.*

Oriska
August 25th

Brian O'Brien sat on the front porch of Han Yery's cabin in silent companionship with his friend. Han's wife, Tyonajanegen, could be heard talking to their sons, Cornelius and Paulus, in the kitchen. Attired for comfort, both men wore clean linen shirts, deerskin breeches, and moccasins.

Han Yery and Brian became battle companions when Brian owned a neighboring farm and defeated a raiding party of Ottawa during the French and Indian War. After his wife died, Brian sold his farm and started his freighting company. Brian transported the produce from Han's farm to market, continuing a close relationship between the two men.

"My friend, your family's resilience is impressive. Less than a month ago, Tyonajanegen and your sons fought alongside the militia at the Battle of Oriskany," said Brian.

"As America's ally against the British, the Oneida Nation was bound to fight. As a sachem, my duty was to lead the warriors." Smiling ruefully, Han Yery shook his head and continued, "Unfortunately, my family refused to allow me to go alone."

"Well, speaking as one of the men trapped in the ambush, without your intervention, none of us would have survived," remarked Brian.

Han Yery said, "In return for our aid, Congress has supplied ample powder and ammunition to defend Oriska and equip a war party to drive the Abenaki and Ottawa allied to the British from our territory."

"Has your harvest been affected by the fighting?"

Han Yery replied, "No. The people gathered the crop, and the corn and beans were stored in our barns."

"Since the siege of Fort Stanwix has been broken and the invasion repulsed, the British have retreated to Quebec. My batteaux convoy will be departing the day after tomorrow to return General Arnold and the relief force to reinforce the defense of Albany against Burgoyne. Will the Oneida war party be joining us?" asked Brian.

"No. A portion of Oriska's crop will be loaded for transport to the Northern army in compliance with our agreement with Congress. I will ride to Kanonwalohale to consult our principal sachem, Shenandoah, concerning our response to Burgoyne's army."

"There will be a fight, and the Oneida shall be welcome."

Laying down his pipe, Han Yery said, "You are wise in how the British will wage war against the continentals. What is your advice as to how the Oneida may best serve?"

"The British will rely upon the Abenaki and Ottawa warriors to kill the patriot scouts, blinding the continentals to their movements. The Oneida will be invaluable in driving your enemies back to Quebec and scouting the British movements."

"What of engaging the British regulars in combat?"

"That would be a mistake. General Burgoyne's regulars are experts fighting in close formation in the open field. Each man is trained for years to load and fire their muskets three times a minute in the blinding smoke and chaos of receiving volley fire from an enemy. When the enemy breaks and runs, they press home a mass bayonet charge to kill or capture them."

Han Yery passed his tobacco pouch to Brian and said, "This will be the last time we can enjoy a smoke until we defeat the British."

The odor of burning tobacco could be detected for miles and therefore forbidden in war.

Refiling his pipe, Brian asked, "How many warriors will be in the war party?"

"I have over one hundred volunteers but will take only sixty. The remainder will be needed to safeguard Oriska. I expect more volunteers from Kanonwalohale. The council of sachem shall decide how many warriors can be spared from the defense of the Oneida Nation. Fortunately, the Crown's Seneca and Mohawk had returned to their territories after Ledger retreated to Quebec."

Tyonajanegan emerged through the front door wearing a loose linen shift, her hair unbound and her feet bare.

Brian took several puffs on his pipe and asked, "Tyonajanegan, do you support the warriors leaving Oriska now that the other Haudenosaunee Nations who fight for the British know the Oneida are our allies?"

"After the Mohawk and Seneca were defeated at the Battle of Oriskany, our former brothers will not raid Oneida territory armed only with spears, bows, and tomahawks," Tyonajanegan answered.

"Han Yery, when do you leave?" asked Brian.

"Tomorrow."

"So soon? You were wounded at Oriskany."

Moving his wounded arm with no pain, he smiled at his wife and replied, "O'Brien, my wife is the Nation's chief healer for a good reason!"

"Your wife's gifts are obvious. Tyonajanegan, please forgive me if I do not intend to test your ability in the upcoming fight."

Smiling in reply to the compliment, Tyonajanegan walked behind her husband, placing her hands on his shoulder. Han Yery turned his head and smiled at his wife, "My son Paulus will accompany the war party. Cornelius will remain in Oriska."

"Paulus has proven his bravery and is ready to follow you into battle. The warriors of Oriska have shared the warpath with Cornelius and will follow him in your absence," Tyonajanegan agreed and returned inside.

"I have received a message from General Schuyler requesting me to see his factor in Albany after delivering General Arnold and the relief force of continentals to the Northern Army. The General has purchased additional munitions in Albany to improve the chances of stopping the invasion."

"Who did Congress appoint to replace Schuyler as the new commander?"

"General Horatio Gates. He was a former British officer who retired to the colonies."

"Do you think he will appreciate General Schuyler's gift?"

"I am sure the continentals will."

"Have you heard from Tom?"

"Yes. Your godson has been recruited by Morgan's Rifles and shall be with the Northern Army defending Albany."

"O'Brien, together, no one will ever be able to take this land from us."

Northern Army
Gates' Field Headquarters
Stillwater, New York
September 8th

Waiting for Kosciuszko's recommendation of where to site his defenses,

Gates had reoccupied the army's former encampment at Stillwater, New York.

As fortune would have it, Gates was brimming with good news to impart in his weekly letter to Congress, for which he intended to take full credit. Alone in his office, Gates couldn't help laughing out loud as he thought. *The providential improvement in the present circumstances was due solely to Schuyler's decisions and actions which ultimately cost him his command!*

General Arnold had returned today with the 1,200 continentals Schuyler had dispatched to break the siege of Fort Stanwix by the British and their Haudenosaunee allies. Schuyler forced the British to retreat to Quebec and dispersed loyalists to their homes and villages. The militia of the Mohawk River Valley had been freed to join Albany's defense.

Schuyler had published in every New York paper Burgoyne's declaration releasing his Ottawa and Abenaki to kill and burn out the settlers of the Hudson Valley, resulting in the death of Jane McRae and scores of others. Schuyler's dissemination of the British's acts of terrorism and murder resonated with every father, brother, and husband in the Mohawk and Hudson River Valleys. Those militiamen steadily arrived in the Stillwater camp, reinforcing his core command of continentals.

John Stark's unprecedented defeat of elite Hessian troops by militia had further instilled confidence in the people of New York that Burgoyne could be beaten.

Washington had been equally outraged by Burgoyne condoning the Abenaki and Ottawa slaughter of women and children. Washington knew from his days defending the Virginia frontier during the French and Indian War that the best unit to counter this threat was Morgan's Rifles and transferred that unit to Gates' command. However, in his letter to Congress, Gates decided not to emphasize Washington's motive for transferring one of his best units to his command. But he had no hesitation in assuring his supporters that the Rifles had enhanced the Northern Army's reconnaissance capability, which in his experience, went hand in hand with victory.

Gates concluded his letter by maintaining that Washington was solely at fault for the costly defeats in Long Island and White Plains for insisting upon exchanging volleys with the British in the open field. *When Burgoyne's army is shattered attacking my defenses, Congress shall appoint me as Commander in Chief, replacing Washington at last!*

He was satisfied with his presentation of the much-improved situation, confident that his supporters would take full credit for replacing Schuyler with him. Leaning back in his chair, Gates mused *the people would reward the man who won America's independence with anything he desired.* Excited, his focus returned to an opportunity to fight a purely defensive battle from an unassailable position that Kosciuszko would identify and fortify. *I intend to impress on my field commanders the importance of engaging Burgoyne's professionals from behind fortifications. I am confident that I will receive their full cooperation.*

Gates signed his letter, sealed the envelope, and called his aide to dispatch a mounted rider to carry his report to Congress in Philadelphia.

Bemis Heights
Three Miles North of Stillwater
September 7th

Riding side by side along the hard-packed dirt road from Fort Edward to Stillwater was two soldiers whose physical appearance could not have been more different.

In his early forties, the older man was an elegant rider, wearing a foreign military uniform, secured by a red waist sash signifying his commissioning by Congress as an officer in the continental army.

The much younger man wore the hunting shirt of the Rifle regiments and rode with the intensity of the hard-won experience of one not borne to the saddle.

Despite the disparity in their appearances, both highly skilled professionals had previously delayed a British invasion for almost three weeks preventing the King's crushing of the rebellion.

"Tom, you are a far better rider than I expected," Kosciuszko said.

"Thanks, Colonel. It is kind of you to say so, but repeatedly falling off this thoroughbred stallion the last few days is an effective teacher.

I am used to riding General Schuyler's geldings which he trusts his young daughter to ride."

Chuckling, the usually taciturn Polish gentleman enjoyed the younger man's courage, tenacity, and pragmatism.

"Tom, is the site you are showing me the best terrain to anchor our defense?"

"Colonel, I'm no engineer, but my father and I drove wagon trains over this road for years, and it's worth a look, sir."

"Agreed, Tom."

***

Standing companionly on a heavily wooded irregular plateau whose slope stopped no more than two hundred yards from the west bank of the Hudson River, Tom O'Brien and Colonel Kosciusko looked contently around the compass. Known locally as Bemis Heights, Kosciusko remarked, "Tom, this meets General Gate's requirements. Are you sure there is no way to bypass this plateau?"

Tom grinned and replied, "This is the only road to Albany, and the ridges further inland reach three hundred feet in height. The bottomland by the Hudson River narrows down to six hundred feet wide between a string of bluffs."

Nodding absently, Kosciuszko was already visualizing his defenses utilizing the east-to-west ravines that crossed the heights.

"Tom, I intend to recommend to General Gates that the army occupy Bemis Heights and the construction of its fortification commence without delay."

Stillwater, New York
The Road from Fort Edward
September 8th

Kosciuszko reined in his stallion to a gentle canter in consideration of Tom, who was still no equestrian. Focusing his inner eye on designing defenses to stymie Burgoyne's engineers from conceiving a successful method of assault, Kosciusko lost his sense of time and surroundings. Unconscious of the proximity of the continental camp, Kosciuszko was startled by a mounted calvary picket blocking the road on the outskirts of Stillwater.

Recognizing Kosciuszko from his distinctive uniform, the officer in charge said, "Colonel, General Gates, ordered that you immediately report to his headquarters upon arrival. The sergeant will escort you."

"Good. Time is of the essence," replied Kosciuszko.

***

Within the hour, Kosciuszko and Tom were traveling down the central road of the encampment lined with tents. Halting in front of the twin marquees serving as Gates' headquarters, guards took charge of their horses, and they were ushered into the General's presence.

Gates sitting at his field desk, busy penning a letter, looked up and said, "Welcome back. Scouts report the British Army should be crossing to our side of the Hudson River in the next few days. Please report your findings."

"I recommend moving the army three miles north to Bemis Heights. It is an elevation whose one-hundred-foot slope flattens two hundred yards from the Hudson River's west shore. I can fortify the site to block the main road to Albany."

"How Colonel?"

"The Heights will be trenched in an inverted "U" three-quarters of a mile long, defended by three cannon batteries. The flat plain by the river will be protected by two lines of earthworks with a flanking battery. A floating bridge of roped batteaux shall be constructed from the encampment to the east shore of the Hudson. The terminus of the floating bridge will be protected by earthworks and a battery of cannons."

"I approve your plan. Once the site is surveyed and the defensive lines are staked out, fatigue parties will be assigned to perform the work and install the cannons under your supervision. Written daily reports are to be delivered to headquarters. You are dismissed."

Walking together from the tent, Colonel Kosciuszko said, "Thank you, Tom. I intend to write General Washington and General Schuyler commending your service here. You are released to return to Morgan's Rifles forthwith. I have already sent Colonel Morgan a note commending your fine work."

"Thanks, Colonel. I appreciate your showing me how the terrain may be employed in combat. I intend to use that knowledge when I return to the Rifles."

"My pleasure. Good luck in the coming days."

Northern Army Encampment
Stillwater, New York
September 8th

"Colonel Morgan, look who finally turned up!"

Interrupted in his discussion with Major Henry Dearborn, Colonel Morgan turned sharply in the intruder's direction. Morgan's angry expression faded into a rare smile when he recognized that Tim Murphy had his old protégé, Tom O'Brien, in tow.

"Murphy, put yourself on report for interrupting a senior officer's conference. Then let me have a moment with O'Brien. Will you excuse me, Major?"

In his mid-twenties, Major Dearborn had fought in Quebec, where he was captured and recently exchanged for a British officer of equal rank. General Gates appointed Dearborn to command a composite light infantry battalion of three hundred chosen men. These men were armed and trained to fight with bayonetted muskets. They would fight in concert with the Rifles to protect them during the arduous loading of their rifles.

Gathering his notes, Dearborn replied, "That's fine, Colonel Morgan. We will continue this conversation tomorrow."

As Dearborn left the tent, Morgan stood up and walked over to Tom placing his left hand on his shoulder and shaking his hand.

"Murphy, stop hopping around like a grounded bird and draw yourself and Tom a tot of rum."

Morgan met Tom's eyes as Murphy went to get the rum and said, "We all heard about your work delaying the building of Burgoyne's Road and commanding the ambush that brought down St. Luc. Murphy told me he'd heard from the rangers you wounded St. Luc from over three hundred yards and ran off a war party of Ottawa three times the size of your command."

Smiling shyly, Tom shook his head slightly and replied, "Colonel, you can't believe everything you hear."

Morgan lost his grin and replied thoughtfully, "You and Colonel Kosciuszko gave us the time to march here. If not for your work, Burgoyne would have caught the Rifles in the open as an independent command and wiped us out. You have done well, and Murphy is bragging to anyone who will listen that his lessons have made you one of the best shots in the army."

Tom nodded and asked, "What does Sergeant Jones think of that?"

Morgan's smile returned, and he laughed, "Jones suggested that Murphy be ordered on a three-day hunting trip to get him out of camp for a while. The entire Rifle Corps is proud of you and has earned this outfit the respect that usually takes a few fistfights to accomplish."

Tom asked, "Your offer is still good to join the Rifles?"

Morgan tightened his hand on Tom's shoulders and replied, "You have been a member of the Rifles since receiving that hunting shirt in Washington's camp. We are all glad to have you back. The Rifles fight in pairs, except Murphy. He has asked for you as his partner. Do you agree?"

"Colonel, I'd be pleased to soldier with Murphy, thanks."

"Tom, we are going to be in for a fight. The British light infantry and Hessian jaegers don't know they can lose. We are going to have to teach them."

Gates' Field Headquarters
Stillwater, New York, September 9th

General Gates stood on a raised platform next to his Marque, wearing the light blue sash of the Commanding General. Facing his senior commanders assembled at attention in ranks in front of the platform, Gates addressed them. "Gentlemen, Colonel Kosciusko and I agree that we shall stop Burgoyne at Bemis Heights. The Heights shall be fortified, blocking the only road to Albany. A floating bridge will be constructed across the river to the east bank to facilitate our pursuit of the British should they retreat to Quebec. The 11th Massachusetts continentals shall guard access to the bridge, gather all the cattle on the east bank, and drive the herd across to the main camp to feed the army."

Colonel Morgan asked, "Where do you want the Rifles, General?"

Gates beamed at the assembled officers and replied, "The militia coming in from the north report that the wounding of St. Luc and death of several Ottawa chiefs by Colonel Kosciusko's men has resulted in most of the Abenaki and Ottawa abandoning Burgoyne. The threat your Rifle Corps was organized to counter no longer exists. But do not mistake me. The Rifles' reconnaissance of Burgoyne's movements and troop strengths shall be critical to finalizing our defensive positions."

Shaking his head and grimacing in disagreement, Morgan said, "General, one of my boys stripped Burgoyne's army of its warriors by shooting St. Luc at three hundred yards. I have at least a score of men just as good. With your permission, my Riflemen will eliminate Burgoyne and his senior officers before this army reaches Bemis Heights. The British soldier is trained not to think but to blindly obey orders. No officers, no orders – no army."

Gates, red-faced, his voice raised in outrage and retorted, "Colonel Morgan, I am well aware of your hatred of the British army. The infliction of a whipping of four hundred ninety-nine strokes was barbaric and unjustifiable! However, I wish to clarify that the deliberate targeting of British and Hessian officers will not be tolerated by me. Anyone who orders such action or acts on that order will be court marshaled."

Into the silence, Brigadier General Poor, a thoughtful veteran from New Hampshire, quietly asked, "General Gates, is the army expecting any further reinforcements?"

Grateful that Poor's question had defused what might have become a severe fracturing of his army, Gates thought, *Either I trust Morgan to run his rifles in his own fashion or return an elite unit and veteran commander to Washington. Never!*

"Thank you, General Poor, for returning us to the business. General Lincoln has been successful in his mission to muster two thousand New Hampshire and Vermont militiamen. Lincoln dispatched three columns to attack Burgoyne's supply line to Quebec, targeting

Skenesboro, Fort Ann, and the portage at Fort Ticonderoga. When General Lincoln rejoins the army, he shall command the right wing consisting of Glover, Nixon, and Patterson's brigades. He marches with five hundred militiamen to further strengthen our defenses."

"What of General Stark and his militia brigade? I hear Stark defeated Burgoyne's best Hessians at Bennington," said Poor.

Annoyed by Poor's reference to Stark, Gates responded dismissively, "Lincoln informed me he communicated my orders to Colonel Stark to immediately march his brigade to join in defense of Albany. I shall wait to see Stark before considering his role in this army."

Major General Arnold blurted out, barely controlling his demeanor, "What of me, General Gates?"

Before independence, Benedict Arnold was a prosperous merchant and shipmaster in his mid-thirties. Arnold had led a militia force that joined in the capture of Fort Ticonderoga and the invasion of Quebec. He had gained a reputation for suicidal courage and aggression in battle by successfully delaying a British invasion fleet in the Battle of Valcour Island in October 1776. Arnold survived, but his fleet was sunk or captured.

Gates appreciated Arnold for his martial aggressiveness but did not trust him. Determined to curb Arnold's insatiable quest for glory, Gates surrounded him with responsible senior commanders. Smiling indulgently, Gates replied, "Of course, General Arnold, as a Major General, you will command the advance guard. That shall consist of the Rifle Corps, the light infantry commanded by Major Dearborn, and continental brigades of General Poor and General Learned."

Satisfied, Arnold nodded, pleased with an opportunity to achieve further glory and recognition to advance his career.

As the meeting broke up, Arnold spoke quietly to Morgan, "Come to my headquarters for a tankard of rum and a frank discussion of what I expect from the Rifles."

Arnold's Field Headquarters
Stillwater, New York
September 9th, 8 pm

Sitting in front of Arnold's campaign tent before a small, banked fire, two men silently stared into the fire, nursing the tankard of rum a servant had served a half-hour ago. Despite their service together in the invasion of Quebec, Arnold, and Morgan had never been comfortable with each other.

Morgan, for his part, recognized Arnold's mindless courage and instinctive tactical ability, as exemplified by Arnold's ambush of the British invasion fleet, which allowed the patriot survivors to retreat from Quebec to Fort Ticonderoga in June 1776.

While a British prisoner in Quebec, Morgan had heard the story from his captors. On his initiative, Arnold built gunboats on Lake Champlain, manning and arming the fleet at his own expense. Arnold ambushed the British off Valcour Island, where Lake Champlain narrowed, negating the maneuverability of the vastly superior British force. The attack won Arnold instant recognition from Congress for his heroic leadership of a doomed command, which delayed the British invasion until the rivers had frozen. Unwilling to risk his ships, General Carlton recalled his forces leaving the continental army in possession of Fort Ticonderoga and the winter months to prepare its defense.

As a soldier, however, Morgan was appalled by Arnold's reckless aggression, resulting in the sacrifice of his entire command.

Arnold appreciated Morgan's control of an elite force of marksmen who, if used correctly, would defeat Burgoyne. Morgan's men were armed with a rifle vastly superior in range and accuracy to the musket-armed British and Hessian regulars. Arnold intended to use those marksmen to advance his military career and influence in Congress.

Confident in his ability to exploit Morgan's blind hatred of British officers, Arnold broke the silence and said, "Colonel Morgan, I disagree with General Gates that we can defeat Burgoyne by remaining behind fixed fortifications. There is wooded high ground on the flank of Bemis Heights. Bemis Heights would be subject to bombardment should the enemy discover and place cannons there. I will convince Gates to release my command to stop the British from reaching that ground. Your men are going to be crucial in that effort."

Morgan took a long swallow from his tankard and said, "My boys can handle Fraser's light infantry, but he will have his regiment, the 20th, who will use bayonet charges to scatter and hunt us down while we reload our rifles."

As anticipated, Morgan's concern for his men must be addressed before Arnold could count on his support.

Arnold shook his head and replied, "Dearborn's men are under my command and will always accompany your Rifles in the field."

"Fraser will have artillery with the advance guard, and Dearborn's bayonets will not protect his men or mine from case shot."

Arnold smiled and said, "Not if the officers and men servicing those cannons are dead."

Morgan smiled in return and said, "Gates?"

Arnold nodded. "I disagree with General Gates's prohibition against targeting enemy officers. Your riflemen give us an advantage that must be used to its fullest. Burgoyne's army outnumbers our continentals and the veteran militia. The raw militia will not fight toe to toe with the British regulars. If Bemis Heights is captured, Albany will be lost."

Nodding, Morgan reluctantly agreed with Arnold to disobey Gate's orders not to target enemy officers. "I will explain the situation to my men and how best they can serve this army and defeat Burgoyne."

Freeman Farm
Burgoyne's Field Headquarters
Western Side of the Hudson River
September 15th

Standing with his senior commanders at the foot of the bridge of boats constructed by his engineers, Burgoyne watched his army cross to the west shore of the Hudson. As each regiment reached land, the men were directed to the site chosen to camp along the river's edge. Known as the Great Redoubt, the encampment was defended by cannon batteries and housed the headquarters, hospital, arsenal, and artillery park.

Choosing to speak informally, Burgoyne decided to commence with the positive. "The rebels foolishly failed to oppose our construction of a bridge of batteaux or crossing of the Hudson River at Saratoga. It is confirmed that Gates has replaced Schuyler. Gates is nothing more than a clerk. Colonel Peters, please continue the briefing."

Lt. Colonel Peters evaded capture at Bennington, and his surviving Queen's Rangers had borne the brunt of scouting since the desertion of most of the Ottawa and Abenaki. After crossing the Hudson, he and his men fought a deadly battle with Morgan's Rifles. The Rangers had lost. A thorough professional, Peters reluctantly began his report, disappointed with his men's inability to fight through the Rifles and adequately scout the rebel's position.

"The rebels have fortified high ground several hundred meters from the shore of the Hudson River. The only road to Albany passes through that terrain protected by a double line of earthworks with interlocking batteries. The loyalist farmers report unoccupied high ground on the left flank of the rebels' defensive line, but Morgan's Rifles prevented my confirming its existence."

In his late thirties, John Peters had been a colonel of the New York militia, a Judge of the Court of Common Pleas, and appointed a member of the Continental Congress in 1774. Peters and his family remained loyal to George the Third and fled to Quebec.

Burgoyne nodded at Peters and resumed the briefing. "Thank you, Colonel. Gates is a defensive commander with an exposed left flank which we will exploit. Bemis Heights shall be bombarded until the rebel defenders flee like rats from a burning building. After tomorrow there will be nothing between Albany and us."

General Philips asked, "What of St. Ledger?"

Burgoyne replied with a smile, "St. Ledger is on the way. He will join us in Albany. His regulars will replace those lost at Bennington."

General Fraser asked, "General, what is the plan of attack?"

"The army will form into three columns and advance simultaneously upon Bemis Heights. General Fraser will lead the advance corps strengthened by Lt. Colonel Breymann's grenadiers and Colonel Peter's Queen's Rangers. The advance corps shall capture the high ground identified by Colonel Peters, and artillery will bombard Bemis Heights.

"General Hamilton shall lead the British line regiments in the center column and demonstrate in front of Bemis Heights to distract the rebels. General Riedesel commands his Hessians, which shall march up the shore road pinning the rebel brigades stationed in the river defenses. He shall also escort the batteaux convoy carrying the army's artillery and provisions. The three columns must coordinate their advance. I will be with General Hamilton's central column.

"Once the rebels are driven from their fortifications, we shall advance with the batteaux convoy to capture Albany before Washington can react. The rebellion shall be crushed before months end."

Morgan's Headquarters
Rifle Corps, September 19th

Standing on the bed of a wagon in the camp center, Morgan towered over a sea of the upturned faces of hundreds of his riflemen and said, "Men, I have just received orders from General Arnold. The Rifles and Major Dearborn's light infantry will perform reconnaissance in force on the left flank to prevent the British from locating and occupying the high ground to our west. Dearborn's light infantry is with us to defend against bayonet attacks when reloading. Don't get separated from them!

"Attention to orders – target British officers and artillerymen foremost. Our advance shall not be supported by cannons. General Gates is not releasing any from the defenses of Bemis Heights."

"That's not very friendly of Gates!" Tim Murphy shouted.

Morgan shouted back, "What do you suggest we do?"

"Keep shooting the crew of any enemy cannon until they die or abandon it."

Morgan nodded and continued, "No one is to leave the woods without my direct orders –a successful bayonet charge will destroy us. Our strength lies in the forest, not the open fields. We will be marching out within the hour. I want to talk to Murphy, O'Brien, and Sergeant Jones. The rest of you are dismissed."

Leading the men into his tent, he signaled each to take a seat and a tankard of rum from his supply. When each had complied, Morgan said, "The British always lead from the front. Murphy's mission is to eliminate the senior leadership of Burgoyne's army. Your targets are Generals, Colonels, and Majors. Tom, you are Tim's spotter. Use your woodcraft to position Murphy close to the British command group and ensure no one shoots him. Sergeant Jones, your job is to prevent anyone interfering with Murphy and O'Brien from carrying out my orders. Except for me, you are the meanest son of a bitch in this command."

Jones was an ageless ogre of a man with a full beard and head of unruly hair never tamed by a brush. Over six feet in height, two hundred pounds of muscle, the quickest Tom had ever seen with a knife and a berserker in combat. Jones had been the senior sergeant of the Rifles since its formation.

Pleased by the rare compliment, Jones replied, "Colonel, I will deliver both boys to you tonight to finish this rum."

General Enoch Poor's Field Headquarters
Officers' Call, September 19th

General Poor, a French and Indian war veteran, was a shipbuilder and merchant from Exeter, New Hampshire, twice elected to the New Hampshire assembly. After participating in the Battle of Lexington, Poor was elected Colonel of the 2nd New Hampshire regiment and joined General Montgomery's invasion of Quebec. After Montgomery's death, Poor led the survivors back to Fort Ticonderoga. In February 1777, Poor was promoted to Brigadier General to command the New Hampshire Brigade and sent to Fort Ticonderoga to join the garrison. As ordered by General St. Clair, the brigade retreated from Ticonderoga. The 2nd New Hampshire, commanded by Colonel Hale, became detached during the retreat and fought with Colonel Francis's rearguard at Hubbardton. The regiment was reformed by the survivors.

Fourteen hundred continentals, graduates of winter training at Valley Forge, stood in their regiments in the dew-covered grass of the sprawling encampment awaiting the order to march to engage the British.

Walking alone down past the first rank of his brigade, Poor sensed the men's nervousness and their anticipation to test themselves against the lobsterback invaders. Reaching the formation center, Poor faced his men and said, "We have participated in every significant trial of arms in the Northern Department. You have performed admirably and with honor."

Colonel Joseph Cilley, commander of the 1st New Hampshire continentals, voiced the brigade's chief concern: "The men do not appreciate being reproached by the militia for retreating from Fort Ticonderoga without firing a shot. The brigade wants to fight the British and Hessians man to man in the open field, not behind fortification like garrison troops."

Cilley, in his mid-thirties, had fought in the French and Indian War as a member of Rodgers' rangers. He served as an officer in the siege of Boston, during the invasion of Quebec, and at the Battle of Trenton. Washington appointed Cilley to command the 1st New Hampshire when John Stark resigned his commission after being passed over for promotion to General.

General Poor replied, "We are under the command of General Arnold. He has informed me of his intention to meet and repulse the anticipated attack upon the left flank of Bemis Heights. You may inform the men that they shall demonstrate their mettle to the militia today."

Bemis Heights Fortifications
Rifle Corps Encampment
September 19th, 8 am

Lounging against the log and earthwork fortification on the extreme left flank of the continental defenses, Tom O'Brien and Tim Murphy were finishing breakfast while enjoying the coolness of the early morning.

Standing and looking out from the rampart, Tim remarked, "Tom, this fog will not ease General Arnold's mind about the lobsterbacks trying to turn our left flank."

"Tim, I have heard we are going out with Dearborn's light infantry to see if the British are as smart as Arnold thinks they are," Tom replied.

Tom smiled as he saw Sergeant Jones stalk grumpily towards his involuntary wards, and Jones yelled at them, "You damned privates are not to do anything stupid and get yourself killed, or the Colonel will not be happy!"

Never one to avoid an opportunity to bate a sergeant, particularly Jones, Tim drawled, "Colonel wants me to shoot Burgoyne, so Tom and I will be getting as close as we can, Sergeant."

Snorting in reply but holding his tongue because he knew that was Colonel Morgan's orders. Jones had drawn a musket with a bayonet from the army quartermaster, which he intended to carry in addition to his rifle.

Noticing the sergeant's additional weapon, Tom raised his extra musket. Since he lacked Jones' reach, weight, and strength, his musket was without a bayonet, allowing faster reloading and firing. That precaution had proven to be critical in the ambush of St. Luc.

From the fog emanated the commanding voice of Colonel Morgan, addressing his officers, "Lt. Colonel Butler, you will command the advance with two companies of riflemen seconded by Major Morris and supported by a company of Major Dearborn's light infantry. You will proceed northwest to the forest where we skirmished with the Hessian jaegers and Queen's rangers yesterday. You are not to cross any open ground until joined by the remainder of Dearborn's lights and the second line of riflemen under my command."

"Understood, Colonel. Captain Swearingen led the scouts out," shouted Butler.

Tim motioned to Tom and Jones and said, "That's us. Remember, we are strictly under Colonel Morgan's orders and no one else. I have a job, and you two will help me achieve it."

Tom and Sergeant Jones looked at Tim, who had changed from the wise-cracking fun-loving boy to a cold professional military sniper, one of the first to proudly serve and protect his country from all enemies.

Tom and Jones nodded and followed Murphy into the fog-shrouded woods

General Hamilton's Center Column
Outskirts of Freeman's Farm
September 19th, Noon

After leading his column from camp across an intervening ravine, dense forest, and rough terrain, General James Hamilton's British line

131

regiments emerged into the open fields of Freeman's farm.

In his mid-thirties, Hamilton, a member of the Scottish gentry, commanded troops under General Carlton, expelling the rebel invaders from Quebec.

Hamilton turned to General Burgoyne, who had accompanied the column, and said, "General, I propose an advance picket to cross the open ground toward the flank of the rebel fortifications."

Burgoyne mounted with his aides and staff, nodded brusquely, gestured that Hamilton's recommendation was approved, and ordered.

"General Hamilton, please signal Fraser and Riedesel's columns that I am commencing the attack."

Hamilton transmitted the General's orders to an aide, then shouted, "Major Forbes, picket line forward."

Wood Bordering Freeman's Farm
Captain Swearingen's Rifle Detachment
September 19th, Noon

Perched in a tree on the edge of the fields of Freeman Farm, Tom and Tim observed a single line of red led by a mounted officer emerge from the opposite woods advancing steadily toward their position. Sergeant Jones called from the ground, "First blood to the Rifles. Remember men, officers, and sergeants first. Murphy, yours is the mounted officer."

Tim whispered to Tom as the enemy picket line closed within range, "Tom, when the firing starts, you and I hold this position until we see what will emerge from the woods on our left flank. We don't know the size of the force following the pickets. Swearingen is a soldier, not a hunter. If he breaks cover, we are not following. That is not our job. Agreed?"

"Yes, Tim."

"Agreed, sergeant?" asked Murphy.

The grunt from the brush below signified Jones's disgust to obey a private's orders.

As the mounted officer passed into range, Murphy shot him from his saddle, signaling the hidden riflemen to commence fire.

Freeman's Farm
Perimeter Wood
September 19th, 1 pm

"Murphy, what the hell happened?" roared Colonel Morgan.

Morgan, accompanied by Major Morris, Major Dearborn, and Lt. Colonel Wilkinson, a senior aide of General Gates, gathered below Tim and Tom's firing platform.

"Tom, you tell them. I'm too busy doing my job," Murphy said with authority.

Tom nodded, looked down into the eyes of the agitated senior officers, and described the chaos of the last hour.

"Colonel Murphy dropped the mounted officer commanding the British pickets. The boys picked off the other officers and sergeants. Captain Swearingen and Lieutenant Moore broke cover, following the surviving lobsterbacks into the far woods. Swearingen and Moore, with the scouts, entered the trees and were repulsed by an unbroken line of regulars who fired a volley killing Sweringen, Moore, and many of those who followed them. The survivors scattered to whatever cover they could find."

Colonel Morgan turned to look accusingly at Dearborn.

"Where were you!"

Unflinchingly meeting Morgan's glare, Dearborn responded in kind.

"Colonel, my men and I obeyed your orders. We held our position in the woods to protect your riflemen, who continued to do their jobs. Fraser's advance corps and a column of regulars were following the picket line. Queen's Rangers chased your retreating riflemen across the field. A column of British regulars emerged minutes later, advancing toward our position. Outnumbered, with Fraser's advance corps on my flank, I retreated with my men and the Rifles who followed your orders."

Tom continued, "Tim dropped a ranger officer, and the other Rifles which remained undercover made the rangers chasing our men pay by dropping a dozen of them. The rangers retreated, and our men regained the woods. We were too few to oppose the advancing column of regulars, so Major Dearborn ordered the retreat, and the command fell back to our present position."

Morgan nodded stiffly and said to Wilkinson, "I dispatched a messenger to General Gates with a report of the position and strength of the British column."

Lt. Colonel Wilkinson replied, "General Poor's continental brigade is currently advancing to contest the column of British regulars."

Morgan turned to Major Morris and ordered, "Morris, use your turkey call to signal our men to gather here under the protection of Major Dearborn's light infantry. Fraser will be on Poor's flank, and the Rifles and light infantry must defend it."

Freeman's Farm
General Poor's Field Headquarters
September 19th, 2pm

"General Poor. Colonel Morgan and Major Dearborn are here to see you."

"Thank you, Captain. Please show them in."

Morgan walked into the hastily erected lean-to equipped with a camp table, noting the brigade's regimental commanders surrounding it.

Poor addressed the gathering, "Gentlemen, we will soon learn whether the continental army can stand toe to toe with British regulars. We are roughly equal in size, and the British will be at a disadvantage advancing into our fire. The world is watching."

Cilley, the brigade's senior Colonel, volunteered, "General, the men look forward to using the bayonets General Schuyler sent from the Albany arsenal."

Looking around the circle of faces, Poor prompted them, "Emphasis to your men that their training to deliver three volleys a minute and the discipline to receive the British volleys without breaking shall decide this battle. We must avoid a general melee at all costs. Since entering service, every British soldier has participated in daily bayonet drills. Our men shall keep their bayonets sheathed until ordered to draw and fix. Colonel Morgan, would you continue the briefing."

Morgan said, "Reassure your men that the Rifles and Major Dearborn's light infantry will be on your left flank, holding the woods west of Coulter Farm against whatever comes."

Colonel Cilley asked Wilkinson, "What of supporting artillery? The British are bringing up three and six-pound batteries to support the advance. Has General Gates agreed to release any cannons from the defense of Bemis Heights?"

"No, Colonel." Wilkinson's sharp reply and unwillingness to meet anyone's eyes expressed his discomfort as Gates' representative.

"Wilkinson, those cannons are going to murder us. Are you going to stand with us to report to Gates the effect of his decision?" grated Cilley.

Wilkinson abruptly departed in silence.

Watching the twenty-year-old Wilkinson gallop away on a spirited thoroughbred, Morgan snorted, "A twenty-year-old Lt. Colonel who doesn't know one end of a musket from the other. Gates can sure pick 'em." Turning back, Morgan continued, "General Poor, in the absence of our counter batteries, I recommend a company of my Rifles is stationed with each of your regiments to silence the British cannons."

Seeing the relief on the faces of his regimental commanders that their men would not be subject to being raked by enemy case shot without hope of a respite, Poor replied, "Recommendation granted."

Freeman's Farm
September 19th, 3 pm

General Burgoyne sat on his horse behind the rear rank of his brigade of regulars exchanging volleys with the regiments of Poor's brigade standing in opposing lines less than fifty yards away. Engulfed in a cloud of smoke and deafened by the constant musket fire Burgoyne was shocked by the stalwart performance of the continentals. Burgoyne grated through clenched teeth, "General Phillips, the 62nd is done. The damned rebels have captured Hadden's battery of six-pounders and dragged the cannons behind their lines. We must retake them before they are turned on by our men. You will lead the 20th to stabilize the lines of engagement and recapture those guns."

"Yes, sir. I recommend that you fall back. The rebel riflemen in those nearby trees killed or wounded the artillerymen that serviced the captured cannons."

"Philips, your concern is appreciated, but our lines must be stabilized, requiring my presence here."

As Burgoyne turned to his adjutant, the man slumped in his saddle and fell lifeless. Burgoyne looked down at the bloody body of his friend and said to his aide, "Captain Robertson, check him." Turning to face another staff officer, he motioned him close enough to be heard. He said, "Captain Smith, you are to give General Riedesel my compliments and request him to send as many men as he can spare to attack the rebel's flank to reduce the pressure on the center column. Be quick about it!"

Burgoyne then turned and dropped his eyes to Captain Robertson, who had dismounted to examine the fallen officer. Robertson shook his head slightly and said, "I am sorry, sir. The Colonel is dead."

Nodding, Burgoyne became aware of the agitated state of his surviving staff and guards. They had now been stationary for over a minute within the killing zone of a known marksman. Recognizing that courage was expected but not foolishness, he spurred his horse toward the advance corps, followed by his entourage. He shouted over his shoulder, "Good luck Philips. I will discuss with General Fraser what can be done to attack the flank of the rebel line to break this stalemate."

***

Across the battlefield, Tim Murphy cursed softly, "Dammit, Tom. In another couple of seconds, I would have got another one. At least I got Burgoyne."

Continuing to scan the chaos of movement shrouded in smoke, Tom observed a horseman spur away from the fallen man, followed by a pack of mounted officers toward the position where General Fraser had been reportedly seen.

"Sorry, Tim. I don't know whom you hit. But it wasn't Burgoyne. I believe he is the rider leading the mounted party across our front. You did silence that battery. There are no more mounted officers to our front."

Tim smiled and said, "What do you think? Should we follow Burgoyne to our left flank?"

"No. Burgoyne's reinforcing the attack here. General Poor has extended our flank with Connecticut militia, supported by a company of Rifles. The continentals need us here to demoralize the British by eliminating their officers."

"Agreed. Go down and talk to Sergeant Jones and see how things stand on the ground."

Climbing down from his perch Tom was enveloped in the stinging smoke and painful din of the firing line.

"I don't see any of Dearborn's light infantrymen, sergeant," Tom said.

His face burned by gunpowder and his hunting shirt greyed by the perpetual fog of war, Jones replied, "You are not as stupid as you look, O'Brien! A messenger from Dearborn asked Colonel Morgan to release his men to reform his unit. General Arnold has ordered Dearborn's light infantry and Lattimore's militia to defend the perimeter of Coulter Farm against any reinforcement from Fraser on our left flank. Colonel Morgan agreed and gave Dearborn two companies of rifles to protect his flanks and suppress any artillery support Fraser may employ."

Tom recognized their position in the defensive line had been weakened but trusted Morgan's decision was necessary. Ever practical, Tom focused on the current situation and asked, "Sergeant, Murphy, and I are staying here. Let us know which units Colonel Morgan wants us to focus on."

Jones growled, "O'Brien. You'll know when I do." Handing Tom a small sack, Jones continued, "This contains some smoked jerky the Colonel dropped off for the unit. Get back to work before I get the impression that you are giving me orders."

Hiding his grin, Tom was touched by the motherly concern of the terrifying sergeant. Looking into the sack, he saw dried food, a flask of water, additional rifle ammunition, and powder, all critical to his wards' survival.

Upon returning, Murphy asked, "What did the old bear blame us for now?"

"The sergeant said he misses us and will buy us a drink when this is over."

Receiving the expected chuckle, Tom handed Tim a piece of jerky and took one himself. Chewing the dried meat, they silently scanned the pandemonium of thousands of men killing each other distinguished only by the color of their uniforms.

Coulter Farm
September 19th, 3 pm

Occupying the perimeter woods, Major Dearborn had deployed his men into two ranks without bayonets fixed to improve their speed of loading and firing. Satisfied with his preparations, Dearborn was pleased with the silence maintained by his lights and Colonel Lattimer's militia.

In his early fifties, Jonathan Lattimore served as an officer under General Washington's command in the siege of Boston and the battles around New York City.

Pleased but sobered by what would occur next, Dearborn heard the soft rustle of men moving steadily through the underbrush, advancing toward them without apparently detecting their presence. Judging the distance by sound alone, Dearborn waited until the enemy was within point-blank range and yelled, "Fire."

Hundreds of muskets fired in the direction of the movement, eliciting screams from scores of voices, and Dearborn heard a deep baritone shout, "The bastard killed the captain. No Mercy!"

Dearborn shouted, "First company, fix bayonets and charge! Second company reloads and advances."

Leading the first company forward, Dearborn and his men encountered Queen's rangers charging toward them in revenge and efficiently bayonetted or routed them. After pursuing the rangers for about fifty yards, Dearborn ordered his men to return their bayonets to their scabbards and reload. Minutes passed as his second company rejoined after reloading and securing the surviving rangers. Hearing movement to this front, Dearborn ordered, "Form ranks by company. The first rank, hold your fire until you have targets. Second rank no firing until the first rank has fired. No fixing bayonets unless ordered."

As he listened, individual shots rang out along his first rank until the firing became prolonged. Judging the moment of enemy contact, he yelled, "The first line cease firing and reload. The second rank advance and mark your targets."

As the men began to obey, he turned to his aide and said, "You will deliver the following message to General Poor. We have encountered Fraser's outposts and scattered a picket of rangers. We were attacked by enemy light infantry within minutes, and I expect a counterattack by Fraser on your brigade's left flank. I intend to fall back to join the 3rd New Hampshire. I will withdraw across the fields of Coulter Farm in company with Lattimore's Connecticut militia until we join your brigade's firing line."

As the firing intensified, Dearborn reversed the process of his advance by having his second rank fire and then fall back through the first rank that had previously loaded. As the heavily outnumbered continental light infantry was driven into the open fields, British grenadiers charged Dearborn's left flank with fixed bayonets. General Fraser led his regiment, the 24th, against his right flank. Before either flank attack reached Dearborn's men, Colonel Lattimore's militia fired a volley into the grenadiers disrupting the bayonet charge and allowing the first rank of Dearborn's men to fire a volley into Fraser's 24th.

Dearborn shouted, "Well done, Lattimore. Second-rank fire. First-rank fix bayonets. We shall shield Lattimore's militia and our second rank until they reload. Then we will continue to fall back ten paces, the second rank will come forward, fire, and fix bayonets, and the first rank will fall back and reload. This maneuver shall be repeated until the command joins the firing line of the 3rd New Hampshire. Remember your training."

Yard by yard, always facing the British, the first battalion of continental light infantry and the Connecticut militia crossed the fields of Coulter Farm in a fighting retreat.

As the Dearborn' and Lattimore's men joined the 3rd New Hampshire firing line, Dearborn met General Poor, who said, "Major Dearborn, that was a masterful withdrawal. The discipline of your light infantry inspired the militia to stay and fight. Your bayonets and the militia's firepower have prevented Fraser from turning our left flank."

Exhausted and light-headed from the adrenaline, Dearborn replied, "Thanks, General. The men were magnificent. Where do you want us?"

Briefly studying the current tactical situation, Poor replied, "Lattimore's militia will mix into 3rd New Hampshire. The continentals will stiffen their resolve. Your lights will extend the 3rd New Hampshire line. Colonel van Cortland of the 2nd New York will refuse the line to guard the brigade's flank. Fraser's men must cross open fields and advance into our fire. Today we bleed Burgoyne's finest units of their strength."

Colonel Scammel nodded toward the opposite woods at the gathering of enemy troops and asked, "Reinforcements?"

Frowning for the first time that day, Poor replied, "My aide advises that there has been resistance from General Gates to release General Learned's brigade from the Bemis Heights fortifications. General Arnold, however, recognizes the dire necessity to hold Fraser here and intends to order Learned to march to our relief."

Bemis Heights
Gates' Headquarters
September 19th, 3 pm

General Arnold had been waiting over a half-hour outside Gates' Marque after being summoned from the battlefield by Lt. Colonel Wilkinson. Pacing back and forth, Arnold listened to the increasing frequency and intensity of the musket fire, which he recognized as the moment of maximum effort with victory in the balance.

Wilkinson abruptly opened the tent flap and stepped out, motioning Arnold to enter. Walking into Gates' office, Arnold saw the Commanding General hunched over his field desk, munching on a sandwich and writing a dispatch.

"General Arnold, Colonel Wilkinson reported that you have ordered Learned brigade to reinforce the left flank of Poor's brigade in disobedience of my orders. Is that correct?"

Standing at ease in front of Gates' field desk, Arnold looked at the space above the seated Gates and barked, "That is correct!"

Surging to his feet, Gates shouted, "If this was a British army, I would have you shot for insubordination! Since it is not, and you are a favorite of Washington, General Arnold shall receive no mention in my official dispatch to Congress. You are dismissed."

Dropping his gaze to stare into Gates' eyes, Arnold replied, "You ought to visit the battlefield before finalizing that dispatch. I'll be there if you think of anything else to say."

General Riedesel's Field Headquarters
Officers' Call
September 19th, 3 pm

Standing behind a log rampart built from the shore of the Hudson River across the road to Albany and through the forest facing the rebel entrenchments of Bemis Heights and adjacent river defense, Riedesel chaffed at his elite soldiers being relegated to merely pinning Gates' attention. Thoroughly agitated, Riedesel's professional restraint broke, and he shared his frustration with his aide.

"We are wasted here. Gates squanders most of his army immobile behind unassailable defenses, revealing him to be a fool, a coward, or perhaps both."

"General, a messenger from General Burgoyne, wishes to see you."

Resuming his professional demeanor, Riedesel replied in a conversational tone, "Of course, Captain."

Escorted by his adjutant, Riedesel recognized one of Burgoyne's arrogant child aristocrats with which he surrounded himself. However, this peacock's plumage was filthy and bloodstained, and the boy looked about to cry. A grandfather himself, Riedesel softened his manner and asked, "Lieutenant, what is your message?"

Consciously straightening his spine and squaring his shoulders, the messenger stammered, "General Riedesel…General Burgoyne requests you march with all haste with every man that can be spared to his aid at Coulter's Farm."

Adrenaline pouring through his body Riedesel slapped the rampart, gestured his adjutant to summon his staff, and replied to the peacock, "Return to General Burgoyne and assure him reinforcements are on the way."

As the boy mounted and galloped away, Riedesel's staff gathered about him, waiting eagerly to join the fight. Glancing at his map, Riedesel decided upon his action and said, "General Burgoyne needs our help to attack the enemy's right flank and strengthen General Phillips's central column of regulars. Captain Pausch, you will take your battery of cannons escorted by infantry and reinforce General Phillips's assault. I will take the regiment Von Riedesel and two companies of the regiment Von Rhetz and work my way behind the rebel's right flank.

"General Specht, you will continue to guard the army's supplies and reserve artillery pending my return. Time is of the essence!"

Riedesel's Relief Column
5 pm

Riedesel double-timed his relief column a mile through the rough country Gates had failed to fortify. Riedesel struck Poor's right flank with the men of the Von Rhetz regiment singing Hessian hymns accompanied by the regimental band. That assault shattered the Connecticut militia, which fell back into the woods.

Captain Pausch's horse-drawn battery of four 6-pounder cannons passed behind the firing line of British regulars and halted at the center of the collapsing British formation. Professionalism born from a lifetime of training permitted the artillerymen to unhitch the horses, load, and prime the cannons in mere minutes. Then, fire round after round of case shot into the advancing rebel militia and continentals.

***

Looking down from his perch upon the slaughter resulting from the enemy cannons, Tim shook his fist at the battery protected by Hessian light infantry and jaegers and yelled, "My God, Tom. I have no ammunition, and those bastards are murdering our men!"

Leaning over the platform's edge, Tom yelled, "Sergeant, we need ammunition to silence those guns!"

Instead of Jones, Tom saw Colonel Scammel and heard him say,

"Tom, you and Murphy are to join my regiment. We are falling back to Bemis Heights. Our ammunition is almost exhausted, and Hessians are attacking our flank. Fortunately, their numbers are insufficient to block our line of withdrawal."

Climbing down from their platform, Tom and Tim joined Colonel Scammel, organizing his regiment and the militia to march to Bemis Heights. Tom asked, "Colonel, where is Jones?"

Colonel Scammel looked at the two men he considered the guardian angels of his men this day and said sadly, "I am sorry, men. The sergeant shouted to the other riflemen, and they all joined the militia in a charge on the collapsing formation of British regulars. The sergeant and the militia were cut down by cannon fire from the Hessian relief force."

Cursing quietly, Tim shook his head, looked at the Colonel, and replied, "We ran out of ammunition. A hundred more rounds, and we would have silenced that battery. The sergeant's charge would have broken the British!"

"The Rifles kept us in this battle for five hours with no supporting artillery," Scammel replied. "We bleed Burgoyne's line regiments all day. Now it is time to withdraw to Bemis Heights to regroup. Morale is high, and the men are confident. We stood toe to toe with their regulars, and all they accomplished was the occupation of some farmland. Bemis Heights is secure, and there will be no pursuit by the enemy with the fall of darkness."

2nd New York, Courtland Farm
Left Flank of Continental Line
6 pm

After General Learned's brigade had been repulsed by the British, the regiments protecting the extreme left flank were compelled to withdraw rapidly, causing Colonel Philip van Cortlandt and the 2nd New York continentals to be cut off from the safety of Bemis Heights.

Falling back into the woods, Colonel van Cortlandt squatted, encircled by his company commanders, and quietly addressed them.

"The regiment is to retreat to the abandoned sunken road and conceal itself in the underbrush. Only silence and stillness shall ensure our survival."

Leading his regiment to the road, van Cortlandt ordered his officers to direct their men to place their musket on the ground beside them. Then to provide an example, van Cortlandt willed himself to close his eyes and go perfectly still, listening for the enemy.

When darkness began to descend on the woods, van Cortlandt sensed it was safe to leave when a deer walked by him, undisturbed by his presence or his men's.

Moving slowly and quietly, he organized small parties to depart at ten-minute intervals after personally unloading each man's musket. As his party approached Bemis Heights, he was met by a Mohican warrior who whispered, "Colonel van Cortlandt, my brothers have intercepted your advance parties and guided them into the fortification where General Poor's brigade has been stationed."

Nodding, van Cortlandt asked, "And the other regiments?"

"You are the last," the Mohican replied. "The British have not withdrawn to their camp. Each enemy unit has fortified the ground they held after the battle with earthworks. General Gates wants every man within the fortifications if Burgoyne resumes the battle tomorrow. It may be necessary to repulse an attack with the garrison's cannons since ammunition and powder are in short supply."

Grimacing, van Cortlandt said bitterly, "Gates refused to release any cannons yesterday. I am confident that Bemis Heights and the river batteries are adequately supplied. Thank you and your brothers for the help.

I look forward to learning what actions Gates intends if Burgoyne resumes his attack tomorrow."

Northern Army Encampment
General Arnold's Field Headquarters
September 20th, 1 am

Standing before a banked fire in the perimeter woods to the fields of Freeman Farm, Arnold bluntly addressed his senior commanders concerning the current situation.

"That coward Gates will not release any further ammunition or gunpowder from the camp arsenal."

"We have no choice but to continue blocking the British from capturing the high ground on our flank. If it's captured, Bemis Heights shall be a death trap," volunteered Morgan.

Poor and Learned said simultaneously, "I agree."

Nodding, Arnold said with a sly grin, "Facing the British with empty muskets will certainly be glorious!"

***

"O'Brien can you make out anything yet?" asked Colonel Morgan.

Standing with Morgan were Major Dearborn, General Poor, and General Learned under the solitary tree in the area, looking up at Tom, and Tim crouched on its tallest branches.

"Fog starting to thin, Colonel. It looks like the British and Germans have built temporary fortifications where the fighting ceased last night," Tom replied.

General Poor looked at Morgan and Dearborn and said, "They will be able to see us too. I intend that Burgoyne and his commanders observe a battle line prepared to bleed them with volley fire just like yesterday!"

As frank as ever, Morgan snarled, "That is going to be difficult without any ammunition!"

Unfazed by Morgan's outburst, Poor continued his instructions.

"Dearborn, I want all your men to fall into the first rank of the formation with fixed bayonets. I will complete the first rank with any of my continentals and General Learned's equipped with bayonets. When the fog breaks, I intend Burgoyne to see a mile-long rank of bayonets facing his men.

"Morgan, your men shall form a skirmish line two hundred yards ahead of the formation. I want the enemy to anticipate marching in close formation for at least three hundred yards into rifle fire. Let the British remember yesterday's losses your Rifles inflicted upon their regiments."

Morgan nodded grimly and turned to walk to his men when Poor addressed him again.

"I am asking your men to stand exposed without ammunition. Please assure them that my brigade and I will be waiting for the Rifles to rejoin the line and fight the invader hand to hand if Burgoyne advances today."

Dearborn nodded to Morgan, signifying that his light infantry would not abandon the Rifles, men they had fought and died with yesterday.

As the continentals formed in the fields of Freeman Farm facing the Balcarres Redoubt, the Rifles stood in a picket line hundreds of yards in advance of a rank of leveled bayonets flashing in the morning sun.

Balcarres Redoubt
Officers' Call
September 20th, Dawn

Burgoyne chose not to change the uniform he had been wearing at the end of the fighting last evening. Walking amongst the survivors, he conveyed a spirit of camaraderie with those who had remained on the battlefield all night guarding the ground taken from the enemy. Watching how few able-bodied men were constructing redoubts, Burgoyne viscerally felt the cost his army had incurred to reach, at best, a stalemate with the continentals. Faced with the unadorned truth, Burgoyne acknowledged the battle had been lost until Riedesel arrived with his forces to attack the rebels' flank. That mercenary had saved the King's army.

Joined by his senior officers, they climbed together to the top of the earthen walls of the Balcarres Redoubt, thrown up by the light infantry and named in honor of their commander. Removing his telescope from his case, Burgoyne looked toward the enemy camp. Illuminated by the dawn, he was surprised by seeing a single line of those murderous Rifles in front of an unbroken rank of bayonets three miles from his field fortifications.

Slapping his riding crop against his leg in annoyance, Burgoyne sneered, "Well, gentlemen, the rebels appear to be waiting for us to march into their fire again. What are your recommendations,

General Philips?"

The Scots artilleryman replied in his soft burr, "The artillery has been restocked with powder, ball, and case shot. My men will blow a hole through the rebels. We shall be marching to Albany by this afternoon!"

Burgoyne expected no less from his second in command and moved on. "General Fraser?"

The tough highlander staring hard at the rebel battle lines growled, "The advance corps will march through that hole, and heaven help any rebels who are foolish enough not to run!"

Turning to the mercenary, Burgoyne asked, "General Riedesel?"

Stepping away from the group of British commanders, Riedesel scowled and replied, "I recommend an immediate tactical withdrawal across our bridge of batteaux to the east shore of the Hudson River. Once across, a forced march to the mouth of the Batten Kill River. Fortify the site and await General Clinton's reinforcements."

Without being asked, General Hamilton, commander of the decimated line regiments of the center attack column, volunteered, "General Burgoyne, the men are as game as ever and will do their best. But I spent the night with them. They are all physically spent. To attack today would waste the finest army sent to the colonies."

James Hamilton, in his mid-thirties, was a professional soldier who had fought the French in the European wars before his deployment in America. After the war, Burgoyne wrote of Hamilton that he "was the whole time engaged and acquitted himself with great honor, activity, and good conduct."

Surprised by Hamilton's interruption, which prevented his automatic rejection of Riedesel's recommendation, Burgoyne looked at Fraser and Philips for their reaction to Hamilton's words. To his astonishment, his senior commanders' reluctant nods demonstrated their agreement that continuing the attack today would break the spirit of his army.

Looking pointedly at Riedesel, Burgoyne replied, "I will not retreat from this position. General Clinton shall proceed up the Hudson with reinforcements to restore our strength and discourage the militia from reinforcing the rebel army. General Philips."

"Yes, sir."

"You will supervise the construction of the extension of the Balcarres redoubt to include the Freeman Farm's stone house."

Burgoyne turned to Riedesel, "Breymann is to improve his field fortifications and hold his position."

Addressing the assembled officers, Burgoyne said, "We shall hold our positions and regroup while we wait for the arrival of General Clinton. My adjutant has returned from our camp, confirming the wagons carrying rations are on the way. Instruct your company commanders to prepare their men to occupy the redoubts. The wagons will return, carrying the wounded to the hospital and the dead for burial."

As the meeting broke up, Burgoyne's aide motioned him aside and whispered, "A sachem of the Mohawk is here and wishes to offer you his services and one hundred warriors."

Burgoyne shook his head angrily and slapped his riding gloves on his thighs before saying dismissively, "The Seneca and Mohawk abandoned St. Ledger, forcing his retreat to Quebec. Tell him to leave this camp forthwith! Escort him through our lines and order all commands that no Iroquois warriors will be permitted to join my army."

Bemis Heights
Hudson River Defenses
Bridge of Boats
September 20th

Pointing downriver, the duty officer yelled, "General Glover, a batteaux convoy is approaching with an advance party of canoes carrying warriors. Major Morris, one of General Schuyler's staff officers, is in the lead canoe."

General John Glover, in his mid-forties, with a face weathered by thirty years at sea, walked toward the river dock with the rolling gait expected from a lifetime as a Marble Head fisherman. An officer of the Massachusetts militia before the war, Glover marched his regiment to Boston to participate in the siege of the British garrison. A man whose reputation for reliability and competence was held in such high regard that Glover recruited hundreds of professional seamen after independence had been declared, forming an amphibious continental regiment. Glover's men saved Washington's army from capture after occupying Brooklyn Heights by evacuating it across the East River in the first days of the Revolution.

Glover wore his continental uniform with a pink sash over the right shoulder with the white facings, linings, and buttons of a Brigadier General commissioned in Massachusetts. His thick curly brown hair blew in the wind as when his men had rowed Washington's army all night across the ice-chocked Delaware River. That morning Glover led his men to victory in the battles of Trenton and Princeton. Glover served as a brigade commander at Saratoga at the personal request of George Washington.

Major Morris disembarked from the canoe and, after exchanging salutes with General Glover, said, "My apology General. I must immediately proceed to headquarters to deliver an urgent message from General Schuyler to General Gates. I will see you before I return to Albany."

"Carry on, Major. I have a message for you to deliver to General Schuyler," Glover replied.

As the lead batteau pulled along the dock, Glover watched Mr. O'Brien, the Northern Department's teamster, accompanied by a warrior wearing a *kastoweh*, disembark and walk up the pier toward him.

Glover smiled and said, "Mr. O'Brien, you were wearing the same water-stained buck skins three weeks ago when you returned General Arnold and the continentals from Fort Stanwix." Chuckling, Grover asked," Are you ever somewhere other than on this river?"

Brian replied, "No, General. The British are keeping us all busy. We are sorry to have missed yesterday's battle."

Glover said, "Not to worry, the British are still here."

Watching the individual batteau of the convoy land and discharge hundreds of barrels of gunpowder and lead bars for casting into musket balls, Glover turned back to O'Brien and said, "Your timely delivery of General Schuyler's gift will give us a fighting chance to beat them."

"Thanks, General. I want you to meet Han Yery, a sachem of our allies, the Oneida. He escorted the shipment with a hundred and fifty warriors. The Oneida Nation intends to remain and fight the British."

In contrast to O'Brien's weathered work clothes, the Oneida sachem was attired in a newly woven red robe heavily decorated in wampum beads and porcupine needles, forming the symbol of the wolf clan. Hung around his neck was a gold medallion Glover recognized as being awarded during the French and Indian War for conspicuous valor. Meeting Han Yery's measuring stare with his own, Glover liked the sachem's relaxed and casual manner in which he stood cradling his rifle and thought, *this man shall be valuable in the inevitable continuation of this donnybrook.*

"We can use all the help we can get," Glover said. "The British brought the Abenaki and Ottawa south to kill, loot, and burn out the settlers of the Hudson and Mohawk River Valleys. General Burgoyne sought to break the peoples' resolve. He made a mistake. The militia has turned out in their thousands, heavily reinforcing the Northern Army. General Washington also sent his best unit, Morgan's Rifles, to stop the raiding."

Han Yery replied, "The Oneida warriors are here. The Abenaki and Ottawa will kill no more."

Glover nodded in agreement. Observing the severe and sober visages of the lean men crowding the dock convinced the veteran General that this was no idle jest. Their faces were painted black, dressed in deerskin fringed shirts and breeches. Each warrior, uniformly armed with muskets, belted tomahawks, powder horns, and ammunition pouches, gathered around their respective sachems awaiting instructions from Han Yery their War Chief.

Brian asked, "General, has the situation changed since yesterday's battle?"

"No. We stopped the British advance. Last night, the survivors built redoubts of wooden bulwarks in the open fields facing our defensive lines. General Gates is certain that the British shall regroup and continue the assault to outflank our defenses and bombard Bemis

Heights."

"Why not occupy and fortify that ground now?" asked Brian.

"That has been suggested but rejected by General Gates. He believes extending our lines to occupy that high ground would fatally weaken our defenses."

"The solution is to prevent the British from discovering and occupying it," said Han Yery.

"Exactly. When the Abenaki and Ottawa return from their raiding, it is only a matter of time before the ground is found and occupied by the British."

Han Yery met Glover's eyes and said, "The Oneida will ward the forest. The British will never occupy that high ground. None who tries will return."

Reminded of fighting pirates at sea, he felt a shiver down his spine in response to the menace in Han Yery's words. Feeling his confidence grow with the arrival of the powder and Oneida Glover said, "Han Yery, I recommend that you and Mr. O'Brien proceed to army headquarters to discuss your offer with General Gates. My aide, Captain Williams, will guide you. I would appreciate your men's help unloading and storing the munitions shipment."

Nodding, Han Yery spoke briefly to the other sachems in the war party and joined Brian in waiting for Glover's aide.

Following Captain Williams from the river docks, Brian and Han Yery walked through the encampment running parallel for several miles along the Hudson River and road to Albany, twenty miles south. Brian noted the defenses were anchored by a heavily wooded irregular plateau known locally as Bemis Heights. He and his men had often camped here when freighting cargo from the local settlements to Albany.

Less than a year before, Captain Williams of the 1st Massachusetts had been a first-year student at Harvard. Now a hardened combat veteran cited for valor, he proudly wore his red officer's waist sash and enthusiastically described the river fortifications the Hessians had not attempted to assault the day before.

As they moved further away from the river, they entered thick woodlands broken up by farmland and pastures hewn from the forest.

Striding through a city of tents and lean-tos, Brian saw continentals and militiamen in the thousands.

"Captain Williams, do you know where Colonel Morgan's men are camped? My son is with him," asked Brian.

"Morgan's Rifles are camped facing the enemy at Freeman's farm. Once you have spoken to General Gates, the duty officer will provide a guide."

Brian observed, "Captain Williams, there were no militiamen when I returned Arnold and the relief force from Stanwix. Now there are thousands."

Surprised by the effect of his words, Williams' face tightened and flushed with emotion. He grated in reply, "Those men started arriving in camp individually and in groups anxious to avenge the deaths of loved ones or the destruction of their homes and farms wrought by the Ottawa and Abenaki warriors employed by the Crown. They fought side by side with my continentals yesterday and, in their rage, endured and exchanged volley fire with the lobsterbacks until they stopped advancing and started building those redoubts." Closing his eyes, taking several deep breaths, and regaining his calm demeanor, Williams continued, "Excuse my loss of control, but Burgoyne's Ottawa killed my brother and his family."

"Why didn't you drive them back to their camp?" asked Brian.

Frowning, Williams said coldly, "The brigades fighting the British ran out of ammunition despite repeated requests for replenishment. General Gates refused, and Generals Poor and Morgan's Rifles were obliged to withdraw to our defensive lines." Williams continued, "Let me pass you through the headquarters guards."

Entering the headquarters tent, Brian and Han Yery heard Gates say, "General Arnold, I am amazed that you had not secured and transported the powder and ammunition from the camp's arsenal to replenish your men's supply during yesterday's battle. General Poor reported that your entire command faced the British and Hessian advance corps with empty muskets. You and you alone are guilty of gross negligence, which almost lost this battle."

Han Yery stared at Arnold, whom he saw shaking with a murderous rage, his body leaning toward the speaker, gripping his sword with white knuckles.

"That is not true," yelled Arnold. "I repeatedly requested your quartermaster for powder and ammunition in person and by messenger. He refused, citing your express orders to hold all reserve powder for the cannon and troops guarding your headquarters."

Gates stood up from his desk and, caressing the light blue sash of command, replied, "Rightly so! The camp holds the hospital and our supplies, which are always given priority by a professional army!"

"But for my men and I facing the enemy this morning with unloaded muskets, the British would have captured the high ground on your flank. Their cannons would have rightfully blown you out of your hiding place."

Sensing a possible mutiny, which Captain Williams had no intention of witnessing, he interrupted. "General Gates, may I introduce Mr. O'Brien and sachem Han Yery? Mr. O'Brien ably commanded the batteaux convoy, which returned the Massachusetts continentals from Fort Stanwix so they could fight in the battle. Today he delivered a fresh supply of gunpowder and ammunition discharging at the river docks. Han Yery of the Oneida escorted the convoy and brought one hundred and fifty warriors to join us."

As an opportunity to avoid further discourse with Arnold, Gates replied, "Thank you, Captain. Give my regards to General Glover and ask him to expedite the discharge of the munitions for storage in the camp's arsenal. General Arnold, you will immediately prepare and submit the necessary powder and ammunition requisitions to ready your men for combat. I am holding you responsible for maintaining the security of our lines." He turned his back to Arnold and resumed his seat at his field desk. "Arnold, you are dismissed." Glancing at O'Brien and Han Yery, Gates said, "Gentlemen, thank you for your service to the cause."

Taking several deep breaths, his eyes boring into the back of Gates, who had resumed reading his correspondence, Arnold abruptly turned and walked from the tent, motioning Brian and Han Yery to follow.

Joining Arnold outside, the three men stood in silence, watching thousands of continentals and militia drilling with the confidence and competence borne of their hard-won victory over the most feared military in Europe.

"You and your men have arrived late but still in time to be useful. Have you met Colonel Morgan?" Asked Arnold.

Brian shook his head but added, "My son Tom is with Morgan's Rifles. I would appreciate your help in locating their encampment."

"Mr. O'Brien, you're in luck. Morgan is under my command. I will accompany you and Han Yery to meet him. It is imperative that we succeed in preventing any reconnaissance by the British."

Han Yery joined the conversation. "I have heard Mohawk warriors have come east to offer their services to Burgoyne. The Mohawk ambushed and killed hundreds of our friends and neighbors at Oriskany. O'Brien and I intend to avenge those deaths in these woods."

Brian placed his hand on his friend's shoulder, again remembering the hours surrounded by enemies expecting death.

Arnold nodded, preoccupied with his grievances against Gates as they passed through the guards and entered the Rifles' camp.

Standing outside his tent, Morgan waited until Arnold walked to him and said without enthusiasm, "General, what can I do for you?"

"Granny Gates has a mission for you. I have brought you two men who fought at Oriskany to help you accomplish it."

As he shook hands with Brian, Morgan said, "We hear you defeated St. Ledger's invasion and saved the people of the Mohawk River Valley."

Brian smiled, pleased that Morgan recognized them as fellow soldiers, and replied, "I am Brian O'Brien. Let me introduce my friend, Han Yery, a sachem of the Oneida. He and his men fought with us at Oriskany."

"That's what we heard from your son Tom. Before joining the Rifles, he was involved in a fight with an Ottawa war party three times the size of his patrol. He wounded that renegade St. Luc at three hundred yards and successfully drove the war party off. One of Washington's engineers, Colonel Kosciuszko, thinks highly of him."

Brian smiled, relieved that his son was a member of an elite regiment who considered him one of their own.

Into the silence, Han Yery said, "Tom was always a fair shot."

The men laughed, relaxing the formality of their first meeting, and began discussing their mission. Aloof from the camaraderie, Arnold interrupted, "I must arrange for the distribution of the munitions to my troops." Arnold abruptly turned and walked further into the camp, saying over his shoulder, "Colonel Morgan, I expect you to present your recommendation on preventing British reconnaissance at my staff meeting tomorrow morning."

Following Arnold with his eyes, Han Yery shook his head and said, "I will not place my warriors under the command of such a man. They represent the security and strength of the Oneida Nation and will not be squandered."

"Not a problem, Han Yery. We are an independent command. General Arnold will only want to hear of our successes to report to Generals Gates and General Washington," said Morgan.

"What are we up against?" asked Brian.

Leading the men to a wooden lean-to he used in the field when drilling his men, Morgan pointed at the map on his field desk and answered, "Bemis Heights is the anchor of our defenses. The river emplacements defended by three continental brigades are to the right of the heights. Burgoyne would lose his army storming that position, and he knows it. He will continue to station a token force opposite those positions to pin those brigades in place. Our post will be on the left flank, which is heavily forested. The main assault will come from there."

"Do you know where my son is stationed?"

Colonel Morgan looked up from the map.

"Sorry, Mr. O'Brien. I should have told you before commencing the briefing. Tom is in camp with the rest of my men, resupplying their ammunition from the supplies you brought this morning. Han Yery, your warriors, will be camping with the Rifles and Colonel Dearborn's light continental infantry. We will settle your warriors and continue our joint planning. I intend to send out patrols this evening. We will operate jointly. I will show you around the encampment and introduce my officers."

***

"Tom O'Brien, front and center!"

Squatting with a score of other men casting bullets in a huddle of huts used to store the Rifles' munitions, Tom and Tim Murphy looked up and saw Colonel Morgan, a fully armed sachem, and a middle-aged militiaman coming out of the twilight. Upon recognizing the two men who had raised him, Tom shouted and rushed forward into his father's arms.

"Father, Han Yery! I knew you would come after driving the British back to Quebec."

Watching the father and son's reunion, Han Yery felt thankful that his sons had survived the British invasion when so many others had not.

Shaking hands with his godfather, Tom asked about Tyonajanegen, Cornelius, and Paulus. Then he said, "Han Yery, our scouts report a large group of Mohawk warriors departing the British camp today and returning north. After the Abenaki and Ottawa ran amok, Burgoyne wanted nothing further to do with any allied warriors."

Brian nodded and added, "The Mohawk and Seneca also abandoned St. Ledger, forcing Burgoyne's reinforcements to retreat to Quebec, leaving his army unsupported. I am not surprised he doesn't trust the Crown's Haudenosaunee allies."

"The Mohawk shall pay for Oriskany another time. My men and I want to be part of this fight," replied Han Yery.

Tom said, "I asked Paulus about Brant, and he told me he spared his life in the forest before the Battle of Oriskany."

"Yes, Paulus carried my message to Fort Stanwix that the warriors of Oriska would be joining the Tyron militia to reinforce the garrison. Brant is my brother-in-law. He was married to my sister, who died in childbirth. Your father knew my relationship with Brant and understood my decision not to kill him in cold blood. I will not hesitate to take his life to protect my companions."

Tom motioned Murphy to join them and said, "I want you to meet my partner, Tim Murphy. We have been battle companions since the Colonel let me join the Rifles."

Shaking hands, Han Yery took Morgan and Tim to help settle his men allowing Brian and Tom to talk.

Walking into the closest hut for a private moment with his son, Brian said, "I could not be prouder of you. General Schuyler told us how you guided Colonel Kosciusko in his work in delaying the British's march from Quebec and the fortifying of Bemis Heights. General Schuyler and Han Yery agree with your decision to only wound St. Luc. It stopped the Ottawa raids saving the lives of the work parties and countless settlers on the frontier."

"I didn't do anything you and Han Yery have not taught me."

"General Schuyler sent his congratulations and told me that his daughter Peggy misses your visits."

Brian smiled as Tom blushed, reverting to the shy young man he had been before the war.

As Han Yery and Tim Murphy joined them in the hut, Tim said, "The Colonel has asked you and Tom to join him in his tent to plan how to stop the lobsterbacks from scouting our positions. Since the Colonel is generous with his rum during meetings, I'd appreciate your taking me along."

"You're invited, Tim," replied Brian.

"O'Brien. Murphy and I have shared our thoughts on increasing rifle range and accuracy by casting bullets of varied weights and sizes. He is someone worth talking to," added Han Yery.

Taking a closer look at Tim Murphy, Brian perceived a younger version of Colonel Morgan. Tim was in his mid-twenties, over six feet tall, and possessed a professional hunter's weathered visage and piercing gaze.

Brian smiled at Tim and said, "That's high praise. Han Yery is the finest rifleman in the Mohawk Valley."

"Mr. O'Brien, Tom has told me all about you and Han Yery, his godfather. I will enjoy having the opportunity to get to know you both."

Walking together toward Morgan's headquarters tent, they continued to discuss their hunting and combat experiences, developing a camaraderie critical to their mutual survival in the coming days.

***

"Please come in and draw a tankard of rum," Colonel Morgan began. "Tom and Tim, you may join us. I have a favor to ask Mr. O'Brien."

Centrally located in the Rifles' bivouac, Morgan's headquarters consisted of two separate canvas tents, serving as his office and residence.

Drawing the rum from a barrel outside the office tent, Brian respected Morgan for sharing the same living conditions as his men, unlike the comforts he observed in General Gates' headquarters.

"Mr. O'Brien, the British killed my top sergeant yesterday. I would be grateful if you would accept that post. My men were all raised on the frontier, and I'm concerned there may be trouble with the Oneida warriors. I need a man who can maintain control over the camp while Han Yery and I are with the ambush parties."

"I agree with the Colonel," Han Yery said. "I do not want anything to spoil the Oneida Nation's service in this army. Should one of my warriors be at fault, my son will act as my representative. Paulus won the respect of Oriska's war band by carrying word of the relief force marching to Fort Stanwix. He risked certain death by walking alone and unarmed through a forest filled with Mohawk warriors."

"Paulus and I will maintain camp discipline in your absence," said Brian.

"Thanks, Mr. O'Brien. I know my command will be in good hands."

Several days later, at an all-officers meeting held by General Gates, Arnold paid Morgan a rare public compliment announcing that the Rifles had the most orderly encampment in the army in his daily inspections of the militia and continental units.

Burgoyne's Headquarters
Officers' Call, September 21st

Burgoyne mused, *what a difference a day will make in one's perspective.*

After eight hours of uninterrupted sleep, bathed, and in one of his dress uniforms, capped and spurred, he felt his old confidence and optimism return.

Addressing a formation of his officers in front of his campaign tent

Burgoyne began, "Gentlemen, you are to be congratulated. Balcarres, your light infantry has made a good start building the redoubt at Freeman's Farm."

Major Alexander Lindsay, Lord Balcarres, the British light infantry commander, nodded wearily. Dressed in the same smoke-stained uniform he had worn in battle, the Major replied, "Thank you, sir. The men worked all night. When completed, the redoubt will be five hundred yards long, with fourteen-foot- high log walls and earthworks."

Looking at General Philips, Burgoyne motioned him to continue the description of the field fortifications.

"Yes, General. The Great Redoubt has been strengthened by constructing three batteries on adjacent hilltops overlooking the Great Ravine and river road."

Philips said, "General Riedesel, would you brief us regarding your preparations."

"My men are building a two-hundred-yard palisaded breastwork manned by Colonel Breymann's grenadiers to secure the right flank."

Captain Boucherville, commander of the batteau men, concluded the briefing from the rear of the formation, "My men fortified several cabins located between the Breymann's redoubt and Balcarres' redoubt."

Annoyed by Boucherville's breach of protocol but mollified that his men would face the brunt of any assault, Burgoyne nodded tersely in the direction of the rear of the formation and concluded the meeting.

"Completing the field fortifications has been the priority, and I approve General Phillip's plan and the industry of the men. The advance to Albany will continue once the army has been reorganized and the wounded are cared for. Our goal remains to join General Clinton in Albany and unite New York City with Quebec. General Fraser."

"Yes, Sir."

"Your men are excused for all fatigue duty to commence scouting and patrolling the forest between us and the rebels. You will be reinforced by Captain Fraser's marksmen, General Riedesel's jaegers, and Colonel Peters' Queen's rangers. The battle between armies is suspended pending St. Ledger's arrival with reinforcements and General Clinton's capture of the Hudson River Forts. However, to accomplish our goal, we must win the battle of the woods to determine the rebels' weak spots so when reinforced, we may bombard their fortifications into submission."

Battle of the Forest
Saratoga, New York
September 23rd – October 1st

Han Yery sat naked, listening and watching for enemy activity. His body, painted in a mixture of green and brown, rendered him indistinguishable from the heavy foliage in which he had remained motionless since night had surrendered to dawn. Perched in a tree twenty feet above him, Tim and Tom scanned the surrounding forest for movement.

As the sun passed above them, Tom saw Han Yery slowly raise his right arm, point, and then close his hand three times, signifying fifteen men moving toward the ambush party.

As the silence grew, the Oneida warriors slithered noiselessly to the flank of the enemy patrol's line of advance.

As the minutes passed, Tom saw three green-coated Hessian jaeger hunters emerge in a triangle formation from the underbrush squatting as one to listen apparently for any change in the natural sounds of the forest. Each man carried the short Hessian hunting rifle without bayonets and a belted short sword.

Motionless for several minutes, as one, they rose, moving forward noiselessly through the underbrush. Thirty seconds later, a dozen black-capped British light infantry armed with bayonetted muskets followed in single file the path blazed by the Hessians.

As a British captain emerged from cover, Morgan's riflemen and the Oneida warriors opened fire, dropping over a half dozen of the enemy. The wounded captain drew his sword and yelled, "Charge the bastards. They do not have bayonets!"

The survivors ran through a cloud of gun smoke into an unbroken line of leveled bayonets wielded by a score of Dearborn's continental light infantry. Shielded by the continentals, the riflemen and warriors reloaded their weapons and watched the members of the enemy patrol be killed or captured.

As day changed to night, Han Yery's party was replaced by another detachment under the command of one of Morgan's captains and an Oneida sachem, which shifted the ambush site and assumed a similar formation. In the fading light, Tom signaled Han Yery's men to return to camp with the captured weapons and prisoners for questioning. The dead were buried in the woods.

Entering the camp, Tom, Tim Murphy, and Han Yery were met by Colonel Morgan, who addressed the ambush party. "Han Yery, your men have scouted out sites between the lines, which have resulted in our third successful ambush in as many days."

"Colonel, why are there no Ottawa or Abenaki warriors with the enemy scouting parties?" asked Han Yery.

Morgan replied, "I have been informed by questioning British deserters, and confirmed by the prisoners, that most of the Ottawa and Abenaki have returned to Quebec with their loot from raiding the northern settlements. The remaining few know better than risk certain death by entering these woods. The British are blind to our positions and troop strength if they attack."

CHAPTER SEVEN
Clinton's Hudson River Campaign

New York City
Clinton's Headquarters
August 6, 1777

Since General Howe's departure on July 23, 1777, to capture Philadelphia, General Henry Clinton had maintained his headquarters in the abandoned Morris Mansion. Situated on Manhattan Island on the highest point of Harlem Heights, Clinton chose to reside there to escape that heat and humidity of the city. Built in the Federal style, the pillared front porch of the two-story house was the site of an early morning staff meeting called by Clinton.

Sitting together at a long table, Clinton addressed the assembled officers.

"General Vaughan, Colonel Campbell, Captain Wallace. I have received a letter from General Burgoyne. He anticipates reaching Albany by late August. Our scouts confirm Washington is marching south to defend the rebel capital of Philadelphia and the seat of the traitors' government. Once Albany is captured, Burgoyne may march down the Hudson Valley to New York City unopposed by the rebel's main army. I intend to capture the rebels' Highland forts to expedite Burgoyne's reinforcement of this garrison. The Royal Navy would then be able to sail from New York harbor to Albany and return with thousands of Burgoyne's regulars securing the Crown's possession of the entire Hudson River."

Looking at the assembled officers, he appreciated the noticeable relief on their faces. General Howe's drastic reduction of the garrison of New York City in favor of his attack upon Philadelphia had exposed the indispensable port to attack.

General Vaughan commented, "The prospect of Burgoyne's army reinforcing the City's garrison would undoubtedly improve the morale of the loyalist population. General Howe's decision to capture Philadelphia has shaken the wealthier residents' confidence in the Crown."

Captain Wallace of the Royal Navy volunteered, "One of our sloops patrolling the coast reported that the fleet carrying Howe's army was becalmed at sea nowhere near its intended landing site of Head of Elk, Maryland."

"My God, man! Howe departed over six weeks ago. Once he lands his army, it's a fifty-mile march to Philadelphia," exclaimed Vaughan.

Clinton forced himself to maintain his affable continence, despite the precarious position of his command due to Howe's vain intention to outdo Burgoyne by capturing the rebel capital and Congress. He thought, *Howe's assurances that his army could sail to Philadelphia, conquer the rebel capital, and return to support Burgoyne had been utter nonsense.*

Returning his focus to his subordinates, Clinton continued, "I have been informed that we will soon be receiving a significant reinforcement of regulars from England. When they arrive, we will be in a position to aid Burgoyne."

Hudson Highlands
Fall of 1777

The Hudson River below West Point and above New York City, flowing through the Appalachian range known as the Highlands, was guarded by Major General Israel Putman. Putman commanded a force of 1,200 continentals based near Peekskill, New York. Affectionately known by his superiors and subordinates as 'Old Put,' Putman was sixty years of age. He had served as an officer in Roger's Rangers during the French and Indian War and, recently, with distinction at the Battle of Bunker Hill.

Several miles upriver from Peekskill were the patriot's primary river defenses obstructing the navigation of the Royal Navy upon the Hudson River. Those measures entailed the construction of a log and boom iron link chain spanning the Hudson River, preventing enemy ships from sailing further north. The western end of the chain was guarded by Fort Montgomery and Fort Clinton, sited on either side of Popolopen Kill. These fortifications mounted sixty cannons to sink British warships attempting to break the chain. The forts were situated where the river narrowed, and the current was swift, hampering the maneuvering of any vessel proceeding upriver. Clusters of sharpened wooden stakes, known as *chevaux-de-frise,* lined the riverbed, and two Continental twenty-four-gun frigates—the Congress and the Montgomery—plus an armed sloop and two-row gunboats completed the defenses.

Brigadier General James Clinton commanded Fort Montgomery, whose perimeter walls were still being constructed. His brother Brigadier General George Clinton, Governor of New York, commanded the completed Fort Clinton.

On September 29, 1777, General Putman received word of the arrival of British troop transports in the harbor of New York City, carrying a reinforcement for the British garrison. Aware of General Henry Clinton's reputation as an aggressive British commander Putman immediately wrote to Governor Clinton advising him of the possibility of enemy activity being initiated in the Highlands and recommending the muster of the militia.

Upon receiving the letter, Governor Clinton followed Putman's recommendation and immediately rode south from Kingston to assume command of the Highlands forts.

New York City
General Henry Clinton's Headquarters
Senior Officers' Call, October 1st

Notification of the arrival of the ships carrying the promised reinforcements from England caused General Henry Clinton to move his headquarters from the Morris Mansion in Harlem Heights to Fraunces Tavern on Broad Street in the heart of the harbor district. Assuming possession of the entire two-story yellow brick building, Clinton interviewed the garrison officers, leaders of the loyalist militia, and the captains of the frigates currently in port to select a strike force and plan a campaign to capture the Highland forts.

Thirty army, navy, and militia officers Clinton personally selected for the Highland campaign were seated at a dozen tables in the tavern's common room.

Seemly tireless, Clinton paced about the room, holding a letter in his hand and smiling, pronounced, "As I predicted! Burgoyne has run into trouble and has requested our assistance. I intend to take three thousand regulars and five hundred loyalist militia upriver by longboats and batteaux escorted by three frigates. Captain Wallace, you will command the naval squadron. General Vaughan will be my second in command and lead one of the infantry columns. Colonel Campbell shall command the second. Colonel Bayard will command the militia. General Tryon, you will command the rearguard."

After listening patiently until General Clinton had completed his presentation, General Vaughan said, "General, the attack force is twice the reinforcement from England. Most of those men are still recovering from the voyage and are unfit for duty. The rebel forces are at least equal to our own. Has General Howe approved your plan?"

General Clinton responded sternly, "I appreciate your concern Vaughan, but remember, New York is a loyalist city. Any rebels are gone. Washington followed Howe south, and the rebel militia went north to oppose Burgoyne. To expedite Burgoyne joining the garrison, we must provide an unobstructed passage from Albany to New York City. Our spies report that Fort Montgomery is under construction, and neither of the two forts is adequately garrisoned. Putman is a relic of the French and Indian war. I guarantee he will not interfere in accomplishing our mission. The flotilla will depart on October 3rd. Captain Wallace will inform us of the precise sailing time in conformity with the tide and winds. Prepare your commands for departure."

Peekskill, New York
General Putman's Field Headquarters
October 5th

Yesterday Major General Israel Putman was informed of British regulars landing at Tarry Town, and this morning at Verplank's Point, only five miles from Peekskill. Riding to the Hudson River, Putman and his mounted staff stopped on a bluff observing the British flotilla as it discharged more regulars and cannons while others were building a base. Motioning his aide to join him, Putman asked, "Captain McBride, what is the latest count from the scouts?"

McBride, a lanky twenty-year-old continental survivor of the Saratoga campaign, replied, "At least two thousand regulars and hundreds of militiamen. The enemy is building an encampment capable of accommodating an additional one thousand troops."

Turning to his adjutant, Putman ordered, "Colonel Gray, send messengers to Governor Clinton with my urgent request to send continentals from the garrisons of Fort Montgomery and Fort Clinton to Peekskill. Peekskill is the British target. We will be falling back immediately."

Verplank's Point
General Henry Clinton's Field Headquarters
October 5th

His campaign tent was on a slight elevation above the village's pier; General Clinton looked down the river watching the last ten long boats filled with regulars approaching the landing. Their arrival would complete the disembarkation of his strike force.

Relieved that the first stage of his plan had been achieved without casualties, Clinton approached General Tryon, supervising his militia digging the earthworks of a redoubt to protect the fleet of empty longboats and batteaux moored or secured to shore.

"General Tryon, stress to your men that their first responsibility is to defend Verplank's Point and our means to retreat if the forts are not captured. General Putman outnumbers you two to one, so I issued army uniforms to the militia. The rebels shall never attack a redoubt defended by British regulars."

"Understood, General."

Walking back to the pier, Clinton motioned General Vaughan as he disembarked from the last longboat of the convoy to join him and asked, "Any boats lost?"

"No, sir. The escorting frigates deterred any rebel interference. Even the fishing boats ran for shore." Smirking, Vaughan continued, "That was brilliant, General Clinton. With several hundred uniforms, you doubled the apparent strength of our forces which panicked Putman into retreating to Peekskill instead of reinforcing the Highland Forts."

Clinton was annoyed that the success of his plan had been questioned. Vaughan was spared a tongue-lashing by the arrival of a longboat from the leading frigate carrying Colonel Bayard and Captain Wallace. Disembarking and saluting, the two officers stood at attention in front of the silent Clinton.

Still unsettled by Vaughan's unsolicited comment, Clinton brusquely ordered, "Colonel Bayard, you and your militia regiment will occupy the redoubt and continue expanding the fortifications and trenches. Two six-pounder cannons with ample munitions shall remain to discourage rebel interference.

Captain Wallace, you will break the cannons out of your frigate's stores and assist in landing, transporting, and positioning in the redoubt. Assign a midshipman and a gun crew to each."

Sensing Clinton's deteriorating mood, Captain Wallace nodded politely and motioned to one of his aides to comply immediately.

When the aide had left, Clinton studied Wallace and asked, "Captain, are you concerned that the three frigates you command may face the combined firepower of the two forts, two enemy frigates, and several gunboats?"

Maintaining a stern visage Wallace, who was a strict, but amicable officer responded,

"I would be if those cannons were adequately supplied with munitions and operated by artillerymen."

For the first time, Clinton smiled and said, "Outstanding, Captain. Please explain your last statement."

Captain Wallace, a royal naval officer for over thirty years, was pleasantly surprised by a senior army officer who was intelligent. His prior experience in joint operations with the British Army had often endangered his ship and crew due to the ego and recklessness of the General in command.

"My sailors have been mixing with the fisherman and bargemen in the local taverns. It's the joke of the Hudson that Congress assigned two new frigates to guard the chain. The continental navy prioritized crewing the frigates raiding the British merchant shipping at sea. There is no prize money for a captain and crew guarding a fort. The rebel warships remain anchored because neither has enough sailors to set sail."

Clinton barked, "My concern is the firepower of the enemy frigates and not their sailing qualities!"

Wallace continued, "There has been no report of any gunnery practice by the cannons of either the rebel frigates or the forts."

"Lack of powder or ammunition, Captain?" asked Clinton.

"Possibly both, but more likely a lack of trained artillerymen. The continentals have two armies in the field. Washington and Gates have demanded priority upon servicing their cannons in battle. In my opinion, Congress stationed two frigates and scores of heavy cannons to guard the chain to create the illusion of strength in the absence of the manpower and trained professionals to render this position truly formidable."

Regaining his amiable demeanor, Clinton nodded and said, "Excellent, Captain. I agree with your analysis of the rebel's vulnerability. I intend to destroy both forts and bag the Clinton brothers! American aristocrats and the older one is the rebel Governor of New York!"

"Yes, sir."

With a rare smile, Clinton confided to Wallace the importance of the plan's success.

"When my men force the rebels from the forts, your naval forces must seal the river to prevent the Clinton brothers from being picked up by the rebel gunboats and carried across the river. Your frigates must pass under the forts' cannons during my assault to accomplish this."

Disquieted by Clinton's intensity, Captain Wallace nodded in agreement but recoiled professionally from Clinton's orders to unnecessarily endanger his ships to capture rebel politicians. After a moment, Wallace replied formally, "General Clinton, the Royal Navy shall perform its duty in the upcoming action."

Fort Clinton
Commanding Officer's Office
October 5, 1777

George and James Clinton sat together in the fort's headquarters building, reading dispatches. George summarized them: "General Putman reports a flotilla of British frigates and a convoy of longboats carrying thousands of infantrymen sailing north on the Hudson River. What is the latest word from Gates at Saratoga?"

James replied, "When Burgoyne's Abenaki and Ottawa raiders killed the McCrea girl and scores of others, all the able-bodied militiamen joined General Gates and fought at Saratoga. The last word is the British have built temporary fortifications, and the Northern army is pinned there blocking Burgoyne's advance."

Frowning, George grumbled, "The British timing could not be worse! Gates and Washington have reassigned most of our continentals and artillerymen to their respective armies. I relied on my authority to muster the militia to supplement the forts' continental garrisons. Now there's none to muster. We lack the men to defend either fort. James, you're the military man. What is your recommendation?"

"First, we avoid the court-martial St. Clair suffered for abandoning Fort Ticonderoga without a fight. We will each command half the remaining garrison and ambush the British in the forest before they reach the forts."

"Agreed. But the cause would suffer if we were captured."

"What of the continental frigates?" asked James.

"I have no authority over those ships. The captains and crews shall decide how best to maintain their honor and that of the Continental Navy."

***

Mustered outside Fort Montgomery's completed officers' quarters, James Clinton addressed the continentals not reassigned to Washington's army or to the defenses of Bemis Heights.

"Lieutenant Lamb, are you the senior artillery officer of the Highland Forts?"

"Since yesterday, I am the only officer, sir," replied Lamb.

James scowled and demanded, "Explain!"

"Colonel Wilkinson presented an order from Gates assigning Captain Masters and four-gun crews to the Northern army. Wilkinson loaded them on batteaux and sailed for Bemis Heights yesterday afternoon."

Breathing deeply for a few moments, James rasped, "How many artillerymen are there?"

"One gun crew, sir."

"Well, Lamb, I expect an assault by over a thousand British regulars. Fort Montgomery shall be defended. You shall report to me in an hour with a plan to bloody the British. Good luck."

***

Walking from Fort Clinton's headquarters building, George Clinton approached his brother standing on the fort's parade grounds in front of two formations of continentals silently waiting at attention.

"Well, James, how do we proceed?"

"Yesterday, Gates stripped us of all but a single gun crew."

"Congress can certainly pick them. I shall ensure Schuyler enters Congress as soon as practicable. New York must be suitably represented. Your plan James."

"I have organized our continentals into two detachments of one hundred men. Our scouts have identified two approaching columns. My force will include the artillerymen and ambush the closer column in the forest. I recommend you defend Fort Clinton from its perimeter

170

defenses. You should ambush the enemy column as it passes through the narrow strip of land between the lake and the river. I built an abatis between those waters, defended by a redoubt. Your continentals shall be protected; it is only a short distance from our gunboats in the river.

Stony Point, New York
October 6th

Sailing upriver from Verplank's Point, the British assault force landed at Stony Point, New York. Clinton addressed his officers.

"Lt. Colonel Campbell, you will take nine hundred men and march seven miles west around Bear Mountain to attack Fort Montgomery from the northwest. Your column will include Robinson's loyalists, who will guide you. I will hold the balance of the men here. My assault shall commence when I hear the drummers signal the commencement of your attack."

Campbell's Column
One Mile from Fort Montgomery
October 6th

After marching for hours through virgin forest upon deer paths guided by loyalist hunters accompanying his column, Campbell asked, "Robinson, what is ahead of us?"

Beverley Robinson, commander of the loyalist, replied, "There is a fortified line across the path of our advance made of logs with an earthwork. It is defended by an unknown force of rebels. I recommend skirmishers advance well-spaced to determine whether the rebels have cannons."

Campbell replied, "Robinson, I appreciate your caution, but Clinton will not attack until he hears the signal launching our assault upon the rebel defenses. It has taken almost an entire day to reach this position. I will lead."

***

His sword drawn, Campbell jogged slightly forward of a column ten men wide with their bayonetted rifles leveled. Advancing down a path bordered by trees blocked by the silent rebel barrier of logs, he observed no activity. Closing within yards of the wall, Campbell shouted, "It's abandoned. The rebels have run."

Sprinting toward the enemy, Campbell experienced an emptiness before his back struck the ground, which drove the air from his perforated lungs and extinguished his life.

***

Crouching behind the barricade, Lt. Lamb watched his continentals' disciplined volleys and the rapid crack of his howitzer continuing to spew canister harvesting the enemy column. The survivors began to trip and fall over the bodies disrupting the charge. Taking advantage of the enemies' confusion, Lamb shouted, "Ceasefire. Fall back to our secondary position. Leave the howitzer."

Sprinting with his command toward the unfinished walls of Fort Montgomery, Lamb saw General James Clinton step from behind a wooden rampart camouflaged by brush, leading a score of continentals who knelt and fired a volley into a pack of racing lobsterbacks who had navigated the place of slaughter. Lamb and his men ran behind the kneeling musketeers to a camouflaged 12-pounder cannon.

Stunned by the unexpected resistance, the surviving avengers scattered, joining the reforming attack column.

"Back to the rampart. Anyone hurt?" asked James Clinton.

"No, General," replied his adjutant.

Falling back with their bayonets facing the enemy, the continentals of Lamb's ambush party joined James' men in cover. They prepared to fire another volley as the reformed enemy column cautiously advanced.

Drawing his sword and pistol, James joined the crew of the 12-pounder cannon and asked, "Lt. Lamb, are you ready to fire?"

His face was blackened by gunpowder; he replied, "Yes. You shall not be disappointed, sir."

Pleased by his success in inflicting significant enemy casualties, James' smile faded as he perceived the few continentals returning with Lamb's ambush party and said,

"Lamb, I can only leave ten men. The rest must find cover in the fort to support your retreat. Delay firing as long as you can."

Sprinting back with his men to Fort Montgomery's partially built walls, a brief silence allowed James Clinton to hear the exchange of volleys from his brother's defenses a mile away. He ordered, "Find cover and fire only on my command. Lamb and his men will be joining us momentarily."

Boom!

Flinching, despite his expectation, the discharge of the case shot from the 12-pounder cannon was deafening. Stunned, James took several moments to recall Lamb retreating to the fort, and shouted, "There will be no time for a second volley, so fix bayonets. When Lamb and the rear guard arrive, we shall fall back to our gunboats for evacuation across the river."

Focusing his attention on the perimeter forest from which James Clinton anticipated Lamb to emerge, he perceived the absence of gunfire from the direction of his brother's defenses. *George, don't be a hero!*

Lamb and a dozen artillerymen and continentals scrambled out of the trees and sprinted across the open ground into the scant protection of Fort Montgomery. An inhuman cry heralded the appearance of a wave of enraged lobsterbacks and Hessian chasseurs. Absorbing the continental's volley with no apparent effect, the furious attackers forewent an answering volley bent upon settling the matter with the bayonet.

During the fierce hand-to-hand melee which followed, James' chest was pierced by a chasseur's bayonet, causing him to collapse unconscious to the ground. Lamb killed the chasseur and carried Clinton to the river with the help of his men.

"James! I forbid you to get yourself killed." Bending over the prone body of his brother, George Clinton unbuttoned James' torn uniform jacket and began to examine the wound when his brother's eyes snapped open.

James murmured, "Governor, my recommendation is an immediate evacuation across the river."

Chuckling, George replied, "You're the military man, James.

Lieutenant Lamb and I shall assist you to board a beached gunboat."

Helped to his feet, James boarded the boat without assistance, prompting Lamb to say, "That Hessian bastard drove a bayonet into your chest!"

James replied, pulling his torn leather dispatch book from his uniform pocket, "I was lucky. The blade was deflected by this. But why didn't he strike again?"

"Because I sabered him."

"My thanks, Lieutenant Lamb. I owe you the life of my brother," said George.

James nodded and asked, "Lamb, why did the British attack us in an unorganized mob? Our volley at point-blank range killed dozens, and we bayoneted others as they climbed over the rampart."

"When the garrison retreated, I fell back to the hidden 12-pounder cannon and waited for the enemies' advance. Instead of sending out scouts, an officer led a column double-time to point-blank range costing his life and those in the first three ranks."

"That explains it," volunteered George, "My men were not so lucky. The British commander outflanked the redoubt and overran my defensive line inflicting severe losses."

James looked up at the silent cannons lining the walls of Fort Clinton and said, "At least Gates stripping us of powder shall prevent the lobsterbacks from employing our cannons to kill us while retreating across the river."

"James, do the Continental frigate captains know the forts' cannons are harmless?"

"Yes, George."

"Then why are the crews abandoning and setting fire to the Congress and Montgomery?"

"I suggest you attend the Continental Navy's court martial of those captains to hear their explanation."

Crossing the Hudson without incident, the Clinton brothers disembarked from the gunboat. One of General Putman's aides met them and said, "General Putman has sent these horses for you and wagons to transport the garrison to Peekskill."

Governor Clinton asked, "What about the Navy?"

James Clinton replied, "George, not to worry. The Continental Navy has boarded lifeboats and sailed upriver, presumably to the continental encampment at West Point. I recommend we all depart for Peekskill immediately before the cannons of the approaching British frigates come within range."

Mounting their horses, James Clinton gestured to Putman's aide to dismount and said, "Lamb, you are now my adjutant and a Captain. I trust you can ride. George, we must meet with Old Put and decide how best to defend the Hudson Valley if Burgoyne breaks through at Saratoga."

George replied, "James, you meet with General Putman. Send me a message with your recommended plan. I am going to Albany, accompanied by Lamb, to meet with General Schuyler to discuss the political situation. He must represent us in Congress. New York has become a battleground and must be represented by a stronger voice in choosing who commands the continentals defending our people."

British Flotilla
October 6th

Upon hearing the battle, Captain Wallace ordered the watch officer, "Weigh anchor. Signal the squadron to remain at anchor until further orders." Addressing his First Lieutenant, he continued, "We shall sail upriver beneath the cannons of Fort Clinton and Fort Montgomery. Send a messenger to the gunnery officer to prepare the bow chasers to fire upon the river chain and log boom when within range. Go about your duties. Dismissed."

Although Wallace heard occasional cannon fire, none was directed at his frigate.

Passing abeam of walls of the forts bristling with cannons, the ship glided through the water in silence, broken only by creaking masts and humming of the rigging.

"Captain, the lookout in the crow's nest reports the forts appear to be abandoned, and the cannons are all capped," shouted the watch officer.

Boom, boom!

A ship's boy scampered from the bow, slid to a stop, knuckled his forehead, and squeaked, "Captain, the gunnery officer reports the bow chasers have broken the chain." Turning on his heel, he returned to report the captain's receipt of the message.

Wallace asked the watch officer, "Are the enemy frigates and gunboats preparing to fight?"

"The lookouts report the enemy frigates have cut their anchors and attempting to raise sail to escape up the river."

"The rebels waited too long. The wind is against them."

As the minutes passed, Wallace heard, "Captain! The rebels have set fire to their ships and dropped their lifeboats. Shall we fire the bow chasers at the traitors?"

"Lieutenant, you are relieved of duty and restricted to your quarters until summoned by me. I am considering your court-martial for suggesting that a ship of the Royal Navy fire upon seamen fleeing a burning ship. Dismissed."

As Wallace returned his attention to the mission, the same ship's boy returned and said, "The bow watch reports clusters of chevaux-de-frise lining the riverbed ten ship lengths upriver."

"Relay my order to drop the anchor. Be off with you."

Two hours later, Captain Wallace stood on his quarterdeck surrounded by the captains of the other two frigates and his ship's lieutenants and, after hearing their reports, said, "The squadron will anchor in place. Each vessel shall launch its longboats crewed by seamen with axes and ropes to clear the chevaux-de-frise blocking our passage north. I have been summoned ashore to meet with General Clinton. All ships must be ready to sail at a moment's notice."

Fort Clinton
General Henry Clinton's Headquarters
October 7th

Pacing back and forth in front of the fort's headquarters building, Sir Henry Clinton addressed the assembled task force commanders.

"I have successfully fulfilled my duty. The rebel forts are no longer obstructing Burgoyne's advance south. I will return to New York City with the bulk of the troops escorted by a single frigate to resume my primary responsibility of safeguarding the King's most important port in the New World. I leave five hundred men to garrison the rebel forts with Major General Vaughan in command. Captain Wallace shall clear the river of obstacles and sail upriver to capture or burn all enemy shipping. Gentlemen, I know you will prosecute this campaign with the same effort you have shown under my command. General Vaughan, I look forward to receiving your report that your forces have joined with General Burgoyne's and are sailing to New York City."

Chapter Eight

Battle of Bemis Heights

Saratoga, New York
Great Redoubt
British Headquarters
October 3rd

Standing at attention in front of Burgoyne's field desk, General Fraser felt embarrassed and frustrated for the first time in his distinguished military career.

"Fraser, your advance corps is experiencing unacceptable casualties, and I know nothing about the enemy's disposition and strength since the conclusion of the battle weeks ago!"

Standing rigidly at attention and staring without expression over Burgoyne's head, Fraser answered quietly, "Yes, sir."

Recognizing he was taking his frustrations and anxieties out on his best combat leader, Burgoyne grimaced and said, "Sorry, Simon, you and your men are not to blame for the current situation. Please sit and let me pour you a glass of the last of my claret."

A close friend, Burgoyne, had chosen Fraser over several senior officers to command his advance corps to bring the Scotsman to the attention of the King. Sitting quietly and taking the proffered glass of the precious spirits, Fraser nodded his understanding and responded in a conversational tone.

"Morgan's riflemen and Dearborn's light infantry, reinforced by a strong force of Oneida warriors, dominate the entire forest between the lines. Ambush points have been established at every approach to the woods flanking the rebel fortifications. My men and Riedesel's jaegers have been ambushed repeatedly, with our best men killed or captured."

Burgoyne knew an honest analysis by a seasoned combat leader when he heard it.

"It appears to have been a mistake to refuse Brant's offer to lead a force of Mohawk warriors in support of the army." Pouring a second drink for Fraser, Burgoyne asked, "What is your opinion of the current situation?"

Holding his glass of claret, Fraser looked into his friend's eyes, replying, "The only way through those woods is a reconnaissance in force. The combined British and Hessian advance corps, plus any other men you can spare from guarding the redoubts and camp. We must fight through the ambush sites and whatever forces lie beyond to determine what we are against."

After a moment, Burgoyne considered his options, leaning back in his chair, and said, "I accept your assessment and intend to forego any further scouting. The army shall renew our attack upon the rebel's left flank. To solve our supply problem under cover of the assault, the Hessian and the batteaux crews shall harvest the Barber Farm's wheat field. You shall meet with Lt. Colonel Breymann and ascertain the number of the Hessian advance guard available for the attack."

Burgoyne's Headquarters
October 3rd

Standing in his dress uniform before an assembly of his officers, Burgoyne formally broke the seal and opened a dispatch just received from General Howe. Reading its contents aloud, he concluded with his summary.

"General Howe has successfully engaged Washington at Brandywine Creek and has captured the rebel's capital of Philadelphia. Can we do less as the finest army sent to the Americas, Gentlemen? We can end this rebellion by defeating the rebel's army standing before us." Crumbling the dispatch in his fist Burgoyne shouted, "What actions should we take?"

As he expected, his junior officers simultaneously answered, "Attack! Attack!"

When the uproar quieted, General Riedesel stepped forward and said, "Given our inability to scout the enemy lines, we have no idea of the strength or positions of their continental or militia units. Our supply situation is critical. The rebels have successfully disrupted our communications with Quebec. There is no possibility of timely resupply or reinforcement from Carlton in Quebec or Howe in Philadelphia. I recommend crossing the Hudson River and withdrawing to Batten Kills to await further news from Clinton. This army would then have the option to be reinforced or retreat to Fort Ticonderoga to await further instructions from the Crown."

When Riedesel finished speaking. Philips, Fraser, and Hamilton nodded their agreement.

Holding his smile with a noticeable effort, Burgoyne responded quietly but firmly,

"There will be no retreat from rebel shopkeepers and farmers! I intend to attack the rebels' left flank with the entire army. The rebels would be unprepared for such an assault. Once we rout the continentals, the militia and the Oneida will melt away!"

Recognizing Burgoyne's plan as merely a gambler's last desperate throw, the attending officers began respectfully suggesting alternatives.

Fraser repeated his recommendation of a reconnaissance in force.

On October 7, 1777, Burgoyne led a force of two thousand men and ten cannons to penetrate the rebel ambushes and patrols to determine the current disposition and strength of the enemy.

Riedesel's Headquarters
October 6th

Riedesel, for the first time in his distinguished career, experienced despair. Sitting alone in his tent, he thought, *Burgoyne's army is doomed, and its commander is content to see it be lost rather than simply withdraw to the safety of Fort Ticonderoga. Five thousand regulars garrisoning Ticonderoga would make it invulnerable to attack. Ticonderoga could then serve as a base for raids harrying the settlements of the Mohawk and Hudson River Valleys supported by loyalist forces. Most importantly, Howe could retain control of Philadelphia and release thousands of regulars to reinforce Burgoyne and the garrison of New York City.*

It was clear to Riedesel that as Burgoyne's superior, Carlton should have been given the command in the first place. Burgoyne was determined to endanger the entire army rather than retreat. Defeated at Bennington and, frankly, at Saratoga in September, the Crown would appoint Carlton to the command, despite the influence of Burgoyne's father-in-law, the Earl of Derby.

The incompetence and selfishness of Burgoyne were overwhelming. Nonetheless, Riedesel recognized his responsibility to safeguard his soldiers and called an all-officers meeting. Hearing his commanders' voices calling the assembly's attention, Riedesel assumed his professional demeanor, stepped from his tent, and addressed his men.

"Gentlemen, three hundred of our men will join a probing attack of two thousand men led personally by General Burgoyne. Burgoyne intends to fight through the enemy pickets and patrols to ascertain the rebels' numbers and defenses. I shall command our contingent and, accompanied by wagons, harvest the Barber Farm's wheat field to replenish our supplies. The batteaux men shall drive the wagons and assist in the harvest. I anticipate the enemy will not be equipped with cannons since none of their batteries have been withdrawn from the river defenses. Captain Pausch's cannons shall anchor our left flank. The British will cover our front with two twelve-pounder cannons. We will do our duty but shall not advance until I observe the rebel's response. I will not sacrifice you should the enemy prove overwhelming."

Morgan's Field Headquarters
Officers' Call, October 6th

Surrounded outside his tent by his officers and Oneida sachems, Morgan said, "The lobsterbacks are coming. I feel it in my bones. It has been several days since any attempt has been made to penetrate our ambush sites. Today, those sites will be abandoned, and I shall initiate patrols of the woods bordering the left flank of our defensive lines. Only the Rifles shall be used. Han Yery, I do not want your warriors moving through the woods to be mistaken for Burgoyne's remaining Ottawa and Abenaki scouts."

Han Yery replied, "I agree. My warriors are not to be used in open battle. The Oneida have served our allies with honor and shall remain in camp."

Morgan reached out, grasped Han Yery's forearms, and said, "It has been a pleasure fighting alongside you and your men."

Morgan then switched his gaze to Dearborn and asked, "Comments?"

"I agree. My men can guard the camp and continue to train the other regiments in using the bayonet. General Schuyler's recent shipment of munitions included hundreds of French bayonets."

Grimacing, Morgan grated, "I never again want to face the British with an empty rifle. I shall never forgive Gates' refusal to release us gunpowder and ammunition after the Battle of Freeman's Farm. Poor and Learned Brigades' mile-long line of sparkling bayonets gave the Rifles the courage to form a skirmishing line hundreds of yards in advance of the continentals.

"Major Morris, take a company and patrol the perimeter woods. You are to leave this evening and report any enemy movement. Send a messenger each hour to advise me of your situation. I anticipate you will encounter an overwhelming force seeking to find a way around our left flank. You shall fire only in self-defense. Once there is contact with the enemy, fallback. The Rifles and the light infantry will confront the enemy together."

Early Morning
October 7th

Captain Fraser, his surviving marksmen, the remnants of Abenaki warriors, and a small contingent of the 24th advanced from the Balcarres redoubt to guide the advance corps around the left flank of the rebels' defensive fortifications.

Heavy fog reduced Fraser's progress to a crawl. Suddenly, one of the 24th inadvertently stepped on a dead branch, making a sharp noise as it broke. The crack of a rifle was heard, and an advancing marksman collapsed to the ground. "Down," someone shouted, and silence descended upon the combatants.

Captain Fraser's command remained in place until the fog began to lift, and he heard the advance corps emerging from the Balcarres redoubt. Captain Fraser rose from cover as his uncle approached on horseback and said, "I am sorry, General, the enemy must have been here all night. They held their positions after wounding one of my men. To advance without knowledge of their position would have been suicide."

General Simon Fraser was not surprised by the failure of his nephew to penetrate the enemy picket and replied, "Captain, join the column. We are too many to fight. The enemy pickets must fall back to their units. This army can no longer afford to be blind. For better or worse, we will know today."

Bemis Heights
Gates' Headquarters
October 7th

General Gates leaned on the map table and confidently addressed his senior commanders.

"My strategy has borne fruit! General Lincoln implemented my plan to employ the militia to cut the British supply line from Quebec. I have forced Burgoyne to leave his fortifications to forage for food."

Lincoln nodded in reply to Gates' praise recognizing that this formal acknowledgment was to further anger and frustrate Arnold. Gates had intentionally failed to mention Arnold in his official dispatch to Congress of the army's victory in the Battle of Freeman's Farm.

Smiling at Lincoln, Gates continued, "I have ordered Colonel Morgan's Rifles and Dearborn's light infantry to engage the enemy foraging party on our left flank."

Standing within an arm's length of Gates, Arnold barked, "That is not enough!"

Waiting for such an act, Gates stood nose to nose with Arnold and yelled, "You are insubordinate, sir! Notify all commands that General Arnold is immediately relieved of command of the army's left wing." Gates continued to his adjutant, "General Arnold is confined to his tent until I summon him to a Board of Inquiry."

Quivering from rage, Arnold again barked, "I demand to be released to join General Washington and the main army!"

Without glancing at Arnold, Gates resumed his seat and said dismissively, "Sir, I give you no further thought."

Arnold turned and stormed out of the meeting.

Resuming his seat behind his field desk, Gates continued, "Gentlemen communicate to your brigades that I have assumed command of the left wing of the army, and General Lincoln will command the right wing."

Lincoln, sensing the unrest of the continental and militia commanders caused by this disgraceful display, said quietly, "General Gates, may I offer a suggestion with your indulgence?"

Satisfied that he had accomplished his purpose of driving Arnold, Washington's favorite, from the army, Gates contently looked at Lincoln and replied, "Of course, General, please continue."

Lincoln leaned over the map table and pointed to the location of the reported troop movements, "General Gates, I recommend that you dispatch Poor's New Hampshire brigade and Learned's Massachusetts brigade to reinforce Morgan and Dearborn. I agree with your opinion that Burgoyne is desperate and may risk as much as half of his remaining command to seize the Barber wheat fields to harvest the entire crop to prolong this campaign. We cannot risk any delay in defeating Burgoyne. Otherwise, he may be reinforced by St. Ledger, Clinton, or Carlton. Should Burgoyne attack with overwhelming force, Morgan and Dearborn, two of your best units, would be lost."

Immediately sobered by the thought that by assuming Arnold's command Gates, not Arnold, would bear the blame for such a loss,

Gates nodded and said, "General Lincoln, I thank God you have returned to this army. Your recommendation is accepted. You are to issue those orders immediately. As a further precaution, order Ten Broeck's militia brigade of eighteen hundred men to act as a reserve behind Learned's men."

As his commanders left headquarters to comply with his orders, Gates thought, *My defensive strategy shall ensure victory. Howe defeated Washington twice in open battle. I expect Congress to appoint me as Commander in Chief before month's end.*

Morgan's Field Headquarters
October 7th, 10 am

Addressing his officers, Morgan said, "Major Morris and his company intercepted a scouting party of Fraser's marksmen and Abenaki attempting to loop around our defensive line into our rear. A single well-placed shot in the fog has stopped their advance. After observing General Fraser and the light infantry join the scouting party, Morris has fallen back to our lines. Gates has been informed, and the Rifles and Dearborn's light infantry have been ordered to engage the advance corps and turn their flank. General Poor and the New Hampshire brigade will be on our right, and General Learned's Massachusetts brigade will be on Poor's right. Join your companies. Murphy and O'Brien, you are with me."

General Poor's Field Headquarters
October 7th, 10 am

"Gentlemen, we will advance in line, and you are to ensure your men keep their interval. We will again be fighting in the area of the loyalist farms, and I intend to take full advantage of our firepower. Your regiments will march in line abreast with loaded muskets. The first rank will fix bayonets, and the second row shall not. I intend to deliver two volleys of seven hundred muskets before advancing with the first line of bayonets. I shall give the order to fire each volley."

Colonel Cilley, commander of the 1st New Hampshire, volunteered, "Today we pay the British and Hessian back for Colonel Hale and the boys of the 2nd New Hampshire we lost at Hubbardton!"

Barber's Wheat Field
October 7th, 2 pm

Burgoyne advanced about a mile beyond his field fortifications and halted above Mill Brook to observe the rebel lines. While his ten cannons were deployed, he watched the harvest of the Barber wheat field. In preparation for battle, he had stationed Ackland's grenadiers on his left, Riedesel's regulars in the center, and Fraser's light infantry on his right.

Burgoyne watched a continental brigade emerge from the woods and advance against his left flank in two lines abreast. Seriously outnumbered, Ackland's grenadiers accepted the challenge and advanced in line with fixed bayonets to fire a volley to test the enemy's resolve.

Burgoyne felt his luck had held. The rebels had chosen to attack his bravest and most disciplined troops, and should these continentals be routed, the day would be his.

***

Major Ackland was excited to be the target of the enemy brigade which he identified as the New Hampshire brigade led by Poor. Ackland addressed his command, walking out in front of his grenadiers, standing in a line formation.

"At Hubbardton, we were outnumbered and defeated the 2nd New Hampshire and the Green Mountain Boys. Today is an opportunity to trounce the entire New Hampshire Brigade!"

Ackland recognized his men were vastly outnumbered by the enemy watching the rebel formation approach. Still supremely confident, Ackland was sure the rebels would scatter in the face of a bayonet charge by the fiercest men of Burgoyne's army.

Raising his sword, Ackland shouted, "We shall double-time to within a hundred yards of the center of the enemy line, fire a single volley, and then charge with the bayonet. The rebels have always run! Captain Ross will attack the left of the broken formation. Captain Anderson, you will strike the right."

***

Three hundred yards away from the advancing grenadiers, General Poor gave his final orders to his regimental commanders.

"The brigade will receive the enemy's first volley and hold their fire until I give the signal by the brigade drummers. The first rank shall fire. Then, kneel with their bayonets toward the enemy. The second rank will wait until a second signal by the drummers to fire. Then, the first rank is to stand and advance with leveled bayonets to engage the grenadiers. The second rank will reload, then advance behind the first."

Nodding their understanding, Cilley, Reid, and Scammel returned to their regiments to relay Poor's orders to the men.

***

Across the field, Ackland saw that the enemy brigade was not advancing, which he interpreted as fear. Emboldened, Ackland shouted, "Halt, aim, fire charge!"

As the grenadiers broke through the smoke of their volley, they had an unobstructed view of seven hundred leveled muskets whose simultaneous volley moments later decimated their formation. As individual grenadiers continued their charge, the first rank of continentals knelt, and the second rank of seven hundred muskets fired, cutting down most of the remainder.

Despite the overwhelming volleys, individuals, many of them wounded, continued to advance, eager to avenge their fallen comrades. Closing to within twenty yards, they were met with a bayonet charge of the first rank of 3rd New Hampshire continentals led by Colonel Scammel. After a sharp fight, the few survivors were routed back to the Balcarres Redoubt.

As the New Hampshire brigade reorganized its ranks, General Poor sent his aides to summon his Colonels for new orders. After gathering, Poor said, "Gentleman, Hubbardton has been avenged. I have received a messenger from Colonel Morgan, and he requests our support in engaging General Fraser's light infantry and the 24th."

Colonel Scammel said, "General, my men have found Major Ackland, commander of the grenadiers."

"I am surprised he survived."

Colonel Scammel replied, "He was shot in both legs. He was down before the brigade's second volley."

Poor pointed to Colonel Lattimore and ordered, "Your militia will gather our wounded and the British. Organize transport to the hospital. Gather all abandoned bayonets to equip the remainder of the Northern army."

"Yes, sir."

He returned his attention to the assembled commanders, "Join your regiments. We will attack. This ends today."

Barber's Wheat Field
Fraser's Advance Corp
October 7th

Emerging from the forest on the extreme left flank of the rebel's lines, General Fraser was encouraged that his light infantry and marksmen had encountered no rebel ambush sites or outposts. Upon crossing this field, he expected to view the rebel's positions.

"Balcarres. Light infantry forward as skirmishers. Captain Fraser and your marksmen watch our flanks," ordered Fraser.

As the light infantry reached the farm field's midway point, a formation of continentals emerged from the woods advancing with bayonets lowered.

Fraser drew his sword and ordered, "Captain Fraser, you and your men will advance as skirmishers."

"Light infantry, fix bayonets! Loose formation and double time."

As the light infantry trotted forward, the woods exploded in rifle fire, dropping individuals and disrupting the advance.

Reacting instinctively, General Fraser turned his horse toward the enemy riflemen and pointed his sword in the direction free of gun smoke. "Balcarres, fall back double time! Maintain your formation. Fraser, your marksmen, will act as rearguard."

Turning his horse, he galloped to his regiment, the gallant 24th. As he approached, Fraser saw a large formation of continentals advancing toward his men. Calling out, he ordered,

"Major Mackenzie, the 24th must hold. The light infantry and marksmen will pass behind you. I will form a new defensive line to which the 24th will fall back. The entire command will then retreat to Balcarres redoubt. Send messengers to General Riedesel and General Burgoyne. Inform them the rebels have outflanked this command, and we are facing at least four thousand continentals."

Major Mackenzie, a member of another Scottish fighting clan, nodded and calmly replied, "Yes, sir, the 24th will stand."

Fraser smiled, nodded, and rode toward the Balcarres redoubt seeking a position where he could unite his command to duplicate the disciplined withdrawal of the rebel commander at Hubbardton.

General Ebenezer Learned
Massachusetts Brigade
October 7th

A tough-minded solid professional, General Learned advanced in two lines of continentals totaling 1,400 muskets. Emerging from the woods, he saw a single British regiment in line formation blocking his advance and shouted, "Sound officers' call!"

Listening to the drum roll summoning his commanders, Learned took the time to decide whether this was an ambush or a fearless regimental commander who could not count. As Colonels Greaton, Putman, and Nixon arrived, so did a mounted messenger dressed in the hunting shirt uniform of Colonel Morgan's Rifles. Turning to his senior officers, he said, "Pardon me, Gentlemen, I suggest we hear what Colonel Morgan's messenger has to say."

Straightening to attention in his saddle, Tom O'Brien took a deep breath, saluted, and said,

"General Learned, Colonel Morgan's compliments. The Rifles and light infantry surprised and outflanked Fraser's advance corps and forced them to retreat to the British redoubts. They are passing behind the 24th regiment, which is to your front. Colonel Morgan urges you to immediately attack with your brigade before Fraser can form a new defensive line."

Learned looked into the eyes of the young sergeant and saw a veteran whose information could be relied upon. Noticing that his rank insignia was partially detached, Learned smiled and said, "When were you promoted, son?"

Tom smiled and replied, "About ten minutes ago, sir."

Turning to his Colonels, he said, "We will go straight in with fixed bayonets. Double time to fifty yards from the enemy. The first rank will fire a single volley and kneel. The second rank shall fire and charge. This ends today!"

Barber's Wheat Field
Massachusetts Brigade
October 7th, 3 pm

Forcing the 24th to retreat in the face of the advancing Massachusetts brigade, General Learned stood with Colonel Morgan, looking at the chaos of the battlefield when they observed a rider galloping toward them, waving his sword and shouting.

"My God, it is General Arnold! I thought he had been relieved!" said Learned.

Colonel Morgan grimaced, shaking his head and replying, "I have never known Arnold to bother himself about obeying orders."

Pulling his horse up at the last moment, Arnold yelled, "General Learned, your brigade will advance and engage the Hessians in the wheat field in conjunction with Poor's brigade. Colonel Morgan, you and Lt. Colonel Dearborn shall continue your attack on Fraser's light infantry and the 24th retreating behind the Hessian formation."

Seeing Tom O'Brien among Learned's staff, Morgan mounted his horse and motioned him over, and they began to ride together to the Rifles' current position.

"You did fine, Tom. Major Morris will be pleased by your return of his horse."

"Thanks, Colonel."

"Tom, our job is to continue pushing Burgoyne back into his fortifications. We have four thousand continentals and two thousand militia against less than two thousand of his best troops. If we bleed them now, Burgoyne is finished. Find Murphy and tell him he has another chance at Burgoyne."

Freeman's Farm
Learned Brigade
October 7th

After Arnold and Morgan rode away, General Learned continued to scan the battlefield, observing Poor's brigade shatter and rout a battalion of British grenadiers.

To his front, Learned observed the Hessians concluding their harvesting and withdrawing with their loaded wagons in good order toward the British redoubt.

Colonel Bailey asked, "General, didn't General Gates relieve Arnold of command and assume command himself?"

Learned replied, "Arnold is a Major General on the battlefield prepared to lead the attack upon the invaders. If you happen to see Gates, please let me know. Poor, and I intend to attack, capture, or kill any enemy soldier who advances upon Albany. Arnold is simply riding in the direction we intend to go. Join your regiment."

Barber's Wheat Field
October 7th

"My God, General, it is a hot one!" yelled a light infantryman loading his musket with professional ease from his years of service.

"My God, it is!" replied General Fraser. His men were holding, and the 24th would join his lines in minutes. "Balcarres, we provide General Riedesel with a rallying point for his men. We will fall back together."

As Fraser scanned his front, he saw Sir Francis Clark, a senior aide of Burgoyne, galloping toward him and pulling up his horse, saying, "Good afternoon General Fraser, General Burgoyne's compliments!"

"Sir Francis, do you have orders for me?"

"Information, not orders, Sir. General Burgoyne has returned to the Great Redoubt to organize its defense. His field commanders have the discretion to continue the engagement or withdraw to the Balcarres redoubt."

Before Fraser could respond, dozens of rifle shots rang out, and Fraser saw Sir Francis fall lifeless from his horse.

Barber's Wheat Field
General Riesedel's Field Headquarters
October 7th

Standing in the partially harvested field, Major General Riedesel watched a mounted officer gallop from the enemy brigade on his right to the second enemy brigade that had defeated Ackland's grenadiers. In response to his summons, Major Williams of the Royal Artillery, and Captain Pausch of his command, stood at attention for orders.

"Gentlemen, General Burgoyne's forethought to equip us with two twelve-pounder cannons under Major Williams and Captain Pausch's six-pound battery will prevent the enemy from outflanking this command. Major Williams, you will concentrate your fire upon the enemy brigade to our right and Captain Pausch upon the brigade to our left. You and your men will continue to fire until the last moment, spike the guns, and fall back into our lines. Your men will be needed to operate the cannons in the Great Redoubt. Join your gun crews."

As the two artillery officers returned to their respective commands, Riedesel turned to Lt. Colonel Speth and said, "Major Williams and Captain Pausch will not leave their guns. If Williams disobeys my orders, I will not forcibly remove him. Captain Pausch is another story. I have promised his mother to return him home if possible. You will assign one of your officers and two of my jaegers to remind Pausch of my orders. I expect to see him when the command has returned to our lines."

Snapping to attention, Speth said, "Captain Pausch and his men will be with us tomorrow."

Looking again at the advancing continental brigades, his cannons opened fire, tearing bloody gaps in their formations.

Bloody Knoll
Fraser's Field Headquarters
October 7th

General Fraser found himself on a small hill with Balcarres' light infantry fighting Morgan's rifles, who had gotten behind his command and on their right flank.

Calling upon his twenty-five years of combat experience, Fraser recognized the rebels' overwhelming numbers and resolve to achieve victory. He instinctively voiced the orders to salvage as many of his men as possible.

"Balcarres, form a circle using all available cover. Send a messenger to Major Agnew to have the 24th fall back to our position and draw the enemy brigade away from Riedesel to allow the Hessians to retreat to the Great Redoubt."

Barber's Wheat Field
Learned's Brigade

Arnold felt his frustration boiling over as he realized the Hessians were too well-led and disciplined to rout. Step by step, Riedesel's men held their formation, exchanging volley for volley as they retreated from the wheat field. Arnold would not achieve the glory to save his career here.

Scanning the battlefield, he saw that General Fraser had succeeded in rallying the light infantry and the 24th. He was desperately organizing a firing line to absorb the Hessians slowly retreating in his direction.

Galloping to where Morgan was fighting a nest of jaegers, Arnold dismounted and crouched beside him. Pointing at General Fraser, he said, "That man's life or victory."

Nodding, Morgan agreed, "The battle hangs in the balance."

Barber's Wheat Field
General Poor's Field Headquarters
October 7th

After a short discussion with General Arnold, Poor watched him gallop back toward Learned's headquarters as the Massachusetts brigade advanced against the Hessian's formation, taking terrible losses from case shot from the enemies' cannons.

"Colonel Cilley, the 1st New Hampshire will pivot right toward the enemy redoubt following the British line regiment falling back toward the hill that Morgan has identified as an enemy outpost. Fraser and his light infantry attempt to use that position as a rallying point for the Hessian foragers. General Arnold ordered the capture of the enemy field redoubts to concentrate the enemy and pin them inside their encampment against the river. Colonel, the 1st New Hampshire, will lead the brigade in the attack."

Bloody Knoll
Morgan's Field Headquarters
October 7th, 4 pm

Murphy had been with the advance detachment of Rifles and Dearborn's light infantry, which had ambushed Fraser's scouting party that morning. His shot had wounded Captain Fraser's marksman. Murphy had remained with the detachment, fighting with two other Rifles after Colonel Morgan had assigned Tom O'Brien as a mounted messenger.

Murphy and his companions employed their hunting skills to shadow the retreating British light infantry and marksmen fighting a deadly game of hiding and seek. Each duel ends in a single shot signifying the elimination of another of the players.

After hours of pursuing the lobsterbacks, Murphy observed that the survivors had stopped retreating and had concentrated in a heavily wooded elevation, known locally as the 'Bloody Knoll' due to heavy hand-to-hand combat contesting possession of the site during the September 19th battle.

"Murphy, I have a job for you."

Rising from a crouch at the foot of ancient oak, Murphy pressed his back against the tree's trunk, shielding himself from enemy fire. Gazing in the direction of the voice, Murphy drawled, "Colonel be careful. There are some talented boys holding the Bloody Knoll."

To verify his opinion, a rifle bullet splintered the bark from the trunk where Murphy had crouched moments before.

Ignoring the danger, Morgan continued, "Murphy, that officer," pointing to the lobsterback mounted on the grey horse, "is successfully organizing that crowd of British and Hessian regulars on the Bloody

Knoll into a steady rhythm of disciplined fire. That is General Fraser. He is the glue preventing us from breaking those bastards! We lose if he lives. Take your companions and get it done."

Morgan watched Murphy and his men crawl through the brush toward the Bloody Knoll. Gesturing Major Moore closer, he said, "Find Major Dearborn and tell him to muster and organize one hundred men to launch a bayonet attack upon the Bloody Knoll when he hears three drum flourishes. Accompany him and report to me whether the attack is successful and the current situation."

Morris departed noiselessly, and Morgan took a moment to observe Fraser. He mused, *Someday the lobsterbacks and us shall fight on the same side, and our enemies shall fear to ever face us again.*

"What are we waiting for, Morris?" Dearborn asked impatiently.

"The drum flourish, Colonel. I don't see Fraser; he must have joined the 24th, Colonel Morgan wants to know where the 24th is before the Rifles attack the British light infantry."

***

Leaving the forest, General Fraser walked his horse to meet Major Agnew, the executive officer of the 24th, and greeted him, saying, "Well met, Major Agnew. The 24th will be the basis for our rally point on the Knoll."

Fraser suddenly doubled over, and his horse bolted, causing him to fall to the ground.

As Major Agnew and Captain Fraser rushed to the fallen man, General Fraser looked up, his face white and eyes blank, and said, "Alex, take your marksmen and scout a way to the Balcarres redoubt for the 24th. Send a messenger to Balcarres and order the lights to fall back. Major Agnew, dispatch messengers to General Riedesel and General Burgoyne to inform them of the situation. I recommend that the Hessians return to the Balcarres redoubt and not the Breymann redoubt."

As Major Agnew organized a stretcher to carry his general back to the camp hospital, General Fraser heard a drum flourish and thought, *My God! What do the rebels have in store for us now?*

195

***

As the last drum echo died in the light breeze, Dearborn drew his sword and shouted, "Charge, no mercy!"

As Dearborn's men poured up the slope of the Knoll, the British light infantry had simply had enough. Taking to their heels, the elite of the finest British army sent to the Americas abandoned the outpost's fortifications and routed to the Balcarres redoubt.

Barber's Wheat Field
Riedesel's Command
October 7th

General Riedesel's column was isolated and vulnerable to capture with the rout of the British grenadiers and Fraser's light infantry. When the enemy brigade on Riedesel's left had turned to assault Fraser's men, both Pausch's and Williams' batteries could concentrate their fire upon the second enemy brigade advancing to his front. The cannon fire repulsed the advance, and the rebels had retreated beyond the case shot range.

Riedesel ordered, "All wagons carrying the wounded and the harvested wheat shall withdraw to the Balcarres redoubt to take advantage of this reprieve. Summon Captain Pausch and Major Williams."

When the two artillery officers arrived, Riedesel said, "I have just received a messenger from General Fraser. The light infantry and the 24th have fallen back to the Balcarres redoubt. We are alone. All cannons will be spiked and abandoned, and we will join in the withdrawal."

Riedesel's command was the only one to successfully withdraw from the battle in good order facing the enemy.

Barber's Wheat Field
General Learned's Brigade
October 7th

"General Learned. General Arnold appears to be approaching," called out a sentry.

With a deep sigh, General Learned prepared himself for the return of the would-be hero of Saratoga. His brigade's losses had been galling in the assault without artillery support upon the Hessian foragers ordered by Arnold. Learned was in no mood to receive further orders from the man responsible for the cost suffered by his men in this futile assault.

Arriving again in a cloud of dust, Arnold yelled in a highly agitated voice, "General, victory is now within the power of the Massachusetts brigade."

In a voice devoid of emotion, Learned responded, "The brigade has suffered terribly from the enemy case shot. Without artillery or riflemen attached to my command, I could not counter or silence those cannons."

Arnold retorted, "Blame Gates, not my order. Gates refuses to release any artillery from Bemis Heights or the river defenses. General Poor's brigade is attacking the British redoubt, so your brigade may assault the Hessian redoubt without possible enemy reinforcements."

As Arnold finished, both Generals turned to see a rider in one of Morgan's hunting shirts pull up and say, "General Arnold and General Learned, Colonel Morgan's compliments. The Rifles and Dearborn's light infantry have assaulted the fortified cabins and jaeger outpost supporting the Hessian redoubt. The Colonel requests your immediate support!"

General Learned respected Morgan's battle instincts and said to Arnold, "The capture of the Hessian redoubt would render the British redoubt untenable. The enemy would be compelled to fall back to their camp or be outflanked."

Arnold looked closer at the messenger and asked, "What is your name?"

"Sergeant O'Brien, General."

"O'Brien? I meet a Brian O'Brien at Fort Stanwix," Arnold said.

"My father, General."

Losing interest in O'Brien, Arnold turned to Learned and said quietly, "Are you going to obey my orders to advance, General?"

Learned turned slowly toward Arnold and held his gaze for several moments before saying, "General Arnold, the Massachusetts brigade has never failed to advance on an enemy. Colonel Livingston, you will support Colonel Morgan and Lt. Colonel Dearborn's assault."

Arnold galloped across the battlefield toward the Hessian redoubt to achieve the glory he craved. As he approached, he saw Sergeant O'Brien ride to and join a group of riflemen, including Colonel Morgan. Changing direction, he rode up to Morgan and asked, "Colonel, have your men found a way into the redoubt?"

"When we captured the cabins, we found a path leading to the rear of the Hessian redoubt."

"Show me!"

Reluctant to use the path in case of ambush, Morgan pointed it out to Arnold and rejoined his men who had just captured the jaeger outpost.

Returning his attention to the battlefield, Morgan observed the approach of a mounted continental colonel. Recognizing the rider, he greeted him, "Colonel Livingston, you are welcome."

"Colonel Morgan. Colonel Dearborn. General Learned is advancing upon the Hessian redoubt and requests your recommendation on the angle of our separate attacks."

"Major Morris, will you attend to General Learned's request."

When Morris had ridden away, Morgan handed Colonel Livingston his flask of rum and said, "You have a good bunch of boys. Your brigade advanced into the enemy cannons, withstood that barrage, and withdrew in good order. I'm sorry Gates stripped you of the support of the Rifles."

Livingston took a drink from the flask and, after returning it, said, "Your men saved us at Freeman's Farm. Gates continues to refuse to release cannons to his brigades in the field. But for Gates, Learned would have broken the British. Cannons would have blown that redoubt to pieces."

Morgan nodded, "If we capture the Hessians' redoubt, we can march right into the main camp. Anyone who fails to retreat is dead or captured."

"General Learned agrees. Poor's brigade blocks any reinforcement from the main camp or Balcarres redoubt. Have you seen General Arnold?"

"Yes, he was looking for a way to be the first to enter the Hessian redoubt."

Livingston shook his head, then said, "Arnold is unbelievable," and departed.

Breymann's Redoubt
October 7th

"Major Mengen, have we had any further word from the jaeger outpost or the fortified cabins?"

"No, Colonel Breymann, we appear to be alone."

Breymann's redoubt had been constructed by the Hessians grenadiers on the evening of September 19th. During the intervening weeks, it had become a wall of logs secured by ship's ropes a hundred yards long, ten feet in height, pierced with loopholes allowing the defenders to fire with minimal exposure to return fire.

Breymann's vivid recollection of the battle of Bennington had spurred his preparation of this refuge for his men. The hellish retreat of his command under constant attack by rebel militia had cost a third of his grenadiers to unknown marksmen and meaningless skirmishes in the dark.

Returning to the current crisis, he replied, "Inform the men we will continue to hold this position until relief is sent by General Burgoyne. No retreat. "

A sudden racket caught his attention, and Breymann saw a mounted continental Major General gallop into the rear of his redoubt, screaming and waving a sword. While his men decided whether to kill or capture the madman, hundreds of rebel riflemen and bayonet-armed continental light infantry assaulted the fortifications.

While Breymann tried to absorb this new situation, his body was slammed to the ground by a terrible force, and he saw and heard no more.

Breymann's Redoubt
October 7th, 5 pm

"General Arnold, are you all right?"

In terrible pain and barely conscious, Arnold recognized the voice and snapped, "Colonel Morgan, report!"

Smiling to himself, Morgan replied, "General Arnold, you lost consciousness when your horse was killed charging into the redoubt. Your leg was broken when your horse fell on you. The same leg was further shattered by a musket ball. The redoubt is in our control, and the grenadiers are dead, captured, or have routed."

Partially delirious from his wound, Arnold asked, "Gates?"

Morgan frowned and snorted, "Now that the fighting is over, Gates has sent reinforcements. General Ten Broek and General Patterson brigades, over four thousand men! General Gates, however, remains at headquarters at Bemis Heights."

Arnold snarled, "What is Lincoln's intention with eight thousand men under his command and Burgoyne's forces pinned against the Hudson River?"

Morgan replied, "Gates has recalled General Lincoln to Bemis Heights. Without a senior field commander on the battlefield and Gates's reluctance to join the army in the field, the brigade commanders are consolidating our position here. They intend to assault the British fortifications tomorrow. With the capture of this redoubt, the Balcarres redoubt is outflanked."

Arnold screamed, "The Balcarres redoubt should be captured now!"

Morgan tersely responded, "In obedience to your orders, Poor's brigade assaulted the Balcarres redoubt and suffered heavy casualties. Since then, the redoubt has been reinforced by Riedesel's Hessians and cannons. We are done today. General Learned's men will be transporting you to the camp hospital."

Watching Arnold and other wounded from the enemy redoubt being loaded onto wagons, Morgan pondered what had been accomplished here and questioned whether the loss of life would bring independence from the Crown any closer.

Great Redoubt
Burgoyne's Headquarters
October 7th

Burgoyne ordered the Balcarres redoubt abandoned that evening, and all troops, cannons, and supplies evacuated into the Great Redoubt.

The Great Redoubt had been built north of the village of Saratoga, situated on a bluff overlooking the Hudson River. Defended by entrenched batteries on three hills surrounding the site, the fortification housed the hospital, arsenal, artillery park, and supplies.

Strolling through the cluster of hospital tents, Burgoyne credited himself for the medical staff's disciplined competence amongst the chaos of hundreds of wounded men pouring in from the battlefield. His duty done, Burgoyne motioned his staff officers to follow him out into the open and addressed them.

"The Great Redoubt is to be evacuated immediately. The army shall occupy the village of Saratoga and guard the bridge of boats to Fort Edward and the road to Ticonderoga. We must be gone before first light."

"John, what of the wounded? Most would not survive the move," said General Phillips.

"General Phillips, you are the last person I would expect to question my efforts to save this army!" shouted Burgoyne.

Startled by Burgoyne's rudeness to Phillips, one of the most respected officers in the British army, Balcarres said formally, "Sir! What of General Fraser?"

Into the silence, Riedesel answered, "My wife is caring for General Fraser, to whom she has become quite fond. Unfortunately, the doctors have informed her that his wound is mortal. He has expressed his wish to be buried in the Great Redoubt."

Conscious of the shocked expressions of his officers, Burgoyne regained control of his emotions and replied, "General Fraser's wish shall be honored. Lord Balcarres, you shall oversee your commander's burial. Other duties prevent my attendance."

His visage devoid of color, Phillips interrupted, "General Burgoyne! You have failed to reply to my request to share your plan to evacuate our wounded."

"Fine, General," snarled Burgoyne. "They will not be evacuated. General Gates was at one time an officer of the King. I trust him to remember his duty to care for and safeguard the wounded that must be left behind."

Burgoyne heard Reidesel's voice from the rear of the assembly.

"I shall not leave my wounded. I intend to honor my duty to my Duke and do my utmost to preserve the life of his soldiers. I recommended withdrawal to Saratoga to prevent the crippling of this army by your negligent assault with no reconnaissance. My men shall camp separately. Henceforth the Hessians are subject to my sole command!"

Expecting his officers' outraged outburst in response to Reidesel's insubordination, the complete silence was stinging support to the fat general's opinion that patronage, not ability, had placed this army under his command.

***

Standing with his brigade commanders on Bemis Heights, General Gates trained his telescope upon the abandoned British and Hessian redoubts and asked, "Colonel Morgan, what is the report of your scouts?"

"Burgoyne's army has fallen back to the main redoubt," replied Morgan.

Turning to General Lincoln, the sweating Gates snapped, "Do you guarantee that there is no possibility of any attack upon Bemis Heights?"

Embarrassed by Gates' apparent fear and loss of control, Lincoln calmly replied, "General Gates, I shall not guarantee what I have not personally witnessed."

"Certainly, General. Return to the battlefield and personally conduct an inspection that would permit you to provide such a guarantee."

Straightening to attention, Lincoln turned to leave when he heard Morgan say, "General Lincoln, with your permission, I shall assign Tom O'Brien to accompany you. You two worked well together in Vermont."

"Fine, Morgan. I will meet O'Brien at the stables. General Gates,

I shall be prepared to guarantee Burgoyne's intentions when I return."

Battlefield
October 8th, 6 am

Walking their horses through the fields of the dead, General Lincoln and Tom O'Brien watched soldiers of both armies carry away those who could be saved. Passing by the abandoned Hessian and British redoubts, Tom asked, "How far are we going, General?"

"We have not encountered our scouts yet. I want to talk to them to ensure how close they got to the main British redoubt," replied Lincoln.

Reeling in his saddle, Lincoln fell heavily to the ground as a rifle shot was heard.

Lifting his rifle, Tom saw two jaeger hunters rise from cover. As the apparent marksman began to reload, Tom shot the second ambusher before he could fire. Drawing a musket from his saddle scabbard, Tom killed the second jaeger as the Hessian shouldered his rifle.

Dismounting, Tom started to reload the musket and knelt next to Lincoln, who had struggled to a sitting position and drawn his pistol.

"Sergeant, you are as good as Morgan said you were."

Wrapping his neck scarf around the General's leg wound and tightening it until the bleeding stopped, Tom said, "The bone is not broken, but to prevent further loss of blood, I am lifting you onto your horse and returning you to camp. We've been lucky no one has come to investigate the shooting."

Lincoln was lifted smoothly by the slender rifleman onto his horse. Tom returned the loaded musket to its scabbard, reloading his rifle and taking the reins of Lincoln's mount, and, his own in his free hand, led the General back to Bemis Heights.

Gates' Headquarters
October 8th

Conducting a meeting of his six brigade commanders in his Marque headquarters, Gates' adjutant stepped in and said, "Sir, General Lincoln is here to report."

"Finally! Show him in immediately."

Carried in on a stretcher and laid on the map table, Lincoln achieved a sitting position supported by Tom and said, "I personally guarantee that Burgoyne is in retreat. There is no longer any danger of an attack on your headquarters."

Collapsing back unconscious, Lincoln was carried out, followed by Tom, who heard General Poor say to Gates, "As the only unwounded Major General in this Army, sir, will you be leading the assault on the British camp?"

Reassured of his safety, Gates ignored Poor's question and said jovially, "Transfer all the cannons and crews from the river and Bemis defenses to form a Grand Battery to commence the immediate bombardment of Burgoyne's camp."

***

Regaining consciousness due to the burning pain in his calf, Lincoln slowly opened his eyes. He looked into the skeletal face of Brigadier General John Stark standing at his bedside in Lincoln's headquarters tent.

"I am sorry, Stark. The rumors of my death have been exaggerated."

What might have been a chuckle seemed to originate from the scowling visage peering down at him. Straightening to attention, Stark said, "Major General Lincoln, I am reporting with my command and requesting your orders."

Unconsciously breaking into a smile and sitting up, which hurt, Lincoln said, "Please sit down, John. Congratulation on your promotion. What is the size of your command?"

Surprised but pleased by Lincoln's sincere welcome back into the Continental Army, Stark replied formally, "2,500. The victors of the Battle of Bennington."

"Where are they?"

"Still on the east shore of the Hudson."

"Excellent. Your men are to build field fortifications at the terminus of the British bridge of boats to cut off Burgoyne's retreat to Fort Edward. With the militia of the Hudson and Mohawk Valleys, we now outnumber Burgoyne three to one. We shall capture the King's finest army sent to the Americas."

Stark growled, "My men shall display the Hessian flags and pennons captured at Bennington. I want Burgoyne to know whom they face should they try to cross that bridge."

"John, please sit down. I want to clear the air between us."

"I will sit if you tell me how you got yourself wounded," Stark replied.

"Gates refused to release the cannons and brigades garrisoning his headquarters until I guaranteed Burgoyne had no intention to continue his attack."

"Gates didn't believe Morgan's scouts?"

"Gates is a clerk and hopeless as a field commander. To launch the counterattack, time was of the essence, so I accomplished what was necessary myself," Lincoln replied.

"I heard you reported to Gates on a stretcher before your wound was cared for."

"Who told you that?"

"Sergeant O'Brien, the soldier who saved your life. O'Brien saved many of my men at Bennington by guiding them undetected behind the enemy's redoubt permitting its capture with minimal casualties."

"I always wondered why you allowed my spy to accompany you."

"A feeling, General Lincoln. I am glad we had this opportunity to talk. I realize now that you were the right man to receive the promotion.

I look forward to your return to duty since Gates doesn't seem up to the job. I will speak to Morgan to encourage his aggressive nature to run Burgoyne to earth as soon as possible. I guarantee that Burgoyne is trapped, and no lobsterback will cross the bridge of boats while I live," said Stark.

***

That evening Gate's cannons made their first appearance on the battlefield, shelling the Great Redoubt and disrupting the funeral of General Fraser. Although largely ineffective, the constant bombardment was relied upon by Burgoyne to justify to his senior officers an immediate evacuation and retreat to Saratoga on the evening of October 8th.

Burgoyne informed his officers of their assignments with the ceaseless barrage and a heavy rainstorm in the background.

"Colonel Sutherland, you shall scout the road to Saratoga in company with the light infantry and remaining Abenaki. General Phillips, you shall command the rearguard. All supplies, cannons, and munitions must be transported to Saratoga. This storm is our salvation because the rebel militia shall not attack and face our bayonets.

Gates shall treat our sick and wounded with respect. Time is of the essence. Carry out your duties and keep me informed."

***

Sheltered in one of the abandoned huts built by the batteau men, Burgoyne sat alone with his thoughts, staring into the flames of a roaring fire. Hearing a soft knock, he looked up as his adjutant entered and said, "General Phillips is here to see you with Lady Henrietta Ackland."

Regaining his focus, Burgoyne put on his uniform jacket and ran his fingers through his wet hair to receive the daughter of an English Earl and an acquaintance of his wife.

Lady Ackland entered the room accompanied by her chaplain. She stood stoically, her clothes soaked and long hair hanging in strands. Despite shivering violently, her voice and emotions were in perfect control. Gazing for a few moments at Burgoyne, she said, "General, I have been informed that my husband, Major Ackland, has survived the battle and lies as a prisoner in the rebel camp. I request you issue me a letter of safe conduct to pass with my attendants through the rebel lines to care for my husband."

In awe of the Lady's grace and courage, Burgoyne threw off his lethargy, insisted she take his chair, and wrapped her in his blanket. Rummaging through his map case, he found a scrap of paper and a pencil. Freshening his cup of tea from a cauldron hung over the fire, he insisted she drink while he wrote a note to Gates and added his signature.

Unfailingly polite and courteous to women, Burgoyne held Henrietta's hand and said, "Your courage has inspired me to carry on and perform my duty to the King. I am powerless to offer assistance besides this note to General Gates and a small batteau to travel to his camp."

Finishing her tea and returning the cup, she squeezed Burgoyne's hand and replied, "I am escorted by my chaplain, and we are in God's hands. My husband's valet is a former bosun in the Royal Navy and will safely row us downriver. With my undying thanks, I must leave to reach my husband before it is too late."

Assisting Lady Ackland to her feet, Burgoyne walked her to his adjutant and said, "Escort the Lady and her attendants to the river and provide her a batteau. Goodbye, Lady Ackland, Godspeed. I am confident the Major shall recover under your care."

After taking leave of his unexpected visitors, he returned to his sanctuary, extinguished the fire, and drank the remaining tea. Re-arming himself, he donned his hat, walked out into the rain, mounted, and rode to join his staff waiting in an abandoned barn on the property.

Riding along the road, scouted by his advance guard, Burgoyne observed the consequences of his overconfidence and reliance upon his gambler's instinct. Wrecked wagons, dead horses, abandoned barrels, and boxes of supplies, the detritus of a retreating army. But, he thought, *not defeated!*

Entering the barn, Burgoyne addressed his staff, "Gentlemen, this storm is a blessing. Should the rebels attack us tonight, the battle shall be decided by cannons and the bayonet. We are their superiors, and victory is certain! Once we reach Saratoga on the shore of the Hudson River, the army shall be protected by cannons of the Royal Navy. General Clinton is sailing upriver with a squadron of frigates carrying the garrison of New York City to finish the rebels.

"Until Clinton reaches us, we shall construct a redoubt defended by General Phillip's cannons and the volleys and bayonets of four thousand muskets." Relieved by the chorus of hurrahs from his staff, Burgoyne continued, "Spread out and reassure the men and encourage their maximum effort."

As his staff departed from cover and scattered to carry out his orders, Burgoyne rode slowly into the storm, passing among his soaked and mud-covered men. Overwhelmed by his men's courage and discipline, marching mile after mile without complaint, Burgoyne thought *Victory was still within reach.*

Gates' Headquarters
October 9th

Sticking his head into the Marque's office, Lt. Colonel Wilkinson said, "Lady Henrietta Ackland is here to see you."

Shocked, Gates stuttered, "The daughter of the first Earl of Ilchester? Wilkinson, the Lady, and her party will be escorted to me immediately". Pondering how he could benefit from this surprising turn of events, Gates stood when Wilkinson entered the Marque in the company of a young woman dressed fashionably but ravaged by the storm of the previous evening.

Bowing from the waist, Gates greeted her, "My Lady. How can I be of service?"

Offering her hand, Lady Henrietta waited until Gates had kissed it and said, "General, I am informed that my husband was grievously wounded yesterday commanding the King's Grenadiers. I wish your permission to join him."

Releasing her hand, Gates straightened to his full height and replied, "Your husband is being held at General Poor's headquarters. Wilkinson will accompany you to him with my verbal order to General Poor to provide you with a tent to care for your husband. Of course, your husband shall remain under guard as a prisoner of war."

"Thank you, General Gates. I expected no less from a former King's officer." Reaching into her purse, she removed a wet and stained piece of parchment and, handing it to Gates, said, "General Burgoyne asked me to deliver this to you." Lady Henrietta stood and then anxiously followed Wilkinson out.

Lady Henrietta was reunited with her husband, and her nursing returned him to health. A son John was born in March 1778. The Acklands returned to England in October 1778. Soon after, Major Ackland was killed in a duel with a fellow officer who had spoken disparagingly of the Americans. She later married her chaplain, who had escorted her safely to General Gates.

Saratoga, New York
October 9th

General Riedesel and Balcarres stood in the early morning sunshine watching their men ford the Fishkill, a shallow tributary of the Hudson River.

Riedesel chose to personally command the Hessian light infantry and jaegers of the advance guard, determined to preserve his men from further loss due to the idiocy of the British. Surprisingly he enjoyed working with Balcarres due to the young officer's courage in battle and consideration for his men. Visibly upset by the death of General Fraser, whose funeral he and Balcarres had missed, Riedesel extended his condolences.

"Balcarres, I didn't always agree with General Fraser, but I respected his courage."

Looking down at the shorter man, Balcarres replied, "Baron, General Fraser regretted not taking your advice to launch a joint attack at Hubbardton. Should he die, I was to thank you for saving his command at that battle." After breaking eye contact with Riedesel, he continued, "Excuse me, Baron, my orders are to construct a redoubt on the elevated ground in the curve of the Fishkill and prepare to install the cannons. Are you joining us?"

"No, Balcarres. My command shall also cross the Fishkill and use its protection. We shall defend your flank with a line of trenches and a wall of logs parallel to the Hudson River."

Gates' Field Headquarters
Saratoga, New York
October 9th

Uncomfortable in public, Gates had agreed to conduct a meeting limited to only brigade commanders. He was shocked to leave his headquarters into the open air facing eleven veteran commanders, clearly agitated by the lack of direction and failure to follow up on yesterday's rout of Burgoyne's army.

Turning to Wilkinson, Gates said, "I said only Brigadier Generals!"

"You now command eleven Continental and militia brigades," Wilkinson stuttered.

Stunned, Gates turned, re-entering his Marque, and whispered, "Wilkinson, come in here!"

Taking a seat at his desk, Gates regained the calm and focus which served him as an administrator and asked, "Wilkinson, what has been the effect of the bombardment?"

"The British encampment has been abandoned but for the wounded and sick. General Glover has evacuated them to our hospital. Morgan's scouts have followed the British retreat toward the Hudson River."

"Has Burgoyne retreated over their bridge of boats?"

'No. General Lincoln ordered General Stark to blockade it."

Startled that he had not taken such an obvious precaution to prevent Burgoyne's escape, Gates flushed, and he thought, *only by my capturing the King's army will Congress promote me to the Commander in Chief of the Army.* Submerging his anxiety, he demanded, "What is the status of the pursuit of Burgoyne?"

Confused, Wilkinson blurted, "None. You have not ordered one."

Gates shouted, "I intend to court-martial Arnold and Lincoln for gross negligence for failing to order their brigades yesterday to pursue and attack the enemy!"

"Sir, both Arnold and Lincoln were seriously wounded yesterday. Both are in the hospital and sedated. You are the only able Major General in this army."

"Why was I not told!"

Since Wilkinson knew that was untrue, he replied, "Sir, the Brigadiers of this army are outside and await your orders."

Blinking and sitting until he calmed down, Gates said, "Lift the tent flap and stand behind me when I address them."

Walking out into the half-circle of waiting men, Gates shouted, "My cannons have broken Burgoyne, and he is running for Ticonderoga. I have trapped the British in Saratoga by ordering General Stark's brigade to blockade the terminus of the Burgoyne's bridge of boats. General Clinton has complicated our bagging the fox by capturing the Highland forts. A squadron of British frigates is sailing up the Hudson River with reinforcements. All continental brigades shall march immediately to assault Saratoga. The militia brigades on this side of the river shall garrison our camp. Those on the east shore shall stay in place and reinforce Stark's brigade to prevent the enemy's escape across the river."

General Poor asked, "Will the assault be supported by cannons of the Grand Battery?"

"No. Time is of the essence. We outnumber them three to one. Surrounded and cut off, Burgoyne will surrender. Ready your brigades to march within the hour."

Burgoyne's Field Headquarters
Saratoga, New York
October 11th

Burgoyne addressed the officers of his command, perhaps for the last time. His final hope was that Gates' impatience to achieve victory would provide an opportunity to blood the rebels and salvage some retribution for Fraser's murder.

"Gentlemen, your outstanding achievement in saving the army's artillery has allowed us to achieve victory! General Philips has positioned twenty-seven cannons to crush any assault by the rebels across the Fishkill. Gates knows General Clinton has captured Highland Forts and is sailing north in a squadron of frigates carrying an army to reinforce us. Gates shall be forced to assault this position with the continental brigades we blew to pieces at the Balcarres redoubt. Our cannons will break them. The rebels must be denied any cover or protection as they advance upon our redoubt. All buildings and houses within one mile must be burned to clear our fields of fire."

General Phillip's asked, "General Schuyler's house?"

"First!" replied Burgoyne, soliciting smiles and laughter from the assembly.

Slapping his riding crop against his leg, his officers' demeanor sobered. Burgoyne continued, "The rebels' assault shall be shattered by case shot, and when the continentals rout, I will lead the entire command in a bayonet attack. We shall spare no one. Without his continentals, Gates will retreat since he has no faith in the militia, and they have none in him. Prepare your men. We shall crush the rebellion once and for all!"

Gates' Field Headquarters
Saratoga, New York
October 10th

Smiling and again surrounded by his Brigadiers in the privacy of his office, General Horatio Gates confidently announced, "The current fog shall aid us in ending this affair with an all-out assault upon the enemy redoubts."

I am sure you are pleased that your men shall achieve victory by the bayonet's point!"

Instead of the resounding "Hurrah!" he anticipated, his words were met with silence.

After a pause, General Glover cleared his throat and said, "General, I recommend that my men and General Patterson's be allowed to scout the approaches and lead the assault, since our brigades have not participated in the fighting."

Interpreting Glovers' statement as a criticism of his insistence that two brigades guard his fortified headquarters, Gates took immediate offense and shouted, "With the departure of General Arnold, I believed thoughtless obstruction to my orders had ended. I have informed you that General Clinton is proceeding up the Hudson after his victory over the Clinton brothers and Putman. I will not risk this army's victory by delaying this assault. My strategy has trapped Burgoyne, and here we will finish him. Report to your brigades and prepare for a dawn attack. I will not tolerate any possibility of losing the element of surprise by any scouting before the attack."

Walking with Dearborn back to their joint campsite, Morgan said, "Since we have been excused from the assault to protect Gates and his staff, I am sending O'Brien and Murphy up into the hills to get above the fog and determine if a direct assault can be avoided."

Fishkill Creek
October 11th

In the heavy fog, the brigades of Poor, Learned, Patterson, Glover, and Nixon, numbering 8,300 continentals, surrounded the two redoubts containing five thousand entrenched British and Hessian regulars.

Listening for the drum roll signaling the attack, Glover's adjutant touched him on the shoulder and whispered, "General, we have captured a British deserter who says there are twenty-seven cannons loaded with case shot primed to slaughter us. Burgoyne intends to follow up the cannonade with a bayonet charge. The orders—no quarter."

"Send messengers to the other brigades to fall back. You report to General Gates to explain the situation. This assault is canceled upon my authority."

Glover endured the silence as the minutes passed until he was informed that the other brigades and his own had fallen back beyond the range of the British case shot. Wiping the sweat from his face, Glover moved slowly away from certain death to return to General Gates, the man who was responsible for it.

As his brigade resumed its original position in the Continental defenses, the walls of the enemy redoubts belched flames, and case shot shredded the surrounding ground.

Gates' Field Headquarters
Saratoga, New York
October 11th

Mustered for the second time that day, General Gates stood fidgeting in front of his Marque headquarters, listening to General Glover recounting the near annihilation of the Northern Army.

"Fortunately, my men captured a British deserter warning of Burgoyne's ambush."

"Yes, thank you, General Glover, but it has been five days since the British captured the Highland forts. General Clinton leads a squadron of British frigates whose cannons shall protect Burgoyne until infantry reinforcement reaches him!"

Disturbed by Gates's loss of control, the assembled Brigadiers relaxed when a distinctive voice was heard from the rear of the formation.

"General Gates. Colonel Dearborn and I have found a way through the bluffs to a position above the British redoubt," Morgan stoically reported. "We request the assignment of a battery of cannons and a brigade of infantry to reinforce our position to commence bombardment on Burgoyne's encampment."

"O'Brien and Murphy?" asked General Poor.

"Of course, sir," replied Morgan.

Poor laughed and addressed Gates. "General, my brigade volunteers to reinforce Morgan and Dearborn. Will you release us cannons?"

In the silence, Gates stared at Poor, who returned it, still bitter because of the unnecessary casualties from the absence of artillery support.

"General Poor, you have my approval to consult the Quarter Master to draw whatever artillery and munitions you deem necessary to obtain Burgoyne's surrender." Abruptly entering the Marque, Gates said over his shoulder, "I expect hourly reports. This assembly is dismissed!"

Moments after Gates' departure, pandemonium broke out with the cheering of the Brigadiers, who all rushed to shake hands with Morgan and Dearborn. The emotional release of stress that a costly direct assault had been avoided spread to the army as preparations took place to occupy the high ground located by the Rifles.

Heights above Saratoga
Continental Cannon Batteries
October 12th

Morgan, Poor, and Learned looked down at the ravaged British redoubt, and the survivors of Burgoyne's command huddled within. Poor silently reflected upon the last weeks that had led to this moment and said, "What I cannot forgive is Gates' refusal to release cannons to our brigades at Freeman's Farm, the Barber's wheat field, and the subsequent assault on the Breymann and Balcarres redoubts. Our commands suffered needless casualties to protect Bemis Heights, which was never threatened."

Learned nodded to Poor in agreement and said, "Those British twelve-pounders and the Hessians' battery of six-pounders in the Barber's wheat field accounted for almost all the casualties my brigade suffered in this campaign."

Still bitter, Poor added, "With the cannons on this ridge, we could have blown the Balcarres and Breymann redoubts to splinters, captured Burgoyne's army, and saved the lives of the men wasted by Arnold's last grasp for glory." Addressing Morgan, he continued, "If not for your riflemen, I believe we would have lost the battle on September 19th."

"Thanks, General," Morgan replied. "Let's not forget the Oneida capturing or killing the jaegers and light infantry trying to infiltrate our lines. If successful, the British would be bombarding Bemis Heights."

"General Fraser was a gallant officer," General Learned said.

"Yes, he was," Morgan replied. He walked away from the group and joined his riflemen on the firing line. "Murphy, what is the situation?"

Tim Murphy gestured toward the British redoubt and said, "Tom and the boys have silenced all the cannons in the redoubt facing our position."

Tom said, "Colonel, these men are helpless. What is Burgoyne waiting for?"

Morgan shook his head. "Burgoyne knows he is responsible for giving us a real chance at gaining independence. His career in the British Army is finished."

"But his men, Colonel. You, my father, and Han Yery would never permit this to happen."

"Tom, your father, and Han Yery would not lead men into this situation."

The Convention Army, Saratoga
General Burgoyne's Headquarters
British Camp, October 14th

Sitting at his field desk under a patchwork of canvas stitched together from the tentage salvaged from the abandoned Great Redoubt, Burgoyne pondered, *how had it come to this?*

Four days had passed since the Hessians had mutinied, built, and occupied separate fortifications. Meant only to serve as a temporary refuge until crossing the bridge of boats to the road north to Fort Edward, Burgoyne's line of retreat was now blocked by thousands of militiamen displaying Baum's regimental colors and squadron pennants captured at Bennington. At last, count ten thousand continentals and militia pined his army against the river. Burgoyne's pride had compelled one final act of defiance, commencing a bombardment with his entrenched cannons upon the rebel battery in the surrounding heights. The rebel cannons had rained death and destruction upon his men, and those cursed riflemen had decimated the artillerymen in response. This last refuge had become a tomb, and Burgoyne had requested a ceasefire to commence negotiations for surrender.

Unable to delay this unpleasant experience any further, he left the isolation of his makeshift shelter and regarded the redoubt's interior carpeted by the disheveled and filthy soldiers rationing drinking water from his diminishing supply.

Addressing his officers standing at ease in front of him, Burgoyne began, "Gentlemen, I have called this council of war to discuss whether the finest army sent by our King to the Americas may honorably surrender."

As his second in command and friend, General Philips replied, "General, your officers above the rank of Captain, have unanimously agreed surrender would be honorable. Any further loss is not justified."

Burgoyne tiredly nodded and said, "Major Kingston, you will request a cease-fire under a flag of truce to commence negotiations. Inform Gates he has my pledge that if my soldiers have access to the river for hygienic and medical purposes, the privilege shall be limited to one hundred men at a time supervised by their officer."

***

Two hours later, Major Kingston was admitted into Burgoyne's presence and reported, "General Gates has agreed to the ceasefire and our access to the river."

"Excellent, Major. I didn't expect you so soon."

"Gates insisted on providing me a horse to facilitate negotiations."

"Interesting. General Clinton informed me last month of his

216

intentions to sail from New York City to join us in Albany. While you were in the rebel camp, did you see any activity indicating Gates was preparing for an attack?"

"No, sir. But Gates headquarters is heavily guarded by at least a brigade of continentals and entrenched cannons."

"Kingston, when you were escorted to Gates' headquarters, did you observe the numbers and morale of the rebels?"

Frowning, the Major replied, "I saw thousands of continentals and militiamen. We are outnumbered three to one. My continental escort was respectful, but when the rebel militia saw me, they shook their fists and screamed threats that 'you lobsterbacks were going to pay in blood for the Abenaki and Ottawa slaughter of our families and burning of our property.'"

Leaning back in his chair, Burgoyne admitted to himself, *Trusting St. Luc, that French renegade was a mistake._*"Did Gates suggest how the negotiations were to proceed?"

"Gates intends to deliver written proposals through his Deputy Adjutant General Lt. Colonel Wilkinson. Wilkinson shall return to Gates with your replies unless you insist I deliver them."

"Kingston, inform Gates his suggestion is acceptable, but Wilkinson shall not be permitted into the redoubt. Gates must not learn of the mental and physical state of this army. Does Gates appreciate that I am this army's sole voice, and he is not to approach the Hessians?"

"Gates's only reference to the Hessians was as ruthless mercenaries whom he did not trust and would not parley with."

Burgoyne's Headquarters
Saratoga, October 15th

Amazed how access to the river had improved the health and morale of his army, Burgoyne enjoyed the mild weather and exchanged pleasantries with the Lieutenant and sergeants supervising their men bathing and washing their clothes in the river. He felt renewed wearing his clean dress uniform for the first time since the evacuation of the Great Redoubt.

Burgoyne watched Major Kingston approach, salute, and say, "General Wilkinson has arrived to discuss the two letters you received by messenger this morning from General Gates."

"Escort Wilkinson with General Philips around the redoubts' perimeter walls. Inform General Philips that I want him to describe to Gates' adjutant each of those entrenched cannon's capabilities and point out ample powder and ammunition standing by for use. A crew of Royal artillerymen in their clean and pressed uniforms shall be stationed at each cannon. Our readiness to repulse any assault must be conveyed to Wilkinson and through him to Gates. Otherwise, acceptable terms of surrender shall not be forthcoming. After his tour of our defenses, escort Wilkinson to me. I shall be waiting here."

Kingston's Cambridge demeanor cracked. Grinning broadly, he said, "That was brilliant to prioritize the artillerymen's access to water and Wilkinson seeing our artillery up close."

"Carry on, Kingston, don't disappoint me."

Distracted by the noise of a new company marching from the redoubt to replace the current bathers, Burgoyne walked further down the river, hopeful to glimpse frigates and batteaux of the promised British relief force, and thought, *First Howe abandoned me seeking his glory, and now my friend Clinton. Where shall history place the blame?*

***

Returning to the redoubt, Burgoyne decided to stand beside the ten feet high perimeter walls with eight entrenched cannons, their muzzles protruding above his head.

"General Burgoyne, may I present Lt. Colonel Wilkinson."

Turning in the direction of the voice, he saw a slight, balding teenager unimpressive in every respect and thought. *A clerk's clerk, how did Gates ever beat me?*

Annoyed and unimpressed, Burgoyne snapped, "I have received two letters from General Gates in less than twenty-four hours. The first demanded total surrender, and the second demanded surrendering all arms by no later than 1500 hours today. Both are unacceptable. You are to inform General Gates that my men are prepared to attack with no thought of quarter unless it is agreed that this army is permitted to return to England upon the condition that these troops will not again serve in North America."

Blinking uncontrollably, Wilkinson replied in a whisper, "I will, of course, convey your terms to General Gates."

Motioning Wilkinson closer Burgoyne leaned toward him and said in a whisper, mere inches from his face, "Wilkinson, remind Gates, I expect the sighting of a squadron of frigates carrying General Clinton's relief force. Their arrival will cost Gates his victory and his command! You are dismissed."

***

Passing through the ever-present guards, Wilkinson entered the Marque and saw Gates writing yet another dispatch to Congress at his desk. Gates demanded, "Wilkinson, did Burgoyne mention when Clinton's relief force was expected to arrive?

"Yes, sir."

"What exactly did he say!"

Lt. Colonel Wilkinson was surprised by Gates's intensity and replied, "Only the usual threat, General."

Standing, Gates waived a dispatch at Wilkinson and said, "This confirms that Forts Montgomery and Clinton have been captured. The Continental frigates guarding the river were burned by their crews. General Putman has retreated to Peekskill. I will not lose this victory. Howe repeatedly defeated Washington at Brandywine Creek and Germantown. I am certain to replace Washington as Commander in Chief with Burgoyne's surrender!"

Wilkinson was equally concerned. As his chief aide, if Gates were to replace Washington, Wilkinson was confident he would become a General before year-end.

Wilkinson said, "Burgoyne rejected your demand of unconditional surrender. He insists his army is permitted to return to England upon the condition that these troops will not again serve in North America. Otherwise, combat shall resume."

"Ha! What nonsense! Burgoyne's men will simply be employed elsewhere in the British Empire, and the replaced soldiers shall return to try and crush the rebellion again. But I shall accept. This victory shall empower my supporters in Congress to demand Washington's resignation and my appointment as Commanding in Chief of the Continental Army. I defeated Clinton's attack on Charles Town, South Carolina. I defeated Burgoyne at Saratoga. I shall defeat the British no matter how many troops the King sends. I shall gain our independence and reap the rewards."

"Yes, General. I will advise Burgoyne of your consent to his terms and assist in the drafting of the treaty."

***

Burgoyne spotted the child Wilkinson galloping from the continental lines towards him a surprisingly brief time later. Leaning against the redoubt's parapet wall, Burgoyne descended the dirt ramp to the ground and walked briskly through the guarded gate to intercept Gates' clerk by the river. Now that the rebels were no longer shelling his men, he was confident in any negotiations with Gates, a former British major masquerading as an American Major General.

"Wilkinson, I am through negotiating. Don't bother dismounting if you don't have an original treaty signed by Gates with the terms I demanded."

Dismounting, Wilkinson handed the rolled parchment tied with a cotton cord and silently stood at attention.

Enjoying himself, Burgoyne removed the cord and leisurely read the documents, careful not to smear the fresh ink. Burgoyne was relieved to perceive Gates' spidery signature on the final page. "Wilkinson, I must congratulate you on your penmanship, but you lied to me!"

Breaking into a sweat, Wilkinson removed a handkerchief from his sleeve, wiped his face, and said, "The treaty is signed and provides that your men may return to England upon the condition that they do not return to America."

"Not Enough! I never agreed to capitulation! I shall not sign unless that is struck and substituted with convention."

Relieved, Wilkinson struck out the offending word and began to modify the document when Burgoyne snatched it and tore it in half.

Shocked, Wilkinson looked as if he was about to cry when Burgoyne placed a hand on his shoulder and said, "You shall prepare an original with the correct language, obtain Gate's signature and return."

Picking up the torn parchment, Wilkinson mounted and galloped away.

Laughing, Burgoyne said to himself, *I would give anything to have fought Gates and Wilkinson instead of Morgan and Poor.* Sobering, Burgoyne knew his military career was over, but his father-in-law would preserve his social standing. He felt confident his future professional reputation would continue as an accomplished playwright and member of Parliament.

Burgoyne's Headquarters
Officers' Call
Saratoga, October 16th

Gates relaxed security after the formal surrender, allowing local farmers to sell their produce to the besieged army.

Burgoyne's optimism was renewed after the unexpected supplies and news of the outside world conveyed by loyalist farmers. He again called an all-officers assembly and informed them of the current situation.

"Gentlemen, it is confirmed that General Clinton has captured the Highland forts, and General Vaughn is proceeding north with reinforcements. You have been convened today to ask your opinion whether this army is bound by the signed treaty or whether I may act on this new information."

Most of the officers believed that the army was bound and was concerned that the troops would mutiny if the rebel bombardment and rifle fire upon the redoubts resumed. Burgoyne conceded that achieving his ambition of further recognition from the Crown was finished.

Saratoga
October 17th

Burgoyne's army marched out of their fortifications with the honors of war to surrender their arms to the waiting continentals. Of almost ten thousand men who left Quebec, less than six thousand remained.

Those men are known to history as the Convention Army. The terms of surrender provided that the Convention Army march two hundred miles to Boston, where it was agreed that the British and Hessian regulars would be loaded on transports to sail to England.

Escorted by Glover's brigade, the Convention Army reached Cambridge on November 6th. Lack of food and billeting resulted in an embittered Burgoyne writing to Congress accusing that body of breaking faith with the terms of surrender.

On November 8th, the British garrison at Fort Ticonderoga destroyed the fortifications and retreated to Quebec.

Congress was shocked by Gates's treaty allowing the release of so many professional soldiers for use by the Crown. Citing Burgoyne's allegations that the treaty had been broken, Congress concluded it was no longer binding.

On December 23, 1777, the ships sent to carry the Convention Army to England were refused entry to Boston.

On January 3, 1778, Congress resolved to retain the Convention Army, and it was marched south, where the men were dispersed to prevent rescue by British forces fighting there.

In April 1778, Burgoyne and his aides returned to England. Burgoyne's officers were gradually released on parole, but Philips and Riedesel were not released until 1780 in exchange for General Benjamin Lincoln, who was captured in the fall of Savannah.

The remaining men of the Convention Army were released by Congress in April 1783. The war officially ended with the signing of the Treaty of Paris on September 3, 1783.

December 5, 1777
Versailles, France

Comte de Vergennes, foreign minister of Louis XVI, waited patiently for his King to finish reading the official dispatch from the Continental Congress.

"Vergennes, am I to believe the English rebels' claims in this document?"

Familiar with his King's questioning of any representation from a foreign source Vergennes confidently replied, "Your Majesty, my agents have confirmed that the continental army fought the British and their Hessian mercenaries in two battles and defeated them. Burgoyne's army of ten thousand regulars has been killed, wounded, or captured. New York City remains in British hands, but the continentals still control the Hudson River. Fort Ticonderoga was destroyed by the British before retreating to Quebec. The colonies remain undivided."

Louis' stare softened reflectively for a moment, and he said, "It appears that God has decided, and I intend to act accordingly."

On December 6, 1777, Vergennes and his King met with Benjamin Franklin. A formal treaty of alliance was signed on February 6, 1778, making France America's second ally in its War for American Independence. In 1779 Spain signed the Treaty of Aranjuez, agreeing to support France in the war against Britain.

Morgan's Rifles Camp
Saratoga, October 20th

"Mr. O'Brien, I wanted to thank you for your help running my camp during the fighting. The boys never behaved better. Han Yery, the men of the Northern Army, know the worth of our first allies. With Burgoyne's defeat, the Oneida are released to return to your homes with our thanks." Smiling, Morgan shook hands with Brian and Han Yery, both of whom wore their gifts of Rifles' hunting shirts, and continued, "So, what now that the invasion has been repulsed?"

"Colonel, there is trouble at home. Now that the Hudson River is clear of the British, I intend to return Han Yery and his warriors by batteaux convoy to their homes and families."

"I entrust O'Brien with the strength of the Oneida," said Han Yery.

Tom looked at each man in turn and said, "Colonel, I'm going to have to ask for a leave of absence from the Rifles. Han Yery is my godfather. His wife is the only mother I have known, and his sons are my brothers. Our enemies threaten my home and family, which I am bound to protect."

As kin to Daniel Boone and a follow frontiersman, Colonel Morgan understood the loyalty owed to family, neighbors, and friends in dangerous times.

"Tom, your request for leave is granted. You and your father will always have a place in any force I command."

Brian nodded his thanks to Morgan and asked, "Where to now, Colonel?"

Morgan smiled and said, "Gates has received orders from General Washington to release the Rifles from the Northern Army and rejoin the main army at Valley Forge for the winter."

Brian smiled and said, "You won't miss General Gates?"

Morgan laughed and said, "Who? I fought with Dearborn, Poor, Learned, and Arnold. I didn't see Gates until Burgoyne and those other lobsterbacks surrendered at Saratoga!"

Major Morris stuck his head in the tent and said, "Colonel, Sergeant Murphy requests to see you."

Morgan smiled and shook his head. "Sergeant Murphy? I don't know if I will ever get used to that! Let him come in, but if he wants any rum, he will have to bring it himself."

Tim Murphy walked into the tent with five mugs and a small keg of rum. Setting the mugs down on the map table, he filled each and passed them to the men. He raised his mug and said, "Colonel, I have a request to make, and I believe it's safer for me if you are drinking my rum when I make it."

Morgan took a deep swallow from his mug and said, "You want a leave of absence to accompany Tom and his father."

Murphy looked confused, flustered, and sputtered, "You mean I wasted my rum!"

Morgan smiled and placed a hand on Tim's shoulder, "Han Yery needs your rifle more than General Washington in a winter camp. Your request is granted on the condition that you shall return to my command if I call."

Sobered, Tim and Tom nodded in solemn agreement, and Morgan continued, "Together, we succeeded in turning the world upside down! Now independence is possible." Addressing the gathering, he concluded, "There is more fighting ahead, and each of us shall play a part before victory is achieved."

ABOUT THE AUTHOR

Edward Cuddy was raised in Oneida County, New York, the epicenter of events foiling the British invasion of 1777, which should have crushed the rebellion. A graduate of Fordham Law School and retired litigator, Cuddy is now a full-time writer, telling the story about the people who fought on both sides and how the colonies won independence from the most dominant Sovereign of the time. He was recently inspired by the gallant resistance of the Ukraine people to retain their freedom which parallels the courage and cost suffered by our forefathers and its telling imperative. "1777: The Year of Destiny" is Mr. Cuddy's first book.

OTHER FIRESHIP PRESS TITLES

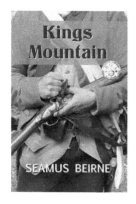

Kings Mountain
by Seamus Beirne

A New World Aflame with the Bonfires of a Budding Revolution.

In the year 1775, Michael Redferne and Isaac Malot break out of a penal colony in Barbados and go their separate ways. Redferne home to Ireland, Malot, a black man, to the Caribbean to captain a pirate sloop. Years later, a shipwreck and the search for a lost child land them, unknown to each other, in South Carolina, a colony in the grip of the American Revolution. From his sharpshooter's perch at the battle of Kings Mountain, Malot, a loyalist, adjusts the small telescope jury-rigged to his Ferguson rifle. Among the patriot enemy advancing into the killing zone, is none other than Michael Redferne. Malot faces a gut-wrenching decision, shoot his old comrade or risk forfeiting his newly won freedom.

The Long Way Home
by Kevin Bannister

The Promised Land for Two Slaves

Set in the turbulent times of the War of Independence, 'The Long Way Home' follows the lives of Thomas Peters and Murphy Steele who are friends, former slaves, fellows-in-arms and leaders of the Black Brigade. Their real-life story is an epic adventure tale as they battle bounty hunters, racism, poverty and epidemic in their adopted country after the war.

For the Finest in Nautical and Historical Fiction and Non-Fiction
www.FireshipPress.com

Interesting • Informative • Authoritative

All Fireship Press books are available through
leading bookstores and wholesalers worldwide.

CPSIA information can be obtained
at www.ICGtesting.com
Printed in the USA
JSHW080928310523
42403JS00002B/20